THREE DOORWAYS DARK

Books by Keith Donnelly

Donald Youngblood Mystery Series
Three Deuces Down (2008)
Three Days Dead (2009)
Three Devils Dancing (2011)
Three Deadly Drops (2012)
Three Dragons Doomed (2014)
Three Daggers Dripping (2016)
Three Divers Deep (2017)
Three Doorways Dark (2022)

Youngblood Stories
Moving Target (2020)

A Donald Youngblood Mystery

THREE DOORWAYS DARK

Keith Donnelly

Hummingbird Books
Kingsport, Tennessee

Hummingbird Books
A division of Harrison Mountain Press
Kingsport, TN 37660

Designed by Todd Lape / Lape Designs

Copyright © 2022 by Keith Donnelly
All rights reserved under International and Pan-American
Copyright Conventions. Published in the United States by
Hummingbird Books, Kingsport, TN.

Library of Congress Cataloging-in-Publication Data available

ISBN 978-0-9993667-8-3

Printed in the United States of America
by Maple Press, York, Pennsylvania

*Dedicated to all those front-line workers
in the war against Covid-19 who risked their lives,
and sometimes gave them,
in the battle against this deadly virus*

Prologue

On a lake halfway around the planet, a world-class sniper was setting up to do a practice run. It would be the first of many. He had set the target on the bank some three hundred yards from his current position on the water. The target was a cutout of a man approximately six feet tall. Earlier, he had shot twenty rounds with the help of a spotter, to zero in the scope. He wanted to go for a head shot but knew it was too risky. Too many factors involved that could easily lead to a miss. Too little margin for error. Anything less than a kill shot would be a failure. He would get only one good shot. A second shot was possible, but an effective second shot was unlikely. One shot, and it had to be on target—a body shot, center mass. He was sure his unaware target would not be wearing a vest.

He was in a fishing boat alone on a deserted part of the lake with a special edition of a Dragunov SVD sniper rifle, a variation of a classic rifle with an accuracy range of over eight hundred yards. The three-hundred-yard shot would normally be a breeze, but calculate in a boat bobbing up and down on a lake and it became much more difficult. He liked the challenge.

The original Dragunov had been around since the sixties, with subtle changes over the years. His was lighter than the original, with a polymer stock, and it was minus the bayonet lug featured on the original. A bayonet on a sniper rifle—he smiled at the thought. Obviously, snipers at that time were not the specialists they were today.

The Dragunov was a rugged and durable weapon, and he had possessed it for a long time, passed down from his father. The ammo was a special load designed to break apart on impact, inflicting maximum damage to the target. Not your typical hollow-point load, these rounds were designed with long distances in mind. They had to be accurate as well as deadly.

He loaded six rounds into the clip and slammed it into the bottom of the rifle. His spotter was a safe distance away with a walkie-talkie. The sniper sighted the target and tried to get comfortable with the movement of the boat on the water. He waited a long time before he took the first shot. He fired at the crest of the boat's movement. He took his time between shots, like a professional golfer on a driving range, pretending each shot was his first.

He put the Dragunov away and picked up the walkie-talkie. The spotter was moving toward the target. When the spotter arrived, the sniper pushed *Send* on the walkie-talkie.

"Is it as good as I think it is?" the sniper said.

"Yes," the spotter said. "Six kill shots, in my opinion."

"Good," the sniper said. "Save the target and set up a new one same time tomorrow."

"It's going to rain tomorrow," the spotter said.

"It could be raining the day I take the live shot," the sniper said. "Stop whining. You are being well paid."

There was a slight delay as the sniper waited for confirmation.

"Okay," the spotter said, resignation in his voice. "See you tomorrow, same time."

The sniper engaged the boat's engines and headed for his cabin. He kept his speed low so the wind chill was at a minimum. The temperature was near freezing and felt much colder on the water. A warm fire, a bottle of vodka, and a willing woman were waiting for him at the cabin. It was tempting to slam the throttle to full speed, but like all world-class snipers, he was a patient man, and the reward at the end of the journey would make it worth the extra wait. In the meantime, he thought of his target, an American who would pay for his sins with his life, thanks to a bullet from his father's Dragunov.

I'm coming for you, he thought. *I'm coming for you.*

1

I was in my second-floor office on a clear morning in late April trying to readjust. Mary and I had just returned from Mexico, where we had spent two fabulous weeks at the beach house of a retired CIA agent and his wife. I was wishing we were still there when the intercom buzzed.

"Tony Price to see you," my junior partner, Gretchen Graves, said.

I pushed the respond button and said, "Send him in."

Tony Price was the local club pro who had taught Lacy, my adopted daughter, to play golf. Lacy turned out to be a natural at the game, winning the Ladies' Club Championship at the Mountain Center Country Club before she went off to Arizona State University to study criminology. Tony's showing up in my office was a real surprise, but then again, my job was full of surprises.

Gretchen showed Tony into my inner sanctum.

"I hope this is a social call," I said.

"Kind of," Tony laughed. "I don't really need a private detective, if that's what you mean."

"Please, sit down," I said, motioning to one of the oversized chairs in front of my desk.

Tony sat. "I'll get to it," he said.

"Let me guess," I said. "You want to try and get your tour card again."

"Not exactly," Tony said. "I want to see if I can qualify for the PGA Championship, and I have a couple of questions for you."

"The answer to the first is yes," I said. "I'll back you financially any way I can. That has to be the first question or you wouldn't be here."

Tony laughed. "I knew you were good, but I didn't know you were a mind reader."

"I'm not. You said you didn't need a private detective, so it had to be about golf. The rest was easy. What's the second question?"

"Well, let me first say that if I win any money, I'll pay you back and give you a percentage of what's left," Tony said.

"If you win any money, you can pay me back," I said. "After that, whatever is left is yours."

"Well, if I get there, I will already have made enough to pay you back. It's a two-step process, and there's decent money if you play well. The last-place guy this year at the PGA made $18,400," Tony said. "So, if I can make it to the championship and make the cut, I can win a good bit of money for myself and my caddie."

"I wish you luck," I said. "Second question?"

"Would it be okay if I ask Lacy to caddie for me?"

I didn't see that coming, yet I wasn't totally surprised. Lacy had held a number of part-time jobs while she was in high school. She had worked with computer whiz Stanley Johns for a few years and learned a lot about programming, software, viruses, hacking, and other skills that were far beyond my understanding. She had helped Doris in the Mountain Center Diner, and she had caddied at the country club the last two summers. The young, tall, attractive, blond caddie had been in great demand. Her tips were pretty impressive. The wolves kept their distance, knowing that her mother was a cop and her father was a private eye who shot first and asked questions later.

"Fine with me," I said. "Think she knows enough not to embarrass herself?"

"She learned some things from caddying at the club," Tony said. "But I know a retired caddie who will teach her the tour ropes. His name is Flip Dawson, and he was on tour for a number of years. He is not physically able to carry a bag anymore, but he is a wealth of knowledge and information. Besides, for a young golfer, Lacy is one of the best I've seen at reading greens. She'll be a real asset."

"Is your game good enough right now?"

"I think it is," he said. "But I'll be practicing a lot this summer, and I'll want Lacy to play a lot of rounds with me so she can get used to my game. Around mid-September, I'll sit down with Flip, and we'll decide if my game is good enough to give it a try. If we feel it is, then I'll sign up for the Tennessee PGA in mid-October. The top five finishers in that tournament win spots in the PGA Professional Championship. The top twenty from that tournament go the PGA Championship at Pinehurst No. 2 in Pinehurst, North Carolina."

"So Lacy would have to miss some school," I said.

"Guess I didn't think about that," Tony said. "You think that's a problem?"

"I'm sure she'll say it isn't," I said.

We discussed the financial end of things. Tony thought ten grand would cover him, and that he would not need it until August. I gave him Lacy's cell-phone number and he left, promising to be in touch.

◆ ◆ ◆ ◆

As I was about to leave the office to get some breakfast, the phone rang and then my intercom buzzed.

"Billy on line one," Gretchen said.

Billy Two-Feathers, best friend, ex-partner, and deputy sheriff in Swain County, North Carolina, didn't call for just any reason.

"Let's have lunch at the diner," he said when I answered.

That was Billy. He didn't call to say, *Hello. How are you? What's been going on?* He left that to me. When he called, he had a purpose.

"Come as soon as you can," I said. "I haven't had breakfast, and I'm hungry."

"I will be there in an hour," Billy said.

◆ ◆ ◆ ◆

We ordered. Doris Black, the owner of the Mountain Center Diner, would not stop gushing over the fact that Billy was in the diner having breakfast for the first time in forever. She finally went away to place our order.

"You didn't come all this way just to have breakfast," I said. "What's up? Everything okay?"

"Relax, Blood," Billy said. "Everything is fine. I wanted to discuss my future with you."

"Your future," I said, taking a drink of coffee. "Let me guess. Charlie has decided to retire, and he wants you to run for sheriff."

Charlie Running Horse was the current sheriff, and I knew how much he admired and trusted Billy. I had supported his campaign when he was first elected. I was really supporting Billy, since Charlie had promised Billy a deputy sheriff job if he won. Charlie won. Billy had closed our satellite office in Cherokee, North Carolina, and become a deputy sheriff.

"I hate it when you do that," Billy said. "Go ahead, tell me the rest of it."

"There's more?"

"Yes," he said.

Doris set our breakfast down and said, "So good to see you, Billy. Now, don't be a stranger. Enjoy. I gave you extra home fries. I know how much you love them."

"Thank you, Doris," Billy said.

I waited until Doris was out of earshot and then said, "Okay, Paul Harvey, tell me the rest of it."

"Who is Paul Harvey?" Billy said, digging into the home fries.

He knew perfectly well who Paul Harvey was. "Out with it," I said, taking a big bite of my feta cheese omelet.

"You are right about the first part," Billy said. "Charlie wants me to run and says that I will win. And I am okay with that, but there is something else I would rather do, if you are agreeable."

"What?"

"Reopen the satellite office in Cherokee," he said.

"Why?"

"I see a big need, and I am tired of law enforcement," Billy said. "There are no private investigators in Cherokee, and many times lawyers are not able to properly defend their clients because the alleged crimes cannot be properly investigated."

"Welcome back," I said. "What about space?"

"The same space we had before will be available at the end of the year," Billy said. "The timing is perfect."

"Convenient," I said.

"Destiny," Billy said.

◆ ◆ ◆ ◆

That evening, I shared my day with Mary, my lover, my wife, and an all-around good cop on the Mountain Center police force, where she was lead detective. We were having our predinner traditional first glass of wine after a hard day's work. I was recovering from wounds sustained in Afghanistan and was just getting used to working a full day. As we sat at our kitchen bar in our downtown Mountain Center condo and began to unwind, I told her about Billy's visit.

"That's great," Mary said. "I'm sure Maggie will be thrilled."

Maggie was Billy's wife. They had one son, named after me. They called him Little D.

"No doubt," I said, nibbling on some honey-roasted peanuts. "Also, Tony Price came to the office today."

Mary looked surprised. "Problem?"

"No," I said.

"So tell me."

I did.

Mary listened. "Interesting," she said.

"Think Lacy will say yes?"

"In a heartbeat," Mary said.

2

I had just returned from Moto's Gym the next morning when Lacy called, much too early for her. There was a two-hour time difference between Mountain Center and Tempe, Arizona, where Lacy was finishing her freshman year at Arizona State.

"You're up early," I said. *Caller ID is great if you're on the receiving end,* I thought.

"Tony Price called," Lacy said.

"I figured. Did you say yes?"

"Are you kidding?" she said. "I'll be home as soon as this semester is over to start working with Tony. He says we'll be playing a lot of golf. He's going to give me a full-time job in the pro shop. Flip Dawson will come down later in the summer and teach me how to be a tour caddie."

"It will be nice to have you home for the summer," I said.

"I can't wait," Lacy said. "I have to go, Don, or I'll be late for class. Love you."

The young, I thought, *always in a hurry.*

◆ ◆ ◆

Gretchen and Rhonda came in later, said hello and goodbye, and went about their business. Gretchen reported that nothing interesting was going on unless I wanted to follow a suspected cheating wife for Rollie Ogle. Rollie, a divorce lawyer you would want on your side, rarely handled husbands. I wondered how he got roped into this one. Regardless, I declined.

Later that morning, I called David Steele, deputy director of the FBI, my on-again, off-again boss when I worked as an FBI consultant. I was lucky he took my call.

"How are you doing, Youngblood?" he said, knowing I had been shot up on the last assignment he gave me.

"You mean besides being bored out of my mind?" I said. "Yeah, I'm doing okay. Got anything interesting?"

"You're on medical leave, Youngblood," he said. "End of story."

"You're a big help."

"Is Mary still pissed at me?" he asked.

"Only when I mention your name," I said.

He laughed.

"Seriously," I said, "she's just glad to have me back in one piece, more or less. She knows you're not to blame. I doubt that POTUS is going to get her vote in the next election."

"I understand that," David Steele said.

"Come on, Dave," I said. "Give me something where I won't get shot."

"Take it easy for a while, Youngblood," he said. "Find something to do. Read a good book. Go to a movie. Call me in a couple of weeks."

◆ ◆ ◆

At lunchtime, I picked up burgers and fries and took them to T. Elbert, my longtime friend and a retired TBI agent. He was amazed and pleased at the same time.

"To what do I owe this honor?" he said. "Did the women kick you out of your office?"

"Slow day," I said. "I thought you might like some lunch. I haven't been here in a while, so—"

He cut me off with the wave of a hand. "No need to explain. Good to see you. I just made iced tea. Let me get a couple of glasses and I'll be right back."

He wheeled his motorized chair into the house and was gone for maybe five minutes. I knew better than to offer help. He came back with a tray perfectly balanced in his lap with a pitcher of tea, two glasses, and a bowl of lemon wedges. I spread out the food, and we got right to it.

"How was your trip?"

"As good as it gets," I said.

"So, how are you feeling?"

"Tip-top," I said. "I've been running and working out at Moto's. I feel great, but I'm bored. I need a new case, and so far, nothing has come around."

"If I were you," T. Elbert said, "I'd enjoy the downtime. You're too famous now for something not to turn up."

"Lacy is coming home in a few weeks," I said. "She is going to spend the summer here working in the country club pro shop and learning how to be a tour caddie."

I told him about Tony Price's visit to my office. "Maybe I'll learn how to play golf," I said.

T. Elbert got a good laugh out of that one—maybe a little too long and loud to suit me.

3

A few weeks later, Lacy came home with her longtime boyfriend, Biker McBride. Biker was a tall, good-looking kid who was focused and hard working. Mary said he was a hunk. Lacy agreed. I said nothing but admitted to myself that he was about as much as I could hope for as my daughter's boyfriend. Marriage certainly seemed likely somewhere down the road. Lacy's best friend, Hannah, was also home with her boyfriend, Alfred, who everyone had called "the Brain" when they were in high school. Now, he was just plain ole Al.

With all the young people in and out, things got noisier and crazier at the downtown condo, so Mary and I decided it was time to move into our newly rebuilt, and mostly refurnished, lake house. We did that, and soon the lake house was also noisier and crazier. Mary reveled in the energy that the young people brought to our new home. Our summer was destined to be a busy one.

Lacy started her job at the pro shop a few days after she got back, and at night we listened to tales from the country club. She and Tony were playing golf early about three days a week, and the reports on both their games were good. Tony was usually under par and Lacy at or near par.

"You got any competition for the Ladies' Club Championship?" I asked one night.

"Maybe," Lacy said.

"No one even close," Biker said nonchalantly.

Lacy stared hard at him. I'd seen that stare from Mary. "Don't jinx me," she said.

Biker looked at me, smiled, and mouthed silently, *No competition*.

"We're going out in the morning," Lacy said. "Why don't you come and watch, Don?"

Since interesting new cases were still nonexistent at Cherokee Investigations, I said, "Okay, I'll do it."

◆ ◆ ◆

The next day, I became a caddie-chauffeur, driving their golf clubs around while Lacy and Tony walked. It wasn't a bad day job. I drank coffee and watched them hit golf balls. They went after the balls they hit, and I followed. Silly game. The grounds crew kept a hole ahead of us, whipping the dew from the greens, making putting a whole lot easier. Lacy and Tony both played well, and at the end of the round Lacy had shot even par and Tony three under. They had teed off at seven o'clock and played the round in three hours.

"Let's go to the restaurant, and I'll buy you breakfast," I said.

"I've got to get to work," Lacy said, and she was off toward the pro shop before we could object.

"Hey," Tony said, "you can buy me breakfast."

We sat at my usual table in the country club restaurant overlooking the eighteenth green. The place was empty, and the food arrived in a hurry. We dug right in.

"Looks like your game is in great shape," I said.

"It's getting there," Tony said. "I left a few shots out there today."

I couldn't see where he left them, but he knew better than I did, so I said nothing.

"I'll tell you one thing," he said. "That daughter of yours can play. She needs to be playing college golf."

"Have you said anything to her?"

"No," he said. "But before Lacy goes back, I'm going to call ASU's women's team coach and tell her that she has a hidden gem on campus. She'd be crazy not to give her a look."

"How's she working out in the pro shop?" I said.

Tony laughed. "Great. Our sales are up twenty percent. All these old guys come in just to stare at her. Then Lacy sells them something they don't need, and everyone is happy. She has worked hard to learn the merchandise. She's a natural."

After we finished, Tony went back to the pro shop and I went to the office with the feeling that his day would be a lot more interesting than mine. I was right, of course.

4

One day in early August, Lacy burst into my office around lunchtime, her face red and tear streaked, a sure sign she was mad as hell. "I just got fired!" she yelled. I heard the door shut behind her. Gretchen was on noise patrol.

"Tony fired you?"

"No," Lacy said, calming a bit. "Tony is playing a match in Johnson City. He doesn't know."

"What happened?"

"This big-deal asshole guest patted my butt and made a suggestive remark," she said. "I smacked the living daylights out of him. He ran to the general manager, claiming he had been assaulted, and the general manager told me to get out, that I was fired. I think he was putting on a show for the guy, but I'm not sure."

"Does Mary know?"

"Yes," Lacy said. "She said she's going out there and straighten it out. She told me to come to the office and tell you."

"Damn," I said. "I'd better get out there before World War III starts. You go on to the lake house. We'll talk more at dinner. Don't worry about this. It's all in-the-heat-of-the-moment stuff. Everyone needs to cool down."

"Don't shoot anybody," Lacy said.

Such a kidder! "I won't even take my gun," I said.

"And don't let Mom shoot anybody," Lacy said. "She's the one I'm worried about."

"Not to worry," I said. "I'll handle it."

I left Lacy and hustled down the back stairs and into my SUV. I was at the club in ten minutes, in time to see Mary get out of her car and head for the entrance. I ran and caught her just inside the door.

She looked hard at me and said, "Stay out of my way."

"You need to take a breath," I said.

"You need to shut up," Mary said as she headed for the general manager's office.

A receptionist was outside the general manager's door. Mary stopped in front of her desk. "Is he in there?"

"Yes, but he's busy," the receptionist said.

Mary leaned over her desk while flipping her badge case open. "You go in there and tell him the police are here," she said. "I want to see him now."

Maybe I imagined it, but I thought I saw color drain from the receptionist's face. Mary's tone was downright frightening. The receptionist sat as if in shock.

"Go now," Mary said.

The receptionist got up hurriedly, went to the general manager's door, tapped on it, and entered. Seconds later, she was back. "You'll have to wait," she said.

Wrong answer, I thought.

"Not likely," Mary said, heading straight to the general manager's door and bursting into his office. I followed.

A young man in a suit sat in front of the general manager's desk. *Salesman*, I thought.

Mary flashed her badge. "Police business," she said to him. "Please leave."

"I'll be in touch," the younger man said to the man behind the desk.

The nameplate on the desk read, *Harvey Shine*. Shine was new to the club, and I had not met him yet. I wondered if he knew who we were. The younger man hurried past us and out the door, which I shut behind him. I leaned against the door saying nothing and trying to look tough. This was Mary's show.

"Would you explain to me, please, Mr. Shine, why you saw fit to fire my daughter this morning after she was sexually assaulted by one of your guests?"

Shine was visible shaken. He got to his feet. "I was told she slapped a guest in the pro shop over a comment he made. There was no mention of sexual assault. I confirmed it with the assistant pro. He did not know what the comment was. The guest said it was harmless and demanded she be fired unless we wanted a lawsuit. I intended to let it blow over for a couple of days and then tell your daughter she could come back."

"Do you know who my daughter is?" Mary said.

"I'm afraid I do not," Shine said.

"My daughter is Lacy Youngblood," Mary said, "your reigning ladies' club champion. I am Mary Youngblood, lead detective on the Mountain Center police force. The hunk at the door is my husband, Donald Youngblood, a famous private detective who works with the FBI. We are members here. Do you think you might have acted a little too hastily?"

"It certainly appears that I did," Shine said, having a hard time forming words. "My apologies. I'm Harvey Shine, by the way."

Mary ignored the introduction. "Take us to the pro shop. I want to talk to your assistant pro."

"Certainly," Harvey Shine said. "Follow me, please."

◆ ◆ ◆

The assistant pro heard only the slap. "I don't know what was said before that," he said. "But Lacy would never have done that without provocation. She told me later that he patted her butt. Her words, not mine. I don't know what he said to her, but the slap sounded like a firecracker going off."

"Then what happened?" Mary said.

"He yelled, 'Bitch, I'll see you fired for this!' Then he stormed out, and half an hour later Mr. Shine came back and fired her."

"Was anyone else in here at the time of the slap?" I said.

"No," the assistant pro said.

So no one can verify Lacy's story, I thought. I wasn't surprised. The asshole would not have been so bold with anyone nearby.

"And your name?" Mary said.

"Jeremy Lake," he said.

I had seen him around but didn't know his name. I had a thought. I looked up and around at the ceiling, and then I saw what I was looking for.

"Do those cameras work?" I said.

"Yes," Jeremy said.

"Do they record?" Mary asked.

"Yes," he said. "They go into a file that I look over at the end of every day."

"Can we go in and view it right now?"

"Sure," Jeremy Lake said.

That's what we did. Jeremy selected a start time close to when the incident occurred and fast-forwarded, then slowed the recording. We saw Lacy arranging clothes on hangers in a far corner. A big guy came past and gave her butt a pat and said something to her. Lacy turned around and slapped him hard. He staggered backward and then appeared to yell at her. He turned and left in a hurry.

"That asshole," Mary said.

"Want me to forward to the firing part?" Jeremy said.

"No need for that," Harvey Shine said. "Not my finest hour."

I shook my head at Jeremy.

"Is that asshole still here?" Mary said.

"He left about fifteen or twenty minutes ago," Jeremy said.

"What was he driving?" Mary said.

I put up my hand to stop Jeremy from answering and pulled Mary gently away for a side conversation.

"No need for that," I said softly, putting my hand on her shoulder. "We can track this guy down if we need to. Why don't you go back to work, and we'll discuss our options with Lacy at dinner tonight."

She took a deep breath and seemed to relax. "You're right," she said. "Good thing one of us is staying cool. I'll see you at the lake house."

Mary left, and I went back to Harvey Shine's office.

"I'm sorry about all of this," he said. "I was just doing some on-the-spot damage control. The guy is from Knoxville and probably will not be back for months, if he ever comes back at all. At least that's what the member said."

"Who was he a guest of?" I said.

He told me. "Not the nicest person," he said.

I let that comment drop, although from experience and observation I had to agree. "So Lacy comes back to work tomorrow, right?" I said.

"Absolutely," Harvey Shine said.

◆ ◆ ◆ ◆

We had dinner on the deck: Lacy, Biker, Mary, and I. I told Lacy first thing that she had her job back. Lacy recounted to Biker what had happened, and Mary and I told what occurred after we found out about the firing.

"So we have the whole thing in a video file," Lacy said. "That's awesome."

"I may go to Knoxville and beat the shit out of this guy," Biker said.

"Not your best idea," I said.

"Only venting," he said.

"If it's any consolation, I'd like to go with you," I said.

"Enough testosterone," Lacy said. "The guy committed the crime, and I found him guilty and dealt out the punishment. End of story. Besides, if anyone is going to Knoxville and beat the shit out of this guy, it will be me."

"I'll drink to that," Mary said.

"Me, too," I said.

5

In late August, the Ladies' Club Championship, a three-day event, was held at the Mountain Center Country Club. Tournament flights, eight of them, were determined by scores from the first two rounds. Lacy chose not to participate in the practice round because she had played the course so much since she returned home.

There had not been one interesting new case at Cherokee Investigations since my return from Afghanistan, and I was struggling to find things to do. Normally, in down times, I would work around the lake house playing Mr. Fix-It. But the lake house was brand-new and solidly built, and it would be years before things started to deteriorate. I had spent so much time at Moto's Gym that he threatened to charge me rent. I was in the best shape of my life, which Mary noticed with great interest. Taking advantage of her attention was challenging with all the young people in and out. Since there was no pill for boredom, a golf tournament with Lacy was just the ticket.

◆ ◆ ◆ ◆

The first round was on Friday, and Lacy shot one over par and had a two-stroke lead at the end of the day, obviously headed for the championship flight. Carts were allowed, but Lacy and her playing partner, a young lady a few years older, both liked to walk, so I ended up driving a golf cart with their clubs. I ferried clubs to and fro, tended flagsticks, and drank a few beers along the way. The whole thing was rather informal. For most of the women, it was a social event, with no one caring who did what. Not so for the women in the championship flight. They were the best at the club and wanted to score like the best. I was impressed with Lacy's focus—every club selection scrutinized, every shot thought out, every putt analyzed.

The second day, Lacy shot even par and opened a five-shot lead, the championship firmly in her grasp. I said nothing, not wanting a lecture on jinxing her. We had a dinner event at the club that night with players, boyfriends of players, husbands of players, and other paying guests, Mary and me included. I had reserved my normal table overlooking the eighteenth green, and that reduced traffic and allowed us a modicum of quiet. Still, many participants found their way to our table to congratulate Lacy on her fine play.

The final day of the tournament was another typically muggy East Tennessee August day. As had occurred the previous two rounds, each player was announced on the first tee. This had been going on since eight o'clock in the morning, when the seventh flight teed off. At 1:10 P.M., the final player of the tournament was announced: "On the tee, ladies and gentlemen, our reigning Ladies' Club Champion and current tournament leader, Lacy Youngblood."

Polite applause came from the light crowd, and I had to admit a blooming pride as Lacy gave a small wave. She bent down, teed up her ball, performed her pre-strike practice swing, addressed the ball, and drilled a drive 250 yards down the middle of the 412-yard dogleg left par four. She walked down the fairway after her ball, Mary with her. I followed in the cart. The day was hot and dry, and carts were allowed in the fairways. I pulled up near Lacy and Mary. Lacy put away her driver and selected an iron. Her next shot was to the center of the green. A twenty-foot putt burned the left edge of the hole and stopped a foot on the other side. Lacy tapped it in for par.

The rest of the round was much like the first hole—fairways and greens and tap-in pars. At the end of the day, Lacy turned in a rather boring scorecard of sixteen pars, one bogey, and one birdie, even par for the second day in a row. She won the championship by eight strokes. After the scorecards were signed and verified, there was a presentation ceremony. Mary and I smiled widely as Tony Price presented the trophy: "Ladies and gentlemen, it gives me great pleasure, for the second straight year, to present this year's Ladies' Club Championship trophy to Lacy Youngblood."

Lacy received ample applause from the eighty or so people who stuck around for the presentation. Afterward, there was a casual buffet poolside, where Mary and I sat at a faraway table while Lacy was the center of attention, receiving separate congratulations from most of the attendees. *Everybody loves a winner*, I thought.

6

In mid-September, Flip Dawson showed up to put the final touches on Lacy's caddie training. Tony said she was ready. Lacy had purchased and read cover to cover *How to Caddie on Tour* by Mick Tarel, a longtime tour caddie. Tony was sure Flip would be impressed.

I drove the cart as Tony got in a morning round with club pros from Johnson City and Kingsport. Lacy was, in golf vernacular, on Tony's bag. Each player had his own caddie, so I was driving an empty cart with Flip as an on-again, off-again passenger. Sometimes he walked with Lacy, and other times he rode with me in the cart.

"Lacy has it down," Flip said as we rode down the long par-five fairway on the fourth hole. "I've been testing her, and she's got the right answer every time. She's a quick study. I hear she's a hell of a golfer in her own right."

"Ladies' club champion," I said with pride. "Back-to-back par rounds in August, the last two days of the tournament."

"I'd like to see her play before I leave," Flip said. "I think one more day on Tony's bag and I will have taught her all I can. The rest is just the experience of doing it."

◆ ◆ ◆

A few days later, Flip rode with me and the clubs while Tony and Lacy played an early-morning match-play round. Whoever won the hole won a point. No points for a tied hole. At the turn, Lacy was one up.

"She can play," Flip said. "No doubt about that. Long hitter for a woman. Tony is going to have a hard time with Lacy hitting from the women's tees."

At fourteen, the number-one men's handicap hole, Lacy had a decided tee advantage. She also had the honors and hit first, a long, straight shot that left her in good position to attack the pin, according to Flip. Tony, trying to make up the distance, drove it long but in the right rough, into tree trouble. Lacy hit first and found the center of the green. Tony's next shot was in the front bunker. He blasted out to within ten feet of the pin, a nice shot that didn't matter. Lacy rolled her fifteen-foot birdie putt into the bottom of the cup for a three, and Tony picked up his par putt. Lacy was two up. They both parred fifteen and sixteen. Tony won the par-three seventeenth when his tee shot landed three feet from the pin and he tapped in. On the eighteenth, Tony hit a monster drive that led to a birdie. Lacy could manage only a par, and the match was halved.

"Thought you had me," Tony said.

"Great birdie-birdie finish," Lacy said. "That's the way to get ready for a tournament, right, Flip?"

"You said it, young lady," Flip said. *Constantly praise and encourage your player*, Flip had told her in private.

◆ ◆ ◆ ◆

In the parking lot, Flip and I shook hands.

"I'll be heading out first thing in the morning," he said. "It was an honor meeting you and Lacy."

"Likewise," I said. "Think Tony is ready?"

"He's certainly got the game," Flip said. "But he has not played in tournament-type competition in a long time. How he responds to that will be the difference."

"Think Lacy is ready?"

"Without a doubt," Flip said. "She was an excellent choice. Smart, good golfer in her own right, and really good looking. She most certainly could be a distraction for some of the other players. I'll tell you this, the final spot for the PGA Professional Championship will be won by either a single stroke or in a playoff. Every shot of every day is important. That's the most important thing for Lacy to understand."

"I hope you'll come down for the tournament," I said.

"I wouldn't miss it," he said.

7

On a Tuesday in mid-October, I was standing on the first tee at Holston Hills Country Club waiting on the next group to be announced and remembering the events that led to my being here. I stood there on an unusually warm morning as Tony Price, Lacy, and the other golfers in Tony's group and their caddies walked onto the first tee to await their introductions for the first round of the Tennessee PGA tournament.

Lacy had flown in from Arizona on Friday night and played a round late Saturday afternoon with Tony. On Sunday afternoon, Flip Dawson, Tony, Lacy, and I had driven to Knoxville. Monday was a practice round, and I had followed the group around in a cart with Flip driving. When he wasn't collaborating with Lacy, he regaled me with stories of the PGA tour and the players he had caddied for. I could tell that Lacy was doing well from Flip's comments. She spent most of the day making notes in her yardage book, recording distances from different spots on any given hole to the center of the green.

"That's exactly right, girl," Flip would say. "Stay right there." Or he would say something like, "Good read," when Tony made a putt.

"She's going to do fine," Flip said to me late in the round. "She's smart and doesn't get flustered." Then he added, "And she's drawing a lot of looks from the other golfers. Best-looking caddie they ever saw, probably."

Then the announcement came that brought me back to the here and now: "Ladies and gentlemen, on the tee, please welcome from Mountain Center Country Club in Mountain Center, Tennessee, head pro Tony Price."

There was sufficient applause from the gallery as Tony leaned down to tee up his ball. Blond, good looking, and with a trim body, Tony was sure to be a hit among the ladies.

"Important shot," Flip whispered.

Tony went through his pre-shot routine, then addressed the ball. The fluid swing I had seen so often remained unchanged as he brought his driver back and unleashed it, resulting in the familiar whack of a perfectly struck golf ball. In the distance, the ball landed dead center in the fairway and rolled maybe another ten yards. Lacy put the driver away, and they began a journey that would last three days. Flip and I followed at a respectful distance wearing IDs that allowed us inside the ropes. Mine was compliments of the head of security after I showed him my FBI creds. He was more than happy to have me there, probably thinking that if anything bad went down, I would be in the spotlight, and not him. "I've heard of you," he had said. "Welcome aboard." Flip's ID was for a roving marshal and rules advisor, thanks to his many years of caddying on the pro tour. We were instantly minor celebrities.

"One hundred seventy-three yards to the center of the green," I heard Lacy tell Tony.

Tony selected an iron, took a couple of practice swings, and then addressed the ball. He waggled the club a couple of times, then hit a smooth, perfect-sounding shot to the front of the green. The ball rolled a few feet and stopped.

"Good shot," Lacy said.

They got to the green, where Tony marked his ball. Then they went about their business of reading the line of the putt, which appeared to be about twenty-five feet. They conferred softly, and Lacy moved away. She removed the pin and walked to the fringe of the green holding it. A new rule gave the player the option of leaving the pin in or taking it out when putting. Tony was old school and always wanted the pin out. He lined up the putt, stroked the ball smoothly, and watched as it tracked toward the hole, catching the right edge and falling in.

"Great birdie," I heard Lacy say.

"That's a big one," Flip said softly.

It was the beginning of an up-and-down day. Tony made a par three on hole two and then bogeyed the par-four third hole. Even par through three holes. He made par on the fourth, then birdied the monster par-five fifth to go back to one under. He birdied the sixth to go to two under, and Flip said, "He's settling in." Tony made the turn at one under after a bogey on the ninth hole. He made one bogey and one birdie on the back, the birdie coming at eighteen. He finished with a one-under seventy-one.

Flip and I waited while Tony turned in his scorecard and Lacy took his clubs to the storage area to wipe them down and check them in. We met at my SUV. Tony looked beat. Lacy looked radiant.

"That was awesome," she said.

"Not the word I would use," Tony said. "*Ordeal* comes to mind. I had to grind out that round. Maybe this was a mistake."

"You did fine," Lacy said. "We might have left a few out there, but it was a good first day. You're in the hunt. You'll do even better tomorrow; I can feel it."

"Listen to your caddie," Flip said. "You had a good day."

"Let's go back to the Residence Inn, shower, have a drink, and go find a place to eat," I said.

"Now, there's a plan I can live with," Tony said.

8

The next day was cloudless, with a sky so blue I knew the humidity from the day before had taken a nosedive. The leaves were changing, the colors not quite to peak but getting there, and the temperature was perfect for playing golf, with a predicted high of seventy.

Tony seemed more relaxed than the day before. He methodically shot par on the front side, with one bogey and one birdie. He consistently hit good putts that were ever so close but would not fall. Lacy kept him loose with a stream of compliments and encouragements.

On the back, things started to get interesting. After a par on number ten, Tony nearly made a hole in one at the par-three eleventh, hitting the pin flush on the first bounce. The ball came to rest a foot from the hole, and Tony tapped it in for a birdie. Two pars later, he hit his tee shot ten feet from the hole on the par-three fourteenth and made that putt for another birdie. He was two under. Tony made par on the next three holes and then, for the second day in a row, birdied eighteen. Lacy was right. Tony was in the hunt.

◆ ◆ ◆ ◆

That night, we had dinner at Ruth's Chris Steak House, within walking distance of our hotel, the downtown Residence Inn. We were tired but excited for Tony, and I thought all of us could use a good meal, my treat.

"That was a fine round today. You're in fifth place," Flip said, raising his pint of draft beer. "Keep it up."

"Thanks, Flip," Tony said.

"To another sixty-eight," I said.

Tony, Flip, and I were drinking drafts, and Lacy iced tea.

"A little bit of bad luck on the putts today," Lacy said. "But you were stroking it well."

"Yeah, I definitely left some shots out there," Tony said.

"Couldn't that be said of almost any round by almost any player?" Lacy said.

"Good point," Tony said. "I will gladly take a sixty-eight any day of the week with no complaints."

We each ordered the eleven-ounce filet mignon with lobster mac and cheese and creamed spinach. Lacy, Tony, and Flip began an intense conversation about the course, and I started to people-watch. Some good-looking women were scattered about. Of course, I ignored them. I was interested in a man at the bar who seemed to be focused on our table. He looked vaguely familiar. Maybe he recognized Tony or Flip or me. Or maybe he was interested in the beautiful young blonde with us. *Too young for you, pal*, I thought. I stared him down, and he looked away. I noticed a few faces that I thought I recognized, and then it dawned on me that some of the players were probably staying nearby, maybe even at the Residence Inn. Maybe the guy at the bar was a player. I lost that train of thought when the food arrived. It was superb, and we ate and talked in a joyful mood of anticipation. Tomorrow could not come fast enough.

Lacy was the first to leave. "I'm going to walk around the square and see what's going on," she said. "I'll see you back at the Residence Inn."

"Be careful," I said.

"I can take care of myself, remember?"

"I know, but still . . ." I let my protest fade away.

She bent down and kissed me on the cheek and patted my shoulder. "Relax, Dad," she said. She pointed at Tony. "What's the word?"

"One shot at a time," he said, smiling.

"Copy that," Lacy said. She turned and walked away.

"Don't think I've ever heard her call you Dad before," Tony said.

"Only when she thinks I'm being unreasonable or over-protective," I said.

"I think that girl can take care of herself," Flip said. He pushed his chair back, stood, and stretched. "I'll see you guys back at the ranch."

That left just the two of us.

Moments later, the guy at the bar stood in front of our table. "Tony Price?" he said.

"Yes," Tony said with a puzzled look.

"I'm Harley Dobbs," the man said. "Remember me?"

"I remember," Tony said. "Not a good memory."

"I reckon so," Harley Dobbs said. "Mind if I sit down? I need to tell you something."

"Go ahead," Tony said.

Harley pulled out the chair previously occupied by Flip and sat.

"I'd better go," I said.

"Stay put," Tony said.

I turned to Harley. "I'm Donald Youngblood. My daughter is caddying for Tony."

Harley offered his hand, and I shook it. "Harley Dobbs. Pleased to meet you," he said. "I saw you-all out there today." He turned to Tony. "I won't take much of your time, Mr. Price. Twenty years ago, you got a raw deal, and I was part of it. But I want you to know I had nothing to do with improving that lie and knew nothing about it before you filed a complaint. My brother, who was my caddie, never actually admitted it, but I know he did it. I wanted to win that spot fair and square. He caddied for me only a few more times, and then I let him go. I just couldn't trust him anymore. Anyway, I've waited a long time to tell you that."

Harley Dobbs seemed sincere, and Tony took the high road. "I appreciate it," he said. "It took guts, coming over here. But that was a long time ago, and it was probably for the best. I got my card the next year and won a tournament. Now, I have a great job, and I'm really enjoying myself."

"You're sure playing good," Harley said. He spoke in a slow Southern country drawl, a good-ole-boy accent.

"Are you in this tournament?" Tony said.

"I am," Harley said. "I'm even par. That's not going to be good enough for the national PGA, but I've enjoyed it so far. It's a great golf course. Anyway, I'll leave you-all to it. Just wanted to clear that up." Harley stood and offered his hand to Tony, and they shook. "Good luck out there."

"You, too," Tony said.

Harley turned and walked away.

"Well," I said, "that was interesting."

"It certainly was," Tony said.

"Want to share the rest of the story?"

"Sure," Tony said.

We ordered another round of beer, and the story began. It went like this:

A young Tony Price sat in the locker room reviewing the nightmare that was the last day of tour school the first time he tried for his playing card. A single stroke had separated Tony from his dream of getting his card and competing on the PGA Tour. To make matters worse, the guy who won the last spot, Harley Dobbs, had cheated to get it; his caddie had, no doubt, improved Harley's lie on the seventeenth hole when he thought no one was looking, then lied about it when Tony turned him in.

"Are you sure about what you saw?" the tour school director had asked Tony.

"Positive," Tony said. "I saw the lie on the way to my ball. I hit first. When I walked back across the fairway, his lie was greatly improved. And before that, I saw his caddie moving his feet around in the rough near the ball."

"I talked to the player and his caddie," the director said. "Of course, they both deny it. For what it's worth, I believe you, but it's your word against theirs, and it looks bad for you because he got the last spot. There is really nothing I can do."

So, Tony had sat and pondered his fate, then packed his gear for the trip home. He had an assistant pro job waiting at a Knoxville country club. The pay wasn't great, but thanks to the extra money from giving lessons and the free golf, it wasn't bad either. He had given himself one chance at earning a tour card. Now, he would go back home and take the job.

As he packed, he noticed the surreptitious looks he was receiving from some of the players. They probably think I'm a rat, he thought. He didn't care. Cheaters did not belong in the game. He took his time cleaning out his locker, and as he did the clubhouse slowly emptied. Bobby Wilkins, a tour veteran, ambled over and sat down next to Tony. Bobby was trying to regain his card after an injury-filled year that had not allowed him to play many tournaments. Tony and Bobby had been paired in an early round.

"Tough day, huh?" Bobby asked.

"I've had better," Tony said.

"Heard you caught Harley improving his lie," Bobby said. "Turned his cheatin' ass in."

"It was either him or his caddie," Tony said. "Probably his caddie."

"Same thing," Bobby said. "Harley's responsible for that dumbass brother of his."

"I didn't look so good turning in the guy who took my spot," Tony said. "But I saw what I saw."

"You did the right thing," Bobby said. "You'll get your card next year. Most of us out here didn't get it on our first try."

"There won't be a next year," Tony said. "I'm done. I have an assistant pro job waiting, and I'm going to take it."

"Well, good luck," Bobby said. "I hope you change your mind. I like your swing. I think you could make it out here."

They shook hands, and Bobby turned to leave.

"By the way," Tony asked, "did you get your card?"

"I did," Bobby said, smiling.

"I'll be rooting for you out there," Tony said. "Hit 'em straight."

The following year, Tony did change his mind and decided to try again. There was no drama; he easily qualified for his tour card. And the rest, as they say, is history.

9

I was up early the next morning having coffee and checking email. I had one from T. Elbert, and that was all. Lacy and I had enjoyed a lengthy conversation with Mary the night before, filling her in on how the day had gone. Mostly, it was Lacy and Mary. I got to say a few words, then Lacy took the phone, and that was that.

A rather loud knock tore me away from my computer. I opened the door to find Tony Price with a rather distraught look on his face.

"I've got a problem," he said. "I just got a call from Holston Hills. Somebody broke into the area where they store clubs and carts and took four sets of clubs, one being mine. They have offered me a brand-new set of clubs, but I can't go into the final round playing clubs I've never swung before."

"Do you have another set of clubs in Mountain Center?"

"Yes, in storage at the club—an old set, but I like them."

"Would they be your best choice?"

"Definitely," Tony said.

"Okay," I said. "Call Jeremy and have him get them ready. Think of anything else you might need that was in your bag. I'll arrange for them to be picked up."

My first thought was to have Rhonda drive them down. After all, she did work for me. Then I had a better thought.

◆ ◆ ◆ ◆

"I have an urgent assignment for you," I said. "Are you free?"

"As a bird," T. Elbert said.

"Okay, fire up the Black Beauty and get to the Mountain Center Country Club posthaste. Here's what I want you to do."

I hung up after explaining the details to T. Elbert. By that time, Lacy was out of the shower, dressed, and talking with Tony.

"Relax," I heard her say. "We've got plenty of time."

"I cannot believe somebody did this," Tony said.

"Don't worry," Lacy said. "It will work out."

Another knock on the door. I opened it, and in came Flip. Tony and Lacy took turns telling Flip the events of the last hour.

Flip shrugged and said, "So we wait on the clubs. Let's get some breakfast."

◆ ◆ ◆ ◆

Two hours later, T. Elbert arrived at Holston Hills with the clubs, and Tony, Flip, and Lacy went to the practice tee. T. Elbert accompanied me to meet the chief of security, Joe Pitts. Pitts was a big guy, probably twenty pounds overweight, with gray flecks in his short, dark hair and hazel eyes that were constantly looking around. *Ex-cop*, I thought. I introduced T. Elbert, and they shook hands.

"The FBI investigating stolen golf clubs now, Youngblood?" Pitts said.

"Maybe," I said. "What can you tell me?"

"Two perps, I'd guess, each taking two bags. They cut the lock with bolt cutters. It wasn't a real serious lock, so it wouldn't have been much of a challenge."

"Did all the clubs belong to tournament players?" I said.

"No," Pitts said. "Two were members."

"Who was the other player?"

He flipped open a notebook. "The players were Tony Price and Harry Jones," he said.

I didn't know who Harry Jones was, but I was betting he had no connection to Tony Price. The theft appeared to be a random act of bad luck.

"Okay, thanks," I said. "My guess is that those clubs are gone for good."

"My guess, too," he said.

◆ ◆ ◆ ◆

T. Elbert and I went to the Men's Grill. A text from Lacy let me know that she, Tony, and Flip were still on the practice tee and that Tony was hitting fine with his old clubs.

"Want something to eat before you go back?" I said.

"Sure," T. Elbert said, looking at a menu.

He finally settled on a cheeseburger with fries and a Coke. I noticed they had Yuengling on tap, so I ordered a pint. While we waited, I told T. Elbert the twenty-year-old story of how Tony had failed in his attempt to secure his tour card. He listened intently. By the time I finished, T. Elbert was halfway through his cheeseburger and fries.

"What are you going to do now?" he asked.

"At one o'clock, I'm going to go out and root for Tony and Lacy to win a spot in the PGA Professional Championship," I said. "Chasing down stolen golf clubs is not in my job description."

"Wish them luck," T. Elbert said. "I'll be heading back."

◆ ◆ ◆ ◆

I was on the tee with Flip at one o'clock, waiting for Tony to be announced. Lacy and Tony huddled off to the side trading whispers. Lacy said something, and Tony grinned. I looked at Flip.

"She has a knack for keeping him loose," he said.

Tony was announced, and Lacy handed him the driver. "Fairways and greens," she said.

He smiled and promptly laced his golf ball straight down the center of the first fairway. The last leg of their three-day journey had begun.

Fairways and greens—that's exactly what Tony did as he made tap-in pars on the first three holes. Then, on the 165-yard par-three fourth hole, Tony hit his tee shot twenty feet from the pin and sank the putt for a birdie. He was one under par. He stayed that way on the front nine. He found the rough twice, both times on par fives, and both times he recovered to make par. It was obvious that playing with his old clubs did not bother him. As we walked the course, I scanned the crowd for anyone who might look like a golf club thief, but no one stuck out.

Tony made the turn at one under. At number ten, he made a three-foot putt for another par. Then, on eleven, a par three, he hit to within fifteen feet and made his second birdie. He scrambled for par at twelve and made tap-in pars at thirteen, fourteen, and fifteen. At sixteen, he found the rough again, managed to get his second shot on the front edge, and two-putted for par. He capped the round with birdies on seventeen and eighteen, both par fives. He had posted a bogey-free four-under-par round. The leader board told it all. Tony Price was alone in fourth place at eight under par, with one group left to finish. His spot was secure. Tony and Lacy were going to the PGA Professional Championship in Florida next May.

Flip and I shook hands with Tony as he headed to the scorer's table.

"I'll be awhile," he said as he passed us.

"Take your time," I said.

"I'm going to take Tony's clubs to the SUV," Lacy said.

"Good job out there today," Flip said.

"Thanks," Lacy said. "I hope I helped a little."

"You did, young lady," Flip said. "And your guy was solid."

As I scanned the leader board, I saw there was a four-way tie for the fifth and final spot for the national tournament. One of the names I recognized: Harley Dobbs.

Then I heard the announcement: "Ladies and gentlemen, there will be a four-way playoff for the fifth and final spot for the PGA Professional Championship. The playoff will start in ten minutes on hole number one."

◆ ◆ ◆

An hour later, we were packed up and on the road. Lacy and Tony were in the backseat replaying the round shot by shot for Flip, as if he hadn't been there. He listened patiently. *How can they remember all of them?* I wondered.

"Fourth place paid three thousand dollars," Tony told Lacy. "You get ten percent of that."

"You keep it," Lacy said. "I have a rich father."

"No way," Tony said. "You're taking it. I could not have done it without you."

Flip turned in his seat. "Take it, young lady, and be proud to get it."

"Yes, sir," Lacy said. "I'll buy something special."

"I cannot believe how much I love those old clubs," I heard Tony say.

"What's not to love?" Lacy said. "We're going to the PGA Professional Championship."

10

Thursday night, Lacy and I took Flip to Tri-Cities Airport to catch a late flight back to Wisconsin. He promised to see us at the next tournament. By the time we got back to the condo, Mary was asleep. By the time I got up the next morning, she was hugging Lacy goodbye and was off to work.

Back at Tri-Cities Airport, an agent I knew let me through security with Lacy. "You carrying, Mr. Youngblood?" the agent said, wanting to know if I had a sidearm.

"No," I said, "not today."

"Can I see some ID, just to cover my butt?"

"Sure." I flashed my FBI creds.

"Great," he said. "Go on through."

Lacy's flight was called as we approached her gate. We stopped in front of the open door that led to the ramp.

"You need to check out the Arizona State golf team," I said.

"I'm way ahead of you, Dad," she said. "I intend to do just that."

"I don't know much about golf, but I know a hell of a lot more than I did before. I had a great time out there. You were awesome."

"Don't get all mushy on me," she said. "I love you, too. I'll see you at Thanksgiving."

She gave me a hug, then a kiss on the cheek, and she was through the door and down the ramp without looking back. *So much like Mary*, I thought. As usual, I went to the observation deck and did not leave until her plane was no longer visible. Afterward, I drove to the club and its lunch celebration for Tony Price. I wasn't going to miss that.

Maybe sixty people were there, a lot of them employees of the club and male and female members who played golf. People were already going through the buffet line. A head table had been set up, and Tony had told me he wanted me there with his wife, the president of the club, and Harvey Shine, the general manager.

When it appeared that everyone had just about finished their food, the president tapped on his water glass with a spoon to get their attention. The glass shattered, which drew a few chuckles before the room became quiet. "They don't make 'em like they used to," he said. More chuckles. "We are here today to acknowledge a first-ever achievement by any Mountain Center Country Club head pro. For those of you who have been locked in a closet or otherwise indisposed, Tony has qualified for the PGA Professional Championship this coming May, with a chance to win a berth in the PGA Championship." Loud applause turned into a standing ovation. "Tony, we are very proud," the president said.

Tony stood briefly. "Thank you," he said. "It was an honor to represent Mountain Center Country Club." He sat down.

"And now," the president said, "a few brief words from an eyewitness, Donald Youngblood, whose daughter, Lacy, caddied for Tony during the three- day event."

I stood. "As many of you know, I'm not a golfer," I said. "I've often wondered about the insanity of hitting a little white ball as far as you can and then going after it, only to hit it again. But my daughter loves golf, and the last few days I spent watching her caddie for Tony gave me a deeper understanding of, and a grudging appreciation for, the game. Tony was rock solid. Only five spots were available to move on to the next tournament, and he nailed down one of them by finishing fourth. You should be very proud of your pro."

I sat down to more applause. One by one, the gathering started to break up. Many guests came by the head table to offer Tony congratulations. I patted him on the back, whispered, "See you soon," and slipped away.

◆ ◆ ◆ ◆

Late that afternoon, I picked up Jake and Junior at our condo and went to the lake house. I could tell the dogs were excited; they knew exactly where we were going. Mary would be along later with pizza, a most-of-the-time Friday tradition. I turned Jake and Junior loose in the side yard. They seemed to be as happy to be there as I was. The grass had made a comeback from the fire. I had spent a lot of my downtime cleaning up around the lake house. The trees were still running behind the grass as far as recovering, and those that could not recover I had cut down. Still, nature was fighting back.

The house looked basically the same inside but still had that smell new homes have when you first move in. The layout was the same, but the furniture was different, a compromise Mary and I both could live with. I was just getting comfortable with being there again. I went out the back door, descended the stairs to the lower deck, and continued down the stairs to the dock. I walked to the end of the dock and, like the village idiot, said, "Hello, lake, I've been missing you." The lake, smarter than I was, remained silent. The day was cooling, and the gentle breeze carried the scent of fall. I looked at the colors across the lake, where the fires had not reached. As always at that time of year, they were spectacular. I had moments in Afghanistan when I thought I would not make it home. I stood there in the silence, gave thanks, and took it all in. I was smart enough to know that I still had a fragile psyche from my brush with death, and that it would take time to heal my mind. I stood until I heard tires on gravel and knew Mary had arrived.

We sat around the island in the kitchen and had a predinner glass of red wine called The One, a full-bodied California red blend bottled by Noble Vines.

"I love this red," Mary said.

"What you love is the fifteen-percent alcohol level."

"That, too," Mary said. "Did you check on Lacy's flight?"

"On the ground," I said. "She texted me. Biker picked her up."

"Good daddy," Mary said. "There will be a reward later."

"I should hope so."

"Now, tell me all about this golf tournament," Mary said. "I really wanted to be there, but Big Bob would have had a cow. I want to hear about our daughter's caddying experience."

"You would have been very proud. Lacy was terrific, and Tony said she had a lot to do with the way he played."

I spent a whole bottle of wine telling the story. I talked, which slowed down my drinking; Mary listened, consuming two-thirds of the bottle. We opened another bottle and transitioned into the pizza and a Caesar salad, which I had tossed while continuing my story. By the time we finished dinner, we were really relaxed.

"Dessert is upstairs," Mary said. "Want it now?"

"Is the Pope Catholic?" I said.

11

We enjoyed one of those glorious fall weekends reserved especially for East Tennessee. Mary and I spent most of the time on the lake puttering on our houseboat, which had miraculously escaped the fire. I fished, and Mary sunned and swam. The water was cold, but she didn't care.

"Come on in, you chicken," she said Sunday afternoon. "It's great once you get used to it."

"I'll pass," I said.

I was happy listening to a Titans game and catching the occasional smallmouth bass. I drank beer and ate sandwiches of Mary's homemade tarragon chicken salad with sliced, toasted almonds. I munched on Doritos, a sinful pleasure I indulged in once in a blue moon. Life was good. As the sun was going down and the temperature cooling, we made our way back to the lake house.

"Why don't you take the week off, and we'll do this every day?" I said.

"Great thought," she said, "but I cannot do that to Big Bob. I've had a lot of time off this year, and he's been a good sport about it. You'll have to tough it out without me."

"No way," I said. "I need to get to the office and see what's going on."

12

I drove in early Monday morning, parked in the back lot, and walked up the back stairs, my calf and hip reminding me that I had been shot earlier in the year. I drank coffee and ate a blueberry muffin I had picked up on my way. I went online to check email, news headlines, sports, and weather while waiting for Gretchen and Rhonda to arrive. They were both in before nine. Rhonda left almost immediately to do a surveillance job. Gretchen came into my office a few minutes later for our morning meeting.

"Exciting news about Tony Price," she said. "I read it in the paper."

"Being there was even more exciting," I said. "I got to follow them around inside the ropes."

"He gave Lacy a lot of credit," Gretchen said.

"Well deserved, I think."

"Proud daddy," Gretchen said.

"Just a little," I said.

"Uh-huh."

"So, tell me what's going on," I said.

"Not much," Gretchen said. "Rhonda's got a lot of work from Rollie, and I'm looking into a runaway daughter for a friend of a friend. I suspect she ran off with her boyfriend and they'll surface soon."

"Need help with that?" I said.

"No," Gretchen said. "Get you own case."

"I would if you'd quit intercepting all of them."

"You're the big gun," Gretchen said. "We're saving you for the big cases."

◆ ◆ ◆ ◆

Later that morning, my intercom buzzed.

"The man on line two will not give his name," Gretchen said. "He said that his father is a friend of Joseph Fleet, and that Joseph Fleet recommended he call you."

"I'll take it," I said. I waited thirty seconds and then picked up. "Don Youngblood. Can I help you?"

"I certainly hope you can, Mr. Youngblood," the male voice said. "You come highly recommended. My name is Jason Gildersleeve."

"As in Congressman Jason Gildersleeve?"

"Yes," he said.

Jason Gildersleeve was an up-and-comer in the Republican Party. He was in his early forties, a good-looking Ivy Leaguer and a great communicator. The press thought him to be a rising star. The Senate and maybe even the White House could be in his future. He had just announced a Senate run for next year. I wondered if he was looking for a campaign donation.

"Let me guess," I said. "You don't want to come to the office, and you don't want to discuss this over the phone."

"Looks like I have the right man for the job," the congressman said.

"Can you give me a one-word clue as to what this is about?"

"Blackmail," he said.

◆ ◆ ◆ ◆

We met that same day for an early dinner at the Mountain Center Country Club. The congressman had chartered a plane and flown into Tri-Cities Airport in time to arrive at the club by five o'clock. We sat at my favorite table in the corner overlooking the eighteenth green. At the moment, we had the place to ourselves. Our cover story would be, should anyone get curious, that he was soliciting funds for his senatorial run.

We had ordered drinks that had just arrived: a martini for the congressman and an AmberBock for me. The congressman picked up his martini and gestured toward me. "To your health," he said.

"And to yours," I said, raising my beer glass.

We drank.

"Now, tell me what this is all about," I said.

"I got this note in the mail," he said as he handed it to me. "It came with a video."

Jason,

We hate to do this but we need the money. Send $100,000 to the P.O. box or we release that old video to the press. You know the one we are referring to. Do this and you will never hear from us again. We promise!

The Twins

I looked at the envelope. The return address was a P.O. in Charleston, South Carolina. It was postmarked exactly one week ago from North Charleston. The congressman had wasted little time seeking help.

"Can I keep this?" I said.

"Does that mean you're helping me?"

"It does," I said, thankful to have something to sink my teeth into.

"Thank you," he said.

"So, you got the note and called your father. He called Joseph Fleet, and Fleet told him to tell you to call me," I said. "That about right?"

"Exactly," he said. "My father and Mr. Fleet go way back. He said you were the man to call. Joseph Fleet contributed heavily to my first campaign."

That did not surprise me. I knew that Joseph Fleet had his thumb on the pulse of the political scene. How much so, I wasn't sure, but I was beginning to feel it was more that I originally thought. He would not contribute heavily to a U.S. congressional campaign without expecting something in return.

"Tell me about the video," I said.

"The video is rather embarrassing. You can watch it if you want." He handed me a manila envelope.

"So, it's sexual in content," I said.

He nodded.

"I need to hear it from you. I'll watch it later if I think I need to."

He took a rather large gulp of his martini. "I met the twins at Princeton at the beginning of my senior year," he began. "Jessica and

Jennifer Johnson: pretty, sexy, spoiled, wild, and from a wealthy family. You've heard of Augustus H. Johnson & Sons."

"I have," I said.

"Well, the current Augustus is the third, and he sired one son and the twins," the congressman continued. "Anyway, I was a party animal, and one night at this party I was pretty high and the twins pulled me away and asked if I'd like to go back to their place with them. Maybe sober, I would have said no. I thought one girl at a time was enough for me. But I was far from sober, so I said yes, and let me tell you, it was a night to remember."

"They made the video that night?"

"No, the video came later," the congressman said. "I didn't see them for a while, and then one of them called and asked if I wanted to get together again. I said sure. I mean, you should have seen these girls—*Playboy* quality. Anyway, I go over that night, and we drink and do some coke, and then one of them says, 'Let's make a video.' I'm three sheets to the wind, so I say sure, and we make it. They have it all set up and ready to go, and some girl comes in to shoot it, so that was their plan all along. I watch it now and I'm disgusted and excited at the same time. But the twins, they were really something."

We finished our drinks and ordered another round. I could see his problem. Even though the video was twenty years old, the press would have a field day—goodbye, Senate seat, maybe.

The congressman took a drink from his second martini.

"Did you watch the whole video?"

"No," he said. "A few minutes, and I had to turn it off. I had almost forgotten what I looked like back then: long hair, beard. That was the Princeton look back in the day."

"How about after the video? Did you see them again?"

"I never heard from them again," he said. "A few weeks later, I tried to call a cell-phone number I had, but service had been discontinued. Then I heard they were expelled from school."

"But at the time, you never had any blowback from the video?"

"None," he said.

"Did you ever have a copy of the video?"

"No. I was supposed to get one, but I never did. I really wanted one at the time because it was, you know, erotic, and I was kind of proud of my performance."

I took a drink of beer and processed what he had told me.

"Should I pay?" he said.

"No. That would look like you have something to hide, that you think what you did, even though it was in private, was wrong. You were of legal age, so what you did sexually behind closed doors was your business. Unless, of course, you decide to run for the Senate. If worse comes to worst, your position should be, 'I was young and stupid and a product of the day. I am a different person now, and I will be a great senator for the state of Tennessee.'"

Jason Gildersleeve smiled. "Want to be my campaign manager?"

"I think you're better off if I remain your private investigator," I said.

"What should I do?"

"Nothing," I said. "Let me look into this."

"If they don't get the money, they might release the video," he said.

"I doubt it. If they do that, they have no chance of getting paid. You will probably get at least one or two more notes before they give up. By that time, I'll have found them and put a stop to it."

"Do you really think you can?"

"I do," I said. "I have resources. Besides, blackmail is a federal offense. That will give me leverage to stop it. I can threaten jail time."

"I've read a lot about you, Mr. Youngblood," Congressman Gildersleeve said. "I know you're a smart guy. In your opinion, could my campaign for the Senate survive this video?"

"Well, more than one politician has survived a sex scandal," I said. "So, yes, I think it could. You'll have to spin it the right way. You might even be able to benefit from it. If your opponents dwell on it too much, it might backfire on them. How would your wife react?"

"My wife knew about the twins before we were married," he said. "She's a spitfire. She would give the press hell about dragging up twenty-year-old dirt. It's my daughters I worry about. They are thirteen and fifteen. My father image would take a serious blow."

"No need to worry about that yet," I said. "I really think I can make this go away, unless there is something you're not telling me."

"I've told you everything," the congressman said. "It would be dumb not to."

◆ ◆ ◆ ◆

That night at the kitchen bar in our condo, I told Mary the whole story. We were waiting for Chinese takeout delivery. Congressman Gildersleeve had finished his second drink and gone back to the airport. A limo had been waiting for him in the country club parking lot. I promised to update him when I had news. I finally had a case that might be interesting.

"Let's watch the video," Mary said.

"I don't think so," I said.

"Why not? He said the girls were hot."

"Because I just met the guy, and I'd feel like a sleaze watching him getting it on with two college girls."

"Prude," Mary said, feigning a pout.

I was sure she was teasing me, but not completely sure. Mary was sexually adventurous. "You watch it," I said. "Maybe you can learn something."

"Not without you," she said. "That wouldn't be any fun."

I shook my head and said nothing.

"How about I show you some fun upstairs?" Mary said.

"Just the two of us?"

"Well," Mary said, "I could invite Wanda. She's been after me for years to do a threesome."

"Let's leave Wanda out of this," I said.

"Let's," said Mary. "I'm not good at sharing."

13

The next day, I went online searching for the form required to rent a post office box. I was curious as to how much personal information was required. Quite a bit, if I remembered correctly. I found it and printed it. I was interested in line eight: Forms of ID. The post office required one photo ID and one non-photo ID. A driver's license was the most common form of photo ID, and a voter or vehicle registration card the most common form of non-photo ID. A Social Security number was not required.

The easiest way of finding out who had rented the P.O. box in Charleston was using my connection with the FBI. I called David Steele. He was in a meeting. I left a message for him to call me back. I had just hung up when I heard the outer office door open and close.

"I'm in," Gretchen said seconds later over the intercom.

"So noted," I said, pushing the respond button. "Come in when you get settled."

A few minutes later, my intercom buzzed again.

"David Steele on line one," Gretchen said.

I picked up. "Thanks for calling me back, Dave."

"I don't like the sound of this already," he said. "You are, no doubt, feeling better and into something."

"Maybe," I said.

"Maybe from you always seems to mean a shitstorm," David Steele said. "What is it this time?"

"It's highly confidential," I said. "If I share more with you, it will have to be off the record."

"Give me a one-line teaser," he said.

"Blackmail of a U.S. congressman."

There was dead air for a few moments. Then David Steele said, "Okay, you have my attention. How do you do it, Youngblood? How do you manage to have these cases drop right on your doorstep?"

"Just lucky," I said. "Anyway, I'd like to pursue this on the fringes for now, without an official sanction from you. I might need John Banks to run down a few things after hours, if that's okay. I may be able to resolve this quickly. If it blows up, you can take me off medical leave and assign it as an active case, with Buckley as the lead agent."

"All right," David Steele said. "I'll let Scott Glass know that you're working something in the shadows and might need a thing or two from John. You keep me posted, Youngblood. There was a time when I was such a by-the-books guy that I would have never agreed to this. You have surely corrupted me."

"Yeah, but we get things done, don't we, Dave?"

"We do indeed, but I was hoping you would take more time before setting off on another adventure."

"I've had all the time off I can stand, Dave," I said. "I haven't been this happy in weeks."

♦ ♦ ♦ ♦

Ten minutes later, Gretchen came in and positioned herself in front of my desk with pad and pen. "I detect a new case in your future," she said.

"And in my present. I need for you to do some research on Jennifer and Jessica Johnson. They're twin daughters of Augustus H. Johnson III."

"The business tycoon?" Gretchen said.

"Yes."

"I'll get right on it. Anything else?"

"No," I said. "You?"

"Not now," Gretchen said.

♦ ♦ ♦ ♦

That afternoon, Gretchen was back in front of my desk.

"What have you got?"

"Sad news," Gretchen said. "Jennifer Johnson was killed in an auto accident two years ago. Jessica was driving. She was drunk. No charges were ever filed against her."

"The old man's influence," I said.

"Maybe they felt killing her twin sister was enough punishment," Gretchen said.

"Good point."

"The only thing I could find on Jessica after the accident was a couple of minor drug busts and a DUI," Gretchen said. "Looks like self-punishment to me."

"Maybe," I said. "Or maybe she's just self-destructive. Nothing else on her?"

"She and her sister grew up in Boston. Private school, prep school, and then Princeton. Really smart, good students, but wild, I guess. Got expelled from Princeton, then got back in and graduated. No early trouble with the law that I could find."

I nodded and said nothing.

"Anything else?" Gretchen said.

"How is Cherokee Investigations doing? Financially, I mean."

"Our financial status report is in your in-box," she said. "I suggest you read it."

"Cliff Notes," I said.

"We're fine."

"Thank you," I said. "You're dismissed."

She laughed, saluted, and went back to the outer office.

◆ ◆ ◆ ◆

I was shutting down when I heard the phone ring in the outer office. Murphy's law. The ringer was turned off in my office, but the line-one light was blinking. Caller ID showed an 801-area code. I recognized the number.

"Youngblood," I answered.

"How are you doing, Youngblood?" John Banks said. "I heard you were shot a few times."

"I'm fine, John," I said. "Thanks for asking."

"I hear you have an off-the-books case that I might be of some help with."

"No heavy lifting, John," I said. "Putty in your hands."

"Lay it on me," he said.

I gave him the post office box number in Charleston. "I need to find out who rented that box. Can you do that?"

"Child's play," John said. "I'll email it to you in a few minutes. What else?"

"Once you identify who rented the box, get as much information on him or her as you can."

"I can do that, too," John said. "Anything else?"

"How about the numbers for the next Powerball drawing?"

"That," John laughed, "will take just a little more time."

I resisted the urge to hang around and wait for the information. It would keep 'til morning. I went home to my wife and dogs.

14

The first thing I did the next morning was check my email. Sure enough, there was one from John Banks. It read,

> Post office box was rented by Harold Keen, a 23-year-old student at the College of Charleston. Keen paid for the box with a check from his personal checking account. The next day, there was a $500 cash deposit into the same account. If I was the great Donald

Youngblood, I might deduce that Keen was paid to rent the box. Further digging found that Keen is a better-than-average student in his chosen field of journalism. He has had a few minor busts for drug possession—pot and pills. I'm working on a current address and photo ID. Let me know if you need anything else.

I replied to John,

Not bad for an FBI geek. The great Donald Youngblood thinks your deduction skills are right on. You deserve a raise. Good luck with that!

I sat and pondered my next move. Normally, I or someone else would sit on the P.O. box waiting for our target to open it. But since I would probably know where Harold Keen lived, I might just go there and ask him what was going on. If I waved the note in front of his nose, showed him my FBI creds, and mentioned blackmail, I was sure he would sing like a canary. On the other hand, someone would surely be checking the box every day for a big payout. I bet Keen had specific instructions on what to do if there was a notification slip to pick up something at the counter. I decided to go to Charleston and bait the trap.

◆ ◆ ◆

That night in our condo, Mary and I were sitting at the kitchen bar and reviewing our day. We were also reviewing an excellent bottle of Cabernet Sauvignon. Reviews for the wine were positive, but Mary's day had been boringly routine. I shared my email from John Banks.
"Good info," Mary said. "Nice to have that kind of access."
"Sometimes, John likes to show off, and I let him," I said. "Never hurts to stroke the troops."
"So, what's your plan?" Mary said, pouring the rest of the wine into her glass.

"Go to Charleston and sit on the box," I said. "Want to come?"

"Will you stroke me if I do?" Mary said in her best Marilyn Monroe.

"You can count on it, Doll," I said in my best Bogie.

15

Big Bob acquiesced to one day off, so Mary and I embarked for Charleston early that Friday. She was thrilled to visit the place that *Southern Living* magazine called the number-one city in the South. Thanks to John Banks, I had Harold Keen's address and photo ID, along with a surprise package for the P.O. box.

We made Charleston in five hours and, early that afternoon, checked into a suite at the Renaissance Hotel on Wentworth. I left Mary reading brochures and headed for the post office on East Bay Street. I knew it was the right one by the zip code written on the envelope containing the blackmail note. I arrived a few minutes after three o'clock carrying my special package, a purple box filled with cut paper and weighing what a hundred thousand dollars in twenty-dollar bills might. The place was moderately busy, with two windows open. An agent at a third window had his head down in paperwork. A small placard in front of him read, *Closed.* I went to him and said in a low voice, "Excuse me."

"This window is closed," he said, never looking up.

"I can see that," I said, continuing to keep my voice low. "I need to see the postmaster."

He looked up. "Regarding?"

I flashed my FBI creds. I now had his undivided attention. "Confidential."

"One minute, please, Agent Youngblood."

The man pays attention, I thought.

They were back in thirty seconds. The postmaster turned out to be a postmistress, and a fetching one at that. She pointed to a door on my right, and I nodded. I went through the door, and she was waiting on the other side.

"Agent Youngblood," she said, "I'm Margie Thomas."

"Nice to meet you, Miss Thomas," I said. She didn't correct me, so I assumed she was single—no ring on the third finger of her left hand.

"This way, please," she said.

I followed her back to her office, admiring her curvy figure as we went. She was about five-foot-four and had dark hair, a pretty face, and a seductive walk that I'm sure she was quite aware of. She went around behind her desk.

"Please sit," she said.

I sat down. She sat down.

"Now, what's this all about?" she asked in a voice that was Southern-girl sexy.

For a second, I almost forgot why I was there, but I recovered nicely. "This is extremely confidential," I said. "For your ears only."

"My ears are open, and my lips are sealed," she said.

Sure they are, I thought. "I assume that you have all your mail and package notices in your P.O. boxes by eleven o'clock or so. That about right?"

"Our goal is ten o'clock," she said.

"Even better," I said, handing her the purple box. "I need a notice put in this P.O. box for this package first thing in the morning. I'll be glad to pay postage."

"That won't be necessary," Margie Thomas said. "We are happy to cooperate with the FBI."

"The FBI appreciates your cooperation," I said. "If the package hasn't been picked up in a week, throw it out. Nothing is in it but cut paper."

◆ ◆ ◆ ◆

That evening, Mary and I walked a few blocks to Hank's Restaurant on Hayne Street. Darkness had settled in, but the evening was pleasant, with just the hint of a breeze. The lights of the historic district gave the city an even more magical feel than it possessed in daylight. We held hands as we walked, a couple of tourists in love, without a care in the world.

"Perfect evening," Mary said, mesmerized. "Let's go for a long walk after dinner."

"Good idea," I said. "We'll need it."

We had a table for two by the window. I had gone by earlier and slipped the maître d' a twenty to make sure it happened. He was only too happy to accommodate.

We ordered a bottle of their most expensive Chardonnay to go with an appetizer of fried shrimp and calamari. I ordered a fried seafood platter for my entrée, and Mary had the pan-seared sea scallops. I drank beer with dinner, and Mary finished the bottle. For dessert, we shared a slice of pecan pie. Our waiter disappeared and reappeared as if reading our minds. The entire experience was five-star.

Afterward, we strolled all the way down Church Street, turned left on Water Street, and walked down to Charleston Harbor. We continued down East Bay Street to where it became Murray Boulevard and kept going, enjoying the cool night air. At Ashley Avenue, we turned right and headed north to Wentworth. A right on Wentworth led us back to the Renaissance Hotel. Saying it was a long walk would be an understatement, but we sure did get to see plenty of nighttime Charleston.

When we were finally inside the hotel, Mary said, "Let's have a nightcap, and then I'll take you to our suite and remind you why you married me, Cowboy."

No mortal man could resist that invitation, so I smiled, nodded, and said, "Your humble servant awaits, ma'am."

16

The next day, we sat in the East Bay post office parking lot with a clear view of the door. I knew what Harold Keen looked like, and I doubted any other purple boxes were being picked up from a P.O. box.

Harold Keen showed up at eleven o'clock. He was driving a blue Prius. He parked in front and went inside. Harold was about five-foot-eight, with a slight build and blond hair. He wore glasses and looked every bit the college student.

"That's him," I said.

He was inside for about five minutes and then came out empty handed. He got in his Prius and drove away.

"Now what?" Mary said.

"We wait," I said.

We waited until the window closed.

"What's going on?" Mary asked.

"I think I outsmarted myself," I said. "Let's go talk to Harold."

◆ ◆ ◆ ◆

Harold lived in an apartment complex in North Charleston. His six-floor building looked relatively new and was located in a decent neighborhood.

"Wonder how Harold is paying for this?" Mary said.

"Let's go ask," I said. "He's on four."

We timed it so that we followed another tenant in, an older, well-dressed woman. She gave us the evil eye. "Where is your swipe card?" she said.

"We don't need one," I said. "We're here on official FBI business." I flashed my creds.

"Oh, my," she said, getting flustered. "Is someone in trouble?"

"No, no," Mary said. "Nothing like that. It's just routine."

We got on the elevator together. The woman punched three and looked at me.

"Six, please," I said.

She smiled and punched six, and the elevator door shut. When she got off at the third floor, she said, "Have a nice day."

As the door shut, I pushed the button for the fourth floor.

Mary laughed. "You are bad," she said. "Now, she'll spend the rest of the day trying to figure out who on six is in trouble with the FBI."

"It will give her something to do," I said.

"Probably make her day," Mary said.

◆ ◆ ◆ ◆

Apartment 4F was at the end of the hall. I stayed back while Mary knocked on the door. I had no idea how she was going to handle this. Mary stood back from the peephole so Harold could get a good look.

"Yes," we heard from the other side of the door.

"Harold Keen?"

"Yes. Who are you?"

"My name is Mary, and I'm helping with a poll on the upcoming presidential election. I just need to ask you a few questions, Harold. We are not asking for a donation or anything like that, just a few questions about who you would vote for and why."

"Hang on," Harold said.

We heard a chain slide, and then the door opened. Mary stood there in jeans and a tank top, blond hair in a ponytail and a big smile on her face. If I were Harold, my heart would have leapt.

"Come on in," he said. "You can call me Harry."

Mary went in, and before Harry could shut the door, I slipped in behind her.

"Wait just a minute," Harry said. "Who the hell is this?"

I had my cred out and in his face. "FBI, Mr. Keen, Agents Youngblood and Sanders," I said. *Courtesy is all.* "Answer a few questions, and we'll be on our way and you'll be free and clear."

"Shit," Harry said. "It's about that damn post office box, isn't it?"

"How did you know?" I said.

"I knew something was hinky about that," he said. "No one pays that kind of money to someone just to open a P.O. box and watch it."

"Who paid what?" Mary asked.

"Some dude," Harry Keen said. "I never saw him. Paid me five hundred dollars to open the box and promised a hundred more every week."

"How did you get hooked up with him?" I said.

"Through school. There's a bulletin board in the business building. People post all kinds of things on it—job offers, things to sell, like that. I check it every morning because I figure that's when people will put stuff out. So, early one morning, there's this note with a phone number for a part-time job that's not physical. Easy money. So I call the number." Harry paused and looked from Mary to me.

"Go on," Mary said. "What did the dude say?"

"He said he would pay five hundred to open a P.O. box and a hundred a week for checking it."

"Weren't you suspicious?" I said.

"Sure," Harry said. "I asked him why he would do that, and he said he was going through a divorce and would be receiving mail that he didn't want his wife or her attorney to be able to find. I asked why he couldn't do that himself, and he said that his wife had hired a private investigator who was following him around. It sounded reasonable, so I said sure."

"How did you receive the initial payment?" Mary said.

"He put it in my mailbox," Harry said.

"So he knows where you live," I said.

"Is that a problem?" he said.

"Might be," Mary said.

Harry looked a little shook.

"What was the drill?" I said.

"Check the box every day as close to eleven in the morning as I could," Harry said. "Some days, my classes would cause me to be as late as noon. It hasn't been that long since I rented it."

"Then what?" Mary said.

We were working well, ping-ponging him back and forth.

"If something was in the box, I was to call and tell him what it was," he said. "Today was the first day anything's been in the box. I called and told him there was a notice that said there was a package too large for the box. He told me to get the package. So I did. He asked what it looked like, and I told him it was a purple box, and he said, 'Shit.' Then he told me to open the box, and there was just cut paper inside. He said to throw it away and get the hell out of there and make sure that I wasn't followed. He said to call him when I got back to my apartment. I called when I got back here, and he asked me if I was sure I hadn't been followed, and I said I was sure. Then he said the job was over and to keep my mouth shut. Did you guys follow me?"

"No," I said. "We had your address."

"How?"

"Your address was on the form you filled out to rent the box, remember?"

"Oh, yeah," he said. "But how did you know the box number?"

"We're the FBI," I said. "We know everything."

That seemed to satisfy him, and he stopped asking questions.

"Give me the number you used to call this guy," Mary said. "And include your personal cell-phone number."

Harry wrote the numbers on a notepad, tore off the top sheet, and handed it to Mary. I gave Harry one of my FBI cards with my cell-phone number on it.

"Did you ever find out this guy's name?" I said.

"No."

"Did you ask?"

"Yes," Harry said. "He said it wasn't important, that I was better off not knowing because of the divorce."

I nodded and looked at Mary. "Anything else, Agent Sanders?"

"I think that about covers it, Agent Youngblood," Mary said.

I looked at Harry Keen. "Be careful about what jobs you take in the future, Mr. Keen."

"I will," he said. "I certainly will."

We walked out of Harry Keen's apartment and heard his door shut behind us. As we went toward the elevator, Mary said, "Well, that was fun, Agent Youngblood."

"It certainly was, Agent Sanders," I said.

◆ ◆ ◆ ◆

We had dinner that night in a restaurant called Slightly North of Broad. The ambiance was better than Hank's and the food superb. I had gone by earlier and arranged for another quiet table in a corner. We ordered a bottle of French Chardonnay and shared the honey-glazed ribs appetizer. Mary had rack of lamb for her main course, and I had shrimp and grits. We skipped dessert and went for a long walk instead.

Back at the Renaissance, Mary went to bed with her current book, and I went into the living area to call John Banks. With the two-hour time difference, I knew it wasn't too late for him.

"Agent Youngblood," he answered. "What can I do for you?"

"Sorry to bother you on a Saturday, John."

"Not a problem," he said. "What's up?"

"I need you to run a cell-phone number for me," I said. "Email it to me later tonight or early tomorrow if you will, please. I'd bet it's a burner phone, but I have to check. If it's not a burner, get me the name and address of the user."

"Will do," he said. "Where are you?"

"In Charleston, South Carolina, with Mary," I said.

"Nice," John said. "I'll be in touch."

17

I was in the office early the following Monday, and Mary was back to work. We had slept in Sunday morning, starting the day off with a bang—Mary's words, not mine. Then we had brunch at Poogan's Porch on Queen Street, returned to the hotel, packed up, and drove back to Mountain Center.

I was sitting at my desk drinking coffee and eating a bacon, egg, and cheese wrap while reading the latest edition of the *Mountain Center Press*. I was reading the police blotter to see if anything interesting had happened while we were away. A man had been beaten unconscious by three other men in the parking lot of the Bloody Duck early Sunday morning. Witnesses said the altercation was, no big surprise, over a woman. The victim was taken to the hospital, while the three suspects fled the scene. The sheriff's department was investigating. Elsewhere, a woman's car was hit by a pickup truck in the Walmart parking lot. The pickup fled the scene, but the woman got the license plate number, and the driver was arrested a few hours later. At the Mountain Center Mall, a man was found passed out in the men's room. Police who investigated found pills in his possession, and he was arrested on drug charges. There were other stories, too, sad or funny, depending on your point of view, that reflected a typical Saturday night for the Mountain Center Police Department. As Big Bob often said, "You can't make this shit up."

Late Saturday night, John Banks had confirmed by email what I expected: the number given to me by Harry Keen came from a burner phone. The burner was purchased at a Walmart in Mount Pleasant, South Carolina. John's attempt to trace it had failed. It was probably at the bottom of the Cooper River by now. I had reached a dead end and would need to turn around and go in a different direction. I sat there drinking coffee and thinking about my next move. I pulled up my contacts on my iPhone, found the one I wanted, and tapped the number.

"Don, how are you?" he said.

"I'm fine, sir," I said. "How are you?"

"Better than expected," Joseph Fleet said. "I'd bet you're working a case right now, for a congressman, maybe."

"You would be right," I said. "Thanks for sending him my way. I was getting bored."

"What can I do for you?" he said.

"Do you happen to know Augustus Johnson III?"

"The third I don't know. I do know his father. Why?"

"I'm looking for an introduction to the family," I said. "If I try to get in without an intro, I probably won't have much luck."

"I would agree," Joseph Fleet said. "But I'm not your guy. Gus Junior and I don't get along. We're on opposite sides of the political spectrum. You'll need to find another way."

"That's fine," I said. "I think I may have another option."

"Sorry I couldn't help, Don," he said. "See you at Thanksgiving?"

"Wouldn't miss it," I said.

◆ ◆ ◆ ◆

Lacy Malone had never known her father, and it was unclear whether or not her mother knew who her father was. Lacy came to live with us temporarily while I searched for her missing mother. I found her mother, who later died of a drug overdose that could have been accidental or on purpose. Lacy chose to see it as accidental, and who was I to argue? Lacy's temporary stay ended up being permanent, leading to an adoption and the emergence of Lacy Youngblood.

During my search for Lacy's mother, I had uncovered the possibility that Lacy's father most likely was John Cross Durbinfield, heir to a vast fortune. John's mother, Elizabeth Durbinfield, went to great lengths to learn if Lacy was her granddaughter. I went to great lengths to be sure she didn't find out. I didn't want Lacy involved with the Durbinfields in any way. When Lacy met Elizabeth, they immediately bonded and accepted each other as grandmother and granddaughter, DNA be damned. Lacy wanted a grandmother, and Elizabeth wanted a granddaughter. They had grown extremely close, and I was thankful for the relationship and glad that Mary and I had let it happen.

I called the Durbinfield residence in the Hamptons, got the butler, and identified myself. Seconds later, Elizabeth was on the phone.

"Don," she said, "is everything okay?"

"Everything is fine, Elizabeth," I said.

"Lacy told me about the golf tournament," she said. "How exciting."

"You would have been proud of her."

"I *am* very proud of her, Don," Elizabeth said. "That granddaughter of mine is one in a million."

"She is that," I said.

"How are you doing, Don? Lacy told me about your adventure in the Middle East. She said you were shot twice."

"I'm fine, Elizabeth. Thank you."

"That's good to hear, Don. Now, quit playing nice and tell me why you called."

"Do you know the family of Augustus Johnson III?"

"I do," she said. "Why do you ask?"

"I need to talk with the husband or the wife about the twins," I said. "Preferably the wife."

"You're working a case?"

"Yes."

"And you're aware that one of the twins was killed?"

"I am."

"Can you tell me what it's about?" Elizabeth said.

"Blackmail," I said.

"Ugly word," she said.

"Indeed. I would prefer you don't mention it."

"Of course not," she said, maybe slightly offended that I would think she would. "I'll see what I can do. I know Katie pretty well. She'll be too curious to say no."

"Let me know," I said.

"I'll call her as soon as we hang up," she said. "How soon can you be here?"

"Tomorrow."

"Let me know when, and I'll send a car. Pack an overnight. I want you to have dinner with me. There is some business we have to discuss."

"Dinner sounds good," I said.

◆ ◆ ◆ ◆

"What kind of business?" Mary said.

We were sitting at the kitchen bar in our downtown condo having our customary glass of wine. The days were getting shorter and cooler, and we had switched from white to red. In less than two weeks, daylight saving time would take a powder and it would get dark really early. I didn't mind, since I loved the winter.

"I don't know," I said. "I'm sure it involves Lacy, and I'm sure it's nothing bad. You can come if you like."

"Can't," Mary said. "I'm investigating that assault at the Bloody Duck."

"Did you talk to Rocky?" Rocky, a friend of Roy Husky's, owned the Duck.

"Yes," Mary said. "They close at two in the morning. The assault was at three."

"Any leads?"

"Too many," she said. "We're sifting through them. I should have it solved by the end of the week, but I need to stay on it."

"How is the victim doing?"

"Not well," Mary said. "When are these guys going to learn that nothing good happens after midnight?"

"Maybe never," I said, taking a sip of my wine.

18

The Youngblood luck was holding. Fleet Industries jet number one was not scheduled for a trip, so Jim Doak flew me to MacArthur Airport in Ronkonkoma on Long Island. We arrived in the early afternoon. Elizabeth Durbinfield's stretch limo was waiting on the tarmac with the trunk up. Her driver, a tall sandy-haired man in an expensive dark suit, was at the bottom of the stairs. He immediately took my overnight and backpack and stowed them in the trunk. He closed the lid a few inches, and it continued by itself until it was completely secure. Without a word, he opened the back door for me. I removed my tan cashmere blazer and slid inside. The door closed behind me.

Once we were clear of the tarmac and heading to the airport exit, the privacy glass slid down. "Mrs. Durbinfield requested that you call her when we leave the airport," he said. "I have instructions on where to take you now."

"Thank you," I said. "What is your name, please?"

"I am Charles Younger Cook," he said. "I go by Younger."

"Younger," I said. "How did you come by that?"

"My father didn't want a junior," he said. "In my family, my father is Charles the Older and I am Charles the Younger. My friends started calling me Younger in school, and it stuck."

"Interesting," I said. "Thank you. I'd better make that call now."

The privacy glass slid up and closed tight, and I punched in Elizabeth Durbinfield's number. I got the butler, of course, and then Elizabeth. "Donald," she said. "How was your trip?"

"Uneventful," I said.

"The best kind," she said.

"Thanks for the ride."

"My pleasure. You met Younger, I assume."

"Yes," I said. "Seems like a nice guy."

"He is," Elizabeth said. "He has been with the family a long time. He is taking you directly to Katie Johnson's estate. She is expecting you. Younger will bring you here when you are finished unless there is somewhere else you might wish to go before dinner."

"Nowhere that I can think of," I said. The only other person I knew in the Hamptons was Carlo Vincente, a semi-retired mob boss, and though we liked each other, I thought it best to stay as far away from Carlo as possible. So Younger drove and I enjoyed the view.

Less than an hour later, we were granted entrance through an ornate gate and drove up a long driveway to the Johnson mansion. It sat on a knoll. The main building had an overhanging entrance supported by four tall white columns that framed a twelve-foot-high double doorway. The doorway, charcoal gray, was the only part of the main entrance that wasn't white. There was a large wing off each side of the main building, mostly brick with white wood trim. As we approached, I counted seven chimneys and two second-story balconies. I didn't bother counting windows, as there were too many. At the end of the driveway was a circle with a fountain in the middle. The grounds, of course, were immaculate. As large as it was, the Johnson estate was smaller than the Durbinfield estate.

Younger drove around the circle and stopped in front. He got out and came around to open my door. I knew to wait. I didn't want to look like an East Tennessee redneck hillbilly who didn't know any better than to open his own limo door. As Younger let me out of the limo, the front door opened and a tall, attractive woman stood waiting for me. I slipped my jacket on.

"I'll park and wait for you, Mr. Youngblood," Younger said.

"Thank you, Younger," I said. *Politeness is all.*

As I walked up the steps, the woman said, "Mr. Youngblood, I'm Katie Johnson. It's a pleasure meeting you. Elizabeth speaks highly of you and your wife and raves about her granddaughter. Please come in." As I followed, she said, "I thought we would have some refreshments on our sun porch."

"That would be nice," I said.

She moved like a model, gracefully and with long strides. The screened-in porch turned out to be a hike. I took in the art collection on the way. I saw a few artists I recognized, none of whose paintings would have been cheap.

"Sorry for the long walk," she said, "but the view is worth it."

"I can use the exercise," I said.

I continued to follow her and admire her sway. Katie Johnson had to be in her sixties but was still gorgeous. I could only imagine what she looked like twenty or thirty years ago.

"You have a beautiful home, Mrs. Johnson," I said, just to say something.

We walked a little farther to a wide-open and airy room.

"Here we are," she said.

The sun porch was large, with a tile floor and windows everywhere that offered a view to the ocean, maybe a half-mile away.

"Great view," I said.

We sat at a round wicker table with a glass top big enough for six. My wicker chair was more comfortable than I imagined it would be. Katie sat in the chair next to me. On the table was a large, round silver tray that held unopened bottles of white and red wine and a pitcher of iced tea. There were sandwiches cut in triangles with the crust off, a bowl of potato salad, and some cookies.

"Would you care for a little snack?" she said, handing me a plate.

"Yes, thank you," I said. *Interview foreplay*, I thought.

I took a sandwich that appeared to be chicken salad, a scoop of potato salad, and a cookie. Katie Johnson did the same.

"Would you like wine or tea?" she said.

"Tea would be fine," I said. "Let me pour. Would you also like tea?"

"I would," she said.

I poured and set the pitcher down. "Great view," I said, taking a bite of my sandwich.

"Isn't it? This is my favorite spot in the house."

We ate and chatted. She obviously knew I was there to ask questions, but I was willing to go at her pace. Besides, I was in no hurry to be anywhere, and the view was spectacular, outside and inside.

When we finished eating, she said, "You're a patient man, Mr. Youngblood."

Goes with the territory, I thought. "Sometimes," I said. I started to ask her to call me Don but stopped short, thinking maybe it was best not to get on a first-name basis with this woman.

"Well, let's get down to business, Mr. Youngblood," she said. "Why are you here?"

"I have some questions to ask about a painful subject."

"The twins," she said. "Yes, Elizabeth mentioned that. What would you like to know?"

"I'd like to know where Jessica is," I said. "I would like to talk to her."

"So would we," she said. "On both counts."

"You don't know where she is?"

"No," Katie Johnson said. "After the accident, she just disappeared. She would call me from time to time to say that she was okay, but I knew she wasn't. She is still in touch with her best friend, Katt Kilgore. Katt sees her from time to time but won't tell me where Jessica is, only that she needs some space. The last time I asked her how Jess was doing, she said she was fine. But I know that's a lie. I can just sense it."

"When was the last time you heard from Jessica?"

"Not for about three months," she said. "I'm really worried. Do you think you could find her?"

Christ have mercy, I thought. *Just what I need, a case within a case.* I was beginning to see why it had been so easy to interview her. Katie Johnson had her own agenda.

"I'm working a case right now that doesn't allow time for another one," I said. "When I'm finished with my current case, I'll be glad to try and locate your daughter."

"How long?" she asked, all business.

You've been blindsided, Youngblood, I thought. Katie and Elizabeth had planned this in advance. "Hard to say," I said. "Maybe days, maybe weeks."

"I want to put you on retainer," Katie Johnson said. The pleasant hostess was gone. I was now facing a matriarch who was not used to hearing the word *no*.

"That's not necessary," I said, looking her straight in the eye. "You have my word that I'll take your case as soon as I conclude the one I'm presently working on."

She was silent for a long moment as she stared back at me, trying to decide whether to push or not. Then she smiled. "Elizabeth said you were a tough nut," she said. "So, we are agreed. You'll take my case as soon as you can."

"Agreed," I said.

She handed me a five-by-seven envelope. "Pictures of Jessica," she said.

I nodded and put the envelope away without looking inside. "When was the last time you heard from Katt Kilgore?"

"Months," she said. "She doesn't return my calls. Another reason I'm worried."

"Do you know where Katt lives?"

"Yes," Katie Johnson said. "Katt teaches art at the College of Charleston in Charleston, South Carolina."

Bingo!

19

Later that afternoon when I arrived at the Durbinfield estate, Elizabeth Durbinfield was out. Smart woman. I was not in a real good mood. She was, no doubt, giving me a chance to cool down. The Durbinfield butler, Grayson, showed me to my massive second-floor suite and informed me that dinner would be served at six on the small porch off the breakfast room. Since I knew my way around from having been there before, he assumed I would not need an escort.

I unpacked and changed clothes. I hung my blazer and dark wool slacks in the closet with my white dress shirt and tie. I put on a familiar pair of old Dockers and a light blue button-down-collar shirt faded by many trips to the laundry. I took off my expensive ankle-top dress boots and replaced them with a well-worn pair of brown lace-ups with thick rubber soles, ugly but comfortable. I looked preppie as hell. I laid out my cosmetics in the bathroom, then unpacked my laptop and set it up on the massive desk in front of a picture window. The window had a distant ocean view. The day was cool and clear, and I could see a long way out.

To the right of the desk was a mini-fridge. I opened it and found a six-pack of AmberBock and two pint glasses: an olive branch. I removed a beer and a pint glass, twisted the lid off the beer, and poured in half. I watched the foam rise and then fall. I took a long drink. The first cold beer swallow of the day was always the best. Then I went online and read the latest news. The press was still treating President Dixon with kid gloves, and all the polls predicted he would win by a landslide in the next election, which was still a year away. I wondered if he even remembered who I was or that he almost got me killed. Probably. The man looked and acted like he remembered everything. Then I read the online sports page from the *Mountain Center Press*. Finally, unable to resist, I checked out Wall Street. The Dow was still setting records, having gone higher than I would have ever imagined. I looked at a number of my holdings. All were doing well.

At five-fifteen, I called Mary.

"Hey, Cowboy," she said. "How's it going?"

"I've been set up," I said. "I now have a second case."

"Tell me all."

I told her about my interview with the lovely and sexy Katie Johnson.

"I warned you about smart, beautiful women," Mary said.

"Of which you are one. A temptation not easily resisted."

"As long as you resist all but me," Mary said.

"Always," I said.

"How much did you tell her?"

"Nothing," I said. "Guess where Jessica's best friend lives?"

Mary paused. I could almost hear the wheels turning. "Charleston," she said.

"Smart and beautiful," I said.

◆ ◆ ◆ ◆

I went down for dinner promptly at six. Elizabeth had not made an appearance, so Grayson was kind enough to bring me another Amber-Bock. I sat, relaxed, and looked out at the distant ocean. There wasn't much to see. Darkness had claimed the day, and I had to admit I was tired. I heard movement behind me and turned to see Elizabeth entering the room. She was almost as tall, and certainly as slim and elegant, as Katie Johnson. Her short silver hair was in a fashionable cut that probably cost two hundred dollars. She had a wineglass in her hand half full of white wine. I stood.

"Donald," she said, "so good to see you." I received a light embrace and a cheek-to-cheek brush. "You are looking fine."

"As are you," I said.

"Please sit," Elizabeth said. "How was your interview with Katie?"

"A bit of a surprise," I said. "I think you set me up."

"I had to dangle a carrot to get you in," she said. "Besides, you're a big boy. You can handle Katie."

"I seem to be putty in the hands of beautiful women, and they are all around me. I now have a second case."

"I think that's a good thing," she said. "Katie lost one daughter, and I would hate to see her lose another. I hope you can help her."

"I'll do my best."

"Good," she said. "Now, tell me what's been happening since I last saw you."

At that moment, Grayson arrived with our food: grilled salmon, wild rice, and a Caesar salad.

I smiled. "You have a good memory. This is perfect."

"It's Lacy who has the good memory," Elizabeth said. "I called her when I knew you were coming."

We began to eat.

"Since you talk with Lacy so much, I expect you know most of what's been going on. Why don't you tell me what you don't know?"

"I know you were wounded in Afghanistan," she said. "I don't know any of the details."

"I was on a mission for the president. I was at the White House three times."

"Really," she said. "I must hear all about it."

I proceeded to eat and tell her about my trips to the most dangerous parts of Mexico and Afghanistan, about my team, about some of the good people I met along the way, and about the ambush. I left out names, and all I said about the mission was that it was successful.

Elizabeth ate and listened. When I finished, she said, "That's quite a story. I'm glad you made it back in one piece."

"For a minute over there, I thought I might not."

We both ate in silence.

"What's going on in your world?" I said.

"Nothing much new. Andrew takes care of the daily rigors of the business, which, by the way, is booming. I have my charities and clubs. Boring stuff, really. The highlights of my week are my phone calls with Lacy. We share everything."

My salmon was disappearing at an alarming rate. I ate some wild rice. Before I could finish my AmberBock, Grayson brought me another.

"You probably know more than I do," I said.

"Undoubtedly," Elizabeth said. "Which brings me to two questions. First, we are losing one of our board members from the Durbinfield Financial Board of Directors. I would like you to fill that seat. I put your name up, and it was unanimous. You sit on the Fleet Industries board, you are a high-profile investigator, you were very, very successful on Wall Street, you have a degree in economics, and most importantly, I trust you."

"You left out tall, dark, and handsome," I said.

"And you still have that rapier wit."

I had finished my meal and sat stunned as I processed the request, another thing today that I had not seen coming. "Can I offer an alternate name?" I said, thinking of my old mentor, A. Ben Shoney.

"No," Elizabeth said flatly. "I will not take no for an answer. You are perfect for the open seat on our board."

"Well, then," I said, "I guess the answer is yes."

"Delightful," she said, almost beaming.

"You said two questions."

"Did you do a DNA test to confirm that John was Lacy's father?" she said.

John was Elizabeth's son who had been murdered in West Virginia. I had stumbled upon the truth of his death while trying to find Lacy's mother. The truth was complicated.

"Why do you ask?" I said.

"I'm revising my will to include Lacy, and I don't want any complications," she said. "I want to attach a DNA report to my will to prove that Lacy is my heir."

"But you're already sure she is."

"Don't play games with me, Donald. You and I both know Lacy is my granddaughter. I would bet everything I own on it."

"Then why bother?"

"I don't want any loose ends," Elizabeth said.

"My position remains the same," I said. "You don't need a DNA report to confirm what you already know, and if you ask Lacy to do a DNA test, she'll think you're unsure, and she'll be hurt."

She was silent for a while. She was used to getting her way, but she loved Lacy completely and didn't want anything to get in the way of that.

"If you pass and there is a problem, I'll take care of it," I said. "Besides, you'll probably live to be a hundred and have great-grandchildren and have to revise your will a dozen times."

She smiled. "Thank you, Donald. I needed some clarity, and you certainly provided it. What a relief. Now, how about a Baileys Irish Cream?"

"Ye certainly know the way to a man's heart, lassie," I said in my best Irish brogue.

Elizabeth Durbinfield laughed out loud.

20

Grayson served us breakfast on the screened-in porch: eggs Benedict, potato cakes, and a mixed fruit bowl. My appetite was fully engaged after an early-morning five-mile run. The day was crystal clear and calm. A few sailboats dotted the distant ocean. The whole scene was an idyllic moment in time.

"Thanks for your help and hospitality, Elizabeth," I said.

"You are most welcome, Donald. You know that you, Mary, and Lacy are welcome here anytime. I relish the time you spend with me. I hope you can come for Christmas."

"Probably not," I said. "I think Mary is planning Christmas at the lake house. You're welcome to come."

"I would love to, but Andrew would have a fit," she said. "It is increasingly difficult to get extended family together for the holidays. Maybe someday we can do it here. I certainly have the room and the staff to handle it."

"I'll see if I can make that happen next year," I said.

"Then you really would be a miracle worker," Elizabeth said.

◆ ◆ ◆ ◆

Younger drove me to the airport, where the Durbinfield jet awaited. Elizabeth insisted that I allow her to assume the responsibility for getting me home. The pilot was efficient, distant, and professional. He didn't say a dozen words the entire trip. I thanked him as I descended the stairs with my overnight and backpack, and he said, "You're welcome. Have a good day." Then he promptly raised the stairway. *Northern hospitality.*

◆ ◆ ◆ ◆

I was back in the office after lunch.

"How'd it go?" Gretchen said.

"Just dandy," I said.

"I hear sarcasm. What happened?"

"I was ambushed," I said. "I now have a second case: find Jessica Johnson."

"Well, you are good at finding people."

"Uh-huh," I said.

She caught me up on the events of the last two days, which were boringly routine, and then went about her business, leaving me to contemplate my next move. I had taken the Johnson case primarily because I was going to have to find Jessica anyway. I needed to know how her sex video got into the hands of the Gildersleeve blackmailer. Two birds with one investigation. I had been rolling an idea over in my mind, and it was time to see if it had any value. I decided to watch the DVD Congressman Gildersleeve had given me.

I buzzed Gretchen. "Disturb me only if we are under attack by aliens," I said.

I put the DVD into my disk drive and muted the sound. I didn't need any more stimulation than I was about to get. Soon, three naked people were on a bed massaging each other's body parts. The lighting and the quality of the production were top notch. It appeared the twins had done this before. The twins were as Congressman Gildersleeve had said: *Playboy*-quality raven-haired beauties with slender bodies and breasts that were large enough but not too large. The kissing began—everywhere. Gildersleeve seemed to be following instructions. I noticed he was well toned and well endowed—probably the reason he was chosen for this little cinema. His hair was long, and he had a light, scraggly beard. He looked a little like a seventies hippie. The thing was, if he hadn't told me it was him, I would never have known it. His face was never fully looking at the camera—mostly side views, sometimes obscured. I watched it all and when it was over felt like I needed a cold shower.

I called Congressman Gildersleeve, talked for a moment with the aide who answered the phone, and was told to hold.

The congressman came on the line soon after. "Any news?" he said.

I told him what I had done so far. "My next step is to track down Jessica Johnson. I need to find out who she gave the video to. What I need is a good, recent headshot or two of you, and I need for you to watch all of the video."

"Why?"

"Because if you hadn't told me it was you on the video, I wouldn't have known," I said.

"You watched it?"

"Had to," I said. "I needed to see if I recognized you. I didn't. I need you to watch all of it and see what you think. Do you recognize yourself? Focus on yourself and not the twins."

"That won't be easy," he said, "but I'll tough it out."

"Great performance, by the way. You should have been nominated."

He laughed. "I think it was the twins who should have been nominated. They were something else. You said you need to talk with Jessica. Why not Jennifer?"

"I assumed you knew that Jennifer is dead."

"I didn't know," he said, sounding genuinely concerned. "I'm very sorry to hear that. What happened?"

"Auto accident," I said. "Jessica was driving. I guess she went off the rails after that."

"That's awful."

"It is," I said.

"So, what's with the headshots?"

"Normally, after looking at the video, I would tell you just to deny it was you. It could be anybody who resembles you on that video. Your opponent wouldn't dare risk trying to say it was you. It would make him look desperate. But in today's world of facial recognition programs, I need to find out if anyone could positively match your face to the video. If they can't, you're home free. Deny, deny, deny."

"Is there someone you can trust to do that?" he said. "The fewer people who know, the better."

"There is," I said. "We have to know."

"Okay," he said. "I'll send the pictures overnight. I hope I don't regret this."

"Better to know than not to know," I said.

"Especially in politics," he said.

◆ ◆ ◆ ◆

"You watched the video without me?" Mary said, feigning annoyance.

"Purely for professional reasons," I said. "If I watched it with you, I would never have been able to finish it."

"Did the twins live up to their billing?"

"And then some," I said.

"How about the congressman?"

"The congressman was impressive," I said.

"As impressive as you?"

"I wouldn't go that far," I said.

"I want to judge for myself," Mary said.

"The video is confidential," I said. "The congressman didn't give it to me so my wife could watch it and get herself worked up."

Mary laughed, grabbed my hand, kissed me, and pulled me toward the stairs. "I don't need anything but you to get me worked up," she said.

21

The next morning, I met Big Bob at the Mountain Center Diner. I was at my usual table, reserved for me by the owner, Doris Black. Rain was coming down steadily, but it had not discouraged the breakfast crowd. The mood inside was cheerful, the hum of a busy place. Big Bob shook the rain off his cowboy hat at the door and headed for my table, politicking along the way.

"Nice of you to recognize the little people," I said.

"Those aren't little people," he said. "They're big supporters."

"You're not up for reappointment for another year."

"Never hurts to get started early. The more people in my corner, the better," he said. "I haven't seen you in a while. What's going on?"

About that time, Doris showed up to pour our coffee and take our orders, so I didn't answer right away. We ordered, and she hurried away.

"I'm working two cases," I said. "One blackmail and one a missing person."

"What can you tell me?"

"Everything," I said. "They are both my cases, with no FBI involvement yet. What I tell you stays between us."

"Goes without saying."

"A friendly reminder," I said.

I brought him up to date on everything that had happened since I met the congressman, though I stopped short of calling him that. I called him a politician.

Big Bob smiled. "So, those twins were hot, huh?"

"Smokin'," I said.

"I'd sure like a look at that video."

"I'm sure you would."

"Professional reasons only," Big Bob said. "Might see something that you didn't."

"Doubtful," I said. "That video is confidential. I won't even let Mary watch it."

Our food arrived, and Big Bob became disinterested in the video. We attacked the breakfast with fervor.

"Man, I would have liked to see you and Mary double-teaming that Harry Keen guy," Big Bob said.

"I'll tell you," I said, "Mary had his head spinning."

"I'll bet she did."

We were silent as our food disappeared. Big Bob ate like he never got a free meal. I paced myself.

"Did you catch those guys who assaulted the guy at the Bloody Duck?" I said.

"Yeah, we caught 'em. Then the victim, Delbert, wouldn't press charges. They were all drunk and knew each other. Delbert told me it would take him awhile, but he would get even. Rednecks," he laughed, "you gotta love 'em."

Our food was almost gone. Doris came by with fresh coffee and hustled away.

"What's your next step?" Big Bob said.

"Go back to Charleston and talk with Katt Kilgore," I said. "See if I can get a lead on Jessica Johnson."

"Well, leave Mary here this time," he grumbled. "I need my best detective full time."

◆ ◆ ◆ ◆

I was in my office when the overnight package arrived. Gretchen walked in and placed it on my desk.

"Aren't you important," she said. "An overnight express letter."

She smiled and walked out before I could think of a clever response. I opened the letter and found three headshots of Congressman Gildersleeve. They were extremely well done and made him look like a movie star. I bet he polled well with the ladies.

I called John Banks.

"Agent Youngblood," he said. "You still working the same case?"

"Yes, I am, Agent Banks," I said. *Formality is all.* "And that information you gave me was most helpful, even though I'm now at a dead end."

"You need something else, I take it."

"Have you ever run a facial recognition program?"

"Facial recognitions are us," he said.

"Cute," I said. "I take it you have the program."

"I do."

"Can I send you a twenty-year-old video and some recent pictures to see if they're a match?"

"Sure," John said.

"Have a cold shower ready when you watch the video," I said. "It's pretty erotic."

"As in pornographic?" he said.

"As in that," I said.

"Overnight it," he said. "I'll get right on it."

I'll bet, I thought. "John?" I said.

"Yeah?"

"No copies."

"Killjoy," he said.

◆ ◆ ◆

I buzzed Gretchen. "Come in when you can," I said.

Five minutes later, she was in front of my desk. I handed her the DVD and the headshots. She stared at the headshots.

"Really good looking," she said.

"Would you vote for him?"

"For anything," Gretchen said.

"Are you speaking for all female voters?"

"Only the ones who are sexually active," Gretchen said.

"Try not to faint while you make copies," I said.

"I'll try."

"And burn a copy of the DVD."

"What's on the DVD?"

"Porn," I said.

"Yuck," Gretchen said. "This is part of the case, I hope."

"It is. When you finish, overnight the originals to John Banks."

◆ ◆ ◆

That afternoon, the congressman called. "I watched the video," he said. "With my wife."

Brave man. "All of it?" I said.

"Yes. And then one thing led to another. You get the idea."

"I do." *Too much information*, I thought.

"Sorry," he said. "Anyway, we both agree that it may not be me. At some point, I thought it was me, and she did, too. And then at another point, I thought it wasn't me, and she agreed. So, we're not sure either way. There was more than one guy around who had the same general look, and it was twenty years ago."

"Okay," I said. "Let's wait and see what the expert says."

◆ ◆ ◆

We were at the bar having a glass of wine and a predinner snack of cheese, crackers, raisins, and nuts. Mary's day had consisted of doing paperwork and more paperwork, with little time for actual investigating. I told her what was happening with the Gildersleeve case.

"So, John gets to watch the video," Mary said with a bogus pout.

"All in the line of duty," I said. "I told him he can't make a copy."

"And do you think he'll listen?"

"Probably not."

"It's not fair," Mary said, drinking more wine. "You've seen it, John Banks is going to see it, and the congressman and his wife have seen it."

"Well, he may be the star," I said.

"More like the supporting male lead. From what you've told me, the twins are the stars."

"Terrific performances, too," I said.

She punched me on the arm.

"Tell you what," I said. "If John tells me it's not the congressman, we'll watch it the next time we go to Singer."

Mary thought about that for a moment. She drank some more wine, emptying her glass. I slid the bottle out of reach. She gave me a hard look.

"Yeah, okay," she said. "Deal. Now pour me some more wine, and maybe you'll get lucky."

I poured.

22

John Banks called midmorning the following day. "It's not him," he said.

Damn! "You're sure?"

"Is the Pope Catholic?"

"He is," I said.

"Well, it's not the guy in the picture you sent," John said. "Did you want it to be?"

"No, I just thought it probably was," I said. "Can you run the guy in the video through the National Crime Information Center?"

"Not without authorization," John said. "If David Steele says to do it, then it's done, but it will take some time unless we just get lucky."

"Forget that for now," I said. Then I had another thought. "What if I have a name for you to run to see if it matches the face?"

"No problem, as long as the name you give me is in NCIC."

"Okay. Thanks, John," I said. "I'll call you if I need you."

◆ ◆ ◆ ◆

In my line of work, I don't get to make too many positive phone calls, but the next call was one of them. The congressman came on the phone soon after I told his aide who I was.

"News?" he said.

"Yes."

"Good news?"

"Mostly," I said.

"It's not me," he said.

"No, it's not you. You can campaign your ass off without worrying about that video."

"What a relief," he said. "I wonder if young people today consider that the stupid stuff they do now might one day come back to haunt them."

"Probably not," I said. "Then again, you probably had no idea that you would be running for the Senate twenty years down the road."

"You got that right." He paused. "You said mostly good news. Explain, please."

"There could still be a video of you out there," I said. "We know one was made."

"So why send the other one?"

"Maybe the blackmailer got mixed up, or maybe your video is lost, or maybe it's in a private collection. Who knows? There could be a lot of reasons."

"What's your best guess?" the congressman asked.

"My best guess is that he couldn't find your video, or it's been destroyed and he tried to run a bluff. Or maybe he thinks it's the right one. He obviously knows Jessica Johnson. Maybe she's in on it, or he knows the history and took the video from her, or took it a long time ago. Like I said, it could be any number of scenarios."

"What now?"

"We wait and see if he makes contact again," I said. "He may not, since he knows you're not playing his game. I may have scared him off. In the meantime, don't worry about it. But if he calls, don't mention that it's not you in the video."

"Why not?" he said. "It could save me some grief."

"Because we don't want him searching for the right video," I said. "Better he sends the wrong one to the press and you deny it's you. Then you have someone run a facial recognition program and prove it's not you. It will look like a smear tactic by your opponent."

"Agreed," the congressman said. "I don't want to have to explain the real video to my daughters, although it could be an object lesson on what not to do when you're young and stupid. Given a choice, that's one talk I'd just as soon not have."

"Let's hope you won't need to," I said. "And one last thing. If he does call, be sure and record it. He'll use a voice synthesizer unless he's totally stupid, and up 'til now he hasn't been."

"Okay, I'll remember to do that. I've got to run. Thanks for all you've done. Mr. Youngblood. I've been very impressed. As of now, we're done. Bill me for your time. If I hear anything, I'll get in touch."

"Sounds good," I said. "Good luck with the election."

"Thanks," he said. "It's a long way from now to then."

◆ ◆ ◆ ◆

"So, I finally get to watch the video," Mary said. "Do I really have to wait until we get to Singer Island?"

Mary was on her second glass of wine and in a good mood. I knew from experience that a third glass could make her militant if I made even the tiniest misstep. It was a tightrope I was willing to walk.

"I'll think about it," I said. "Tell me about your day."

I was trying to get her mind off the video. I knew it was curiosity and the fact that I had seen it and she hadn't that was causing her to push the matter.

"I'm working a stolen car case," she said. "We found the car unharmed and returned it to the owner, but I still have to track down who did it. Probably some teenagers out for a joyride."

"Where was it stolen?"

"Walmart parking lot," Mary said. "Older lady left her keys in the ignition. My guess, whoever stole it just went around looking for a car with keys in the ignition. Pretty good odds you'll find at least one. Anyway, we printed it, and I'll run the prints tomorrow to see if it's anyone in our system. It will probably be a waste of time."

"Sounds like it."

Mary drank a little more wine. "I'm hungry," she said.

"Let's go to the club," I said. "It's fried catfish night."

"I like that idea."

So that's what we did, and the subject of the video did not resurface.

23

Three days later, a Monday, I again heard from Congressman Jason Gildersleeve. I was in the office late by myself when the phone rang.

"He called," the congressman said.

"What did he say?"

"I recorded it for you. I'll give you the number and the code so you can listen to it."

I wrote down the number and code. "Stay there," I said. "I'll call you back."

I dialed the number and, when prompted, put in the code for message playback.

> CONGRESSMAN: Jason Gildersleeve.
> BLACKMAILER (electronic voice): I am still waiting to be paid or I'll release the video to the press.
> CONGRESSMAN: Go ahead and release it. I don't care.
> BLACKMAILER: You don't mean that.
> CONGRESSMAN: I do. It's twenty-year-old news.
> BLACKMAILER: The press will eat you alive. It will cost you the election.
> CONGRESSMAN: I doubt it. It might even help.
> BLACKMAILER: You're a fool.
> CONGRESSMAN: Maybe. We'll see. Do what you have to do. Don't call again.
> BLACKMAILER: You better give it some serious thought. The video will ruin you. Think of your family.
> CONGRESSMAN: My family already knows. I refuse to be blackmailed.
> BLACKMAILER: In case you have second thoughts, I'll call again in twenty-four hours. Then I'll release the video.

That was all there was. I called the congressman back. "You did fine," I said.

"Think he'll release the video to the press?"

"Not unless he gets something for it or he has a personal vendetta against you," I said. "My guess is that he'll try to sell it."

"Who would buy it without confirmation?"

"Some supermarket rag, probably. They might pay ten grand for it, just to be able to say they have a video someone says is you, and to be able to ask you if it's true or not. It's a story even if all they do is ask."

"And then I can spin it like my opponent is behind it," the congressman said. "I can flat-out deny it's me and dare them to prove it is, which we know they cannot do. I like that scenario."

"There are still problems," I said.

"What problems?"

"The main problem is Jessica Johnson. She's still out there somewhere. She could truthfully say that you were on a sex video with her and her twin. Maybe not that video, but another one they made with you. She might even have that video. Also, there could be people who might have heard about the video at the time and would be only too eager to get their fifteen seconds of fame. The video with you on it has to be someplace."

The congressman paused. "You're back on the payroll," he said. "Find Jessica Johnson."

"Okay," I said. "One final thing. If he releases that video, don't get in any kind of dialogue about it with any news agency. Simply say, 'It's not me on that video, and I have no further comment.' Some smart reporter is probably going to ask if you ever made a sex video, and your answer is no, since the twins made it and not you."

"What if I get pushed farther?"

"Say you're through talking about it, that it's not you and you have never made a sex video and you don't want to discuss it further."

Jason Gildersleeve laughed. "You sure you don't want to be my campaign consultant?"

"I need to find Jessica Johnson," I said.

24

The next day, I drove to Charleston. I was now looking for the same person for two different clients, albeit for two different reasons. I felt somewhat conflicted about billing both of them, although they both could certainly afford it. I knew Gretchen wouldn't have any qualms about a double billing, and she was the junior partner in charge of seeing that Cherokee Investigations turned a profit. So, I would find Jessica Johnson and let Gretchen decide who got billed what.

I checked in at the Renaissance in midafternoon on that pleasant November day, unpacked, and headed to the College of Charleston. I didn't have to go far. I walked. I made a right out of the hotel and turned southwest on Wentworth, then crossed King Street. A block later, I crossed St. Philip Street and took a right. I was at the south end of the campus.

I looked like I belonged in my brown loafers, tan slacks, brown belt that matched the loafers, and blue-checked button-down-collar shirt. I had the sleeves rolled up: Mr. Casual. As I walked northwest on St. Philip, I found an attractive older female and asked where the Art Department was. She was happy to give me directions and looked disappointed when I thanked her and walked away. I found the building. An older man who I assumed was a professor was descending the inside stairs.

"Excuse me," I said. "Do you know where I can find Katt Kilgore?"

"Second floor," he said as he went past me in a hurry. Then, over his shoulder, he added, "Her name is on her door."

I climbed the stairs to the second floor and walked down the hall, looking left and right at nameplates. Katt Kilgore's was, naturally, the last door on the right. I went in and found an outer office with a desk for a receptionist but no one sitting at it. My watch indicated that it was quarter after four. Maybe they quit early.

"Anybody home?" I said loud enough for someone in the inner office to hear me.

"In here," a pleasant female voice said.

I went a few steps inside, stopped, and said hi.

"Hello," the attractive female said, standing with a quizzical look on her face.

"Katt Kilgore?"

"Yes."

"My name is Don Youngblood. I wonder if I might have a few minutes of your time."

"Sure," she said. "Please sit down."

Katt Kilgore was a better-than-average-looking brunette with dark eyes and a slender figure. She wore jeans and a white button-up shirt that had a variety of colors of paint on it. The shirt was tied at the waist, and the top two buttons were undone; she was sexy without trying to be. I guessed her at five and a half feet and about 120 pounds. I would have signed up for art in a heartbeat. I sat down.

"How can I help you?" she said.

"I understand you know Jessica Johnson."

Her face clouded. "Is she okay?" I heard concern in her voice.

"I thought maybe you could tell me."

"Did her mother send you?"

"Yes," I said. "I'm a private investigator who sometimes works as a consultant with the FBI."

She thought about that for a few moments. "Why is the FBI interested in Jessica?"

"They're not," I said. "This is a private case."

"Well, that's a relief. I haven't seen Jessica in months. She went off the rails after her sister was killed. I tried to stay close and help her through it, but she told me to leave her alone. Her exact words were, 'Stay the fuck away from me.' So I did. She was heavily into drugs, and that's not my thing."

"Any idea where she might be?"

"Probably around Charleston somewhere," Katt said. "She loves Charleston and said she was never going to leave."

"Know anyone who might know where she is?"

"I don't," she said. "Jessica didn't have close friends. She and Jennifer were so tight they didn't let other people in. I was the exception—for a while, anyway."

I thought about that. Then came a question out of the blue, sparked by what Katt Kilgore just said, like tumblers on a combination safe dial falling into place: *Click, click, click.* "Did you shoot the videos?"

I saw the color drain from Katt Kilgore's face.

"Oh, my God," she said. "This is about those sex videos. The twins swore they had destroyed those. How could you possibly know that I shot the videos?"

"I didn't," I said. "But when you said you were close to the twins, I thought about your being an artist, and that someone had to be behind the camera, and it just kind of made sense."

"Tell me what's happening, please."

"Someone has a video, or maybe all the videos, and is trying to blackmail one of the male participants," I said.

"Oh, my God. That's awful."

"How many videos did you shoot?"

"I don't know," she said hesitantly. "Maybe a dozen."

"Over how long a period?"

"Throughout my junior year," Katt Kilgore said. "The twins were seniors. They graduated and moved. I saw them from time to time, but we didn't hang out. I reached out to Jessica when Jennifer died, but she didn't want anything to do with me. I think I reminded her of the good ole wild times."

"Did you ever participate?"

"No, thank God," she said. "I was tempted once or twice, but the guys had their hands full with the twins, and I'm not into girls. I had a boyfriend at the time, and I can tell you he really benefited. After a shoot, I was ready to rumble."

"Lucky him," I said.

She smiled.

I moved on. "Her mother seems to think you were close."

"That's what Jessica wanted her to think," she said. "I think she used our so-called friendship to hold off her mother. Jessica's mother used to call trying to get information about Jessica. I would be vague, just saying that the last time I saw her, she was fine, which was a lie. I finally quit taking Mrs. Johnson's calls."

"When was the last time you saw Jessica?"

"It's been awhile," she said. "I ran into her in a bar downtown and went over to say hello. She was with some rough-looking guy: big, blond hair. Dye job, I remember thinking. I said hello, and she looked at me and said, 'Do I know you?' She was drunk, but I think she knew exactly who I was. I just said, 'Sorry, my mistake,' and turned and walked away. That was the last time I saw her."

"How long ago was that?"

"Back in the summer," she said. "July, maybe early August."

"Would you recognize the guy if you saw him again?"

"Absolutely," Katt Kilgore said. "He was leering at me the whole time, undressing me with his eyes; it was creepy. Another reason I didn't hang around."

I couldn't think of anything else to ask, so I got up to leave. Katt stood.

"Can I have your email address or cell-phone number in case I have other questions?"

"Certainly," she said, and handed me a personal business card that contained both.

I handed her my card and said, "If you think of anything else that could be useful, let me know."

"I will," she said. "How long are you in town?"

I took the easy way out of that one. "I'm driving back as soon as I leave here."

"Too bad."

I said my goodbye and made a hasty exit. *Why do they always come on to married guys?* I wondered.

❖ ❖ ❖ ❖

That night at the Renaissance, I ordered room service from the Sixty 8 Bar & Table, a small, eclectic restaurant on the premises. The menu was limited, so I settled on a Caesar salad with grilled chicken and two bottles of Stella Artois. I ate in front of my computer, browsing insignificant emails and significant sports. The basketball Vols were playing their home opener, and I was anxious to see how the team looked after losing three starters to the NBA. The seven o'clock game was just getting started.

After finishing dinner, I called Mary.

"Hey, Cowboy," she answered. "How's it going?"

"About as expected," I said. "I checked in, walked to campus, interviewed Katt Kilgore, walked back here, changed clothes, and went for a long run. After the run, I showered and ordered room service. I ate in front of my computer. When I finished, I called you."

"Exciting," Mary said. "What was Katt Kilgore like?"

"Smart and sexy," I said. "But not in your league."

"You are a silver-tongued devil, and you will be rewarded accordingly as soon as you get back. Did you learn anything?"

I recounted my conversation with Katt Kilgore.

"So, what are you thinking?"

"I'm thinking I need to get Katt Kilgore with an FBI sketch artist and get a lead on the man she saw with Jessica Johnson."

"Sounds like a plan," Mary said.

25

The next morning, after my first cup of coffee and a hot shower, I called David Steele. It took a minute or two for him to pick up. I spent that time listening to elevator music.

"Make it fast," he said, a man in a hurry.

I told him what I had in mind.

"I'll set it up," he said. "You'll get a phone call."

After disconnecting, I called Katt Kilgore. She seemed surprised and pleased to hear from me.

"I thought you were leaving town," she said.

"Change of plans. I need a favor."

"Tell me," she said, sounding a bit too flirty.

"I need you to go with me to the local FBI office and sit with a sketch artist and see if you can come up with a face to match the guy with Jessica Johnson the night you saw them at the bar."

The silence from the other end was understandable. Who wants to get involved with the FBI?

"Okay, I'll do it," she said. "But you have to buy me breakfast first."

"Deal," I said.

"Where are you staying?"

"The Renaissance."

"I'll meet you there in an hour," she said.

◆ ◆ ◆

Thirty minutes later, while checking email and various sites on my laptop, I got the call I was waiting for.

"Richard James," a man said, "special agent in charge of the Charleston FBI office."

I resisted a snappy comeback and simply said, "Thank you for calling, Special Agent James."

"I talked with Associate Deputy Director Steele, and he filled me in. You can come in anytime today, the sooner the better."

"Thank you," I said. "We should be there by eleven."

After we disconnected, I put Richard James into my cell-phone directory, knowing I might need him later.

◆ ◆ ◆ ◆

I was at the entrance to the restaurant when Katt Kilgore walked in. She looked even sexier than the day before, wearing a purple peasant-style dress and showing some shoulder and her fine figure as she removed her tan shawl. It was obvious she was not wearing a bra. She wore tan sandals with two-inch heels at the end of some excellent legs. For a moment, my male DNA had me wishing I was still Don Youngblood, man about town. She wasn't dressed for breakfast; she was dressed for something else. I reminded myself I was married to the blond Wonder Woman, and my DNA settled down.

"Thanks for coming," I managed. *Professionalism is all.*

"My pleasure," she said.

We were seated by our greeter at a table for two by a window that looked out on Wentworth Street. A waitress poured coffee and took our order: a Western omelet for Katt and pancakes and bacon for me. We engaged in casual conversation. She made strong eye contact, like she was trying to get inside my head. Every now and then, I looked away, trying not to return any signals. Our food arrived, and we began eating. I decided to take my mind off her looks by probing with a question.

"Did you grow up here?"

"Yes," she said. "I'm a local girl. Most people born here don't leave unless they have to. Where do you live?"

"Mountain Center, Tennessee," I said.

"Did you grow up there?"

"Yes, then went away to school, ended up on Wall Street, and found my way back home."

"And became a famous private investigator," she said.

"Not that famous."

"You're being modest," she said. "I did some homework. There is quite a bit on the web about you. You're not someone to mess with."

I shrugged. "You know the press. They exaggerate everything."

"Or not," she said.

I smiled and said nothing. *Strong, silent type.*

We finished breakfast, and our waitress topped off our coffee.

"I read that you're married," Katt said. "Do you have a picture of your wife?"

I removed the picture of Mary in a bikini at Singer Island that I kept with me as a reminder of what I had waiting for me back in Mountain Center. It also seemed to be a talisman for warding off women with other ideas. I handed it to Katt Kilgore.

She looked at it and smiled. "Interesting picture. She's gorgeous. I'm guessing that your luring me back to your room is not going to happen."

"In another lifetime, for sure," I said. "But not in this one."

"Well, thanks for that. Can't blame a girl for trying. Let's go see what the Charleston FBI office looks like."

◆ ◆ ◆ ◆

The Charleston FBI office looked like the few others I had been in. Phones were ringing and being answered, copies were being made, papers were being filed, and coffee was being consumed. The buzz and energy let you know things were happening. The FBI was busy squelching criminal activity.

More than one set of male eyes tracked Katt Kilgore as she and I headed to the corner office where Richard James resided. James was all business as we introduced ourselves. Katt could have been a seventy-something senior citizen or a ten-year-old girl. His eyes betrayed nothing.

James made a phone call, and seconds later a younger man appeared, the sketch artist. He was visibly interested in Katt Kilgore, who immediately began flirting. He and Katt went happily off to the conference room to do what sketch artists did. With two artists working on the sketch, I was hopeful we would get a really good likeness of the man who had been with Jessica Johnson.

"She's quite a looker," Richard James said after they left.

"I was beginning to wonder if you noticed."

"Oh, I noticed," he said. "And I'm guessing that one is trouble."

Richard James was a quick study. You didn't get to be a special agent in charge of an FBI field office without a certain degree of intuition. I thought he was probably right, but I said nothing.

"No reason for you to hang around if you don't want to," he said. "The process will probably take a few hours. Might go a little faster, since she's also an artist."

"I'm going to head back to my hotel," I said. "Call me when you have something."

"Will do," he said.

26

I walked back to the Renaissance, went up to my suite, and checked email on my laptop. Nothing of interest. I sent David Steele an email update letting him know that Katt Kilgore was now with a sketch artist and we should have something soon. I didn't want to bother him with a phone call, and it gave me something to do. I was in a holding pattern. I hated being in a holding pattern. During those times, I usually called friends and acquaintances I had not talked to in a long time. I decided the day was too nice to ignore: crystal clear, no wind, sixty or so degrees. I changed into my running gear. I ran east on Wentworth Street to East Bay Street, then south on East Bay, which became East Battery Street. Farther down East Bay, the Cooper gleamed calmly to my left and beautifully restored houses sat elegantly on my right. The magic of Charleston had me in its grip, and there was little I could do to resist. I was feeling strong and inspired as I rounded the tip of the Battery, where East Battery became Murray Boulevard. Now, the water on my left was the Ashley River. I pushed on as Murray finally made a sharp right back to the east and became Tradd Street. I ran a short distance and turned north on Ashley Avenue, marveling at how good I felt. It was like that sometimes when I ran. Some days my feet felt like they were in cement overshoes, and other days they felt so light I hardly noticed them touching the ground. I followed Ashley until I ran into Wentworth, then headed east on Wentworth past the College of Charleston and back to the hotel with a final kick. I celebrated, knowing I could still do it. I had run in a giant, irregular circle. I had no idea how far I had been.

Back in my room, I was still trying to recover my oxygen debt when my cell phone played a catchy little tune. "Richard James, FBI," it announced.

"Youngblood," I answered, out of breath.

"You okay?" James said.

"Yeah, just got back from a long run. I don't wait well. What have you got?"

"A damn good-looking sketch with a lot of detail," he said. "Shouldn't be too hard to get a match. We're running it now. I'd say by the time you shower, dress, and walk over here, we should have a match."

"See you soon," I said, and disconnected.

◆ ◆ ◆

I walked into the Charleston FBI office thirty minutes later and found the same hustle and bustle as I headed toward Richard James's office. No one gave me a second glance. Katt Kilgore had obviously gone back to the College of Charleston.

James looked up as I walked in and nodded toward a seat in front of his desk.

I sat. "Anything?"

He smiled.

"You got a hit," I said.

"Of course," he said. "We are, after all, the FBI."

"And so humble."

"Occasionally," he said, "this not being one of those times."

He handed me the sketch. "Meet Kenny Stone, a low-life drug dealer with a high opinion of himself. Smart enough not to do any hard time, dumb enough not to avoid annoying the Charleston Police Department."

"Last known address?"

"North Charleston," Richard James said. "But I'd advise not going up there by yourself. It's a pretty rough area."

"Maybe I can get some backup from the local police."

"Maybe, but don't tell them you're with the FBI, or they'll stonewall you."

"You haven't been playing nice?"

He shrugged. "It's hard to imagine, but they just don't seem to like us."

I smiled and said nothing.

"I'd try the Charleston police, if that's the direction you want to go," Richard James said. "Kenny Stone operates mostly in Charleston, from what we can tell. Never been booked in North Charleston."

"Got a good contact over there?"

"No one interested in doing me a favor," he said.

"Maybe I can just walk in and play dumb," I said. "The hillbilly detective from East Tennessee."

"Doubt that would work, but you never know."

❖ ❖ ❖ ❖

I walked back to the Renaissance and sat in the lobby and texted Mary: **One more night**. All I got back was a graphic of a thumb pointing down. I knew I would hear more about that later. I sat and considered my best approach in getting the Charleston police to help me find Kenny Stone. Worst case scenario, I would walk in cold and take my chances. But first, I played a long shot. As I punched in the number, I could hear T. Elbert saying, *It's not who you are, it's who you know*, a statement I often used myself. Voice mail answered.

"Call me as soon as you can," I said.

I disconnected and waited. I picked up a copy of a pre-owned local paper and scanned it for anything interesting. It contained a funny satirical piece on a local politician becoming a "Florida man," referencing his claim of now being a Florida resident. Evidently, he was smarting from being voted out of office and had responded by leaving the state. I'm sure had I known all the history, it would have been even funnier. I finished it as my cell phone played the tune Lacy had picked out. The man was calling back.

"What's so urgent?" Big Bob said.

"Know anyone on the Charleston, South Carolina, police force?"

"You're in Charleston?"

"As we speak," I said.

"In jail?"

"Not yet," I said. "I might need some local knowledge and maybe some backup."

"I know the chief," Big Bob said.

"I thought you might. Can you give him a call and see if he would be willing to talk with me?"

"I haven't seen him in a while, but I'll see what I can do, if I can even get through to him. I'm sure he's a very busy man. Hang loose. I'll call you back."

◆ ◆ ◆

Half an hour later, Big Bob called. "The chief gave me a name," he said. "A Captain Hall."

"Where is he located?"

"She, you sexist," Big Bob said. "Hester Hall is the captain's name."

He really set me up for that one, I thought. I said nothing.

Big Bob gave me the address. "She'll see you anytime. I laid it on thick to the chief about what a hotshot you are. Try not to make me look bad."

"I'll do my best. Thanks for your help. I owe you one."

"Be careful," Big Bob said.

"You know me. I'm always careful."

Big Bob snorted and hung up.

27

Hester Hall was tall and lanky. She was attractive without being pretty: short, dark hair flecked with gray and dark eyes. Those eyes told me that she had seen a thing or two on her way to making captain. She wore a brown pantsuit with a white blouse and no jewelry except for a ring that was not a wedding band on the third finger of her left hand. She stood as I entered, shook hands with me, and waved me to a chair in front of her desk.

"The chief tells me you're the real deal," she said.

"Whatever that means."

"I looked you up after his call," she said. "You've done some nice work for the FBI."

So much for keeping the FBI connection out of it, I thought. *Damned Internet!* "I think I'm blushing," I said.

"Not that I can tell."

I smiled and said nothing.

"How can Charleston PD help you?" Hester Hall said. She didn't sound thrilled.

"I'm tracking a missing female who was last seen in a Charleston bar in the company of a small-time drug pusher by the name of Kenny Stone. I'm hoping that whoever works narcotics for you might know where he hangs out."

"Kenny Stone," she repeated. She typed something on her keyboard and looked at her computer screen. "Looks like we've run into Kenny on occasion. Who's the female?"

"Daughter of a rich family," I said. "They hired me to find her."

She nodded and looked out her window in thought. Then she picked up her intercom handset and said, "Is Laramie out there?" She listened. "Send him in here." She replaced the handset and looked at me. "My best narcotics guy."

Seconds later, a wiry, tough-looking guy with a gray buzz cut walked in. I guessed him at around five-foot-ten and maybe fifty years old. He glanced at me with pale blue eyes and then looked back to Hester.

"What's up, Cap?" he said.

"Meet Donald Youngblood, private investigator and FBI consultant from Tennessee," she said. "Mr. Youngblood, meet Detective Laramie Sims."

Sims and I shook hands and nodded at each other.

"The chief has asked that we help Mr. Youngblood with one of his investigations," Hester Hall said.

"*The chief*," Laramie Sims said with emphasis. "I see. Sure thing. Anything for the chief."

Hester Hall ignored the sarcasm and moved on. "Do you know a small-time pusher by the name of Kenny Stone?"

"Yeah, I know Kenny."

"Mr. Youngblood would like to ask Kenny a few questions," she said. "Think you can arrange that?"

"Shouldn't be a problem," Laramie Sims said.

"Then get to it," she said.

Laramie told his partner he was going out for a while, and I followed him to his car. He put the key in the ignition but didn't start it.

"Now, tell me why you want to talk with Kenny."

I told him what I had told Hester Hall. He sat and thought about it.

"So, is this woman really a missing person or just doesn't want to be found?" he said.

"I'm guessing the latter."

He gave me the hard cop stare I saw often from Mary. "Now, tell me the rest of it."

I took a moment to think about it, then said, "It stays between us."

"Unless it can't," he said.

"Kenny may also be involved in a blackmail scheme, and the woman may or may not be part of it."

"Busting a blackmailer," Laramie said. "Now you're talking. That would look pretty good on my résumé."

◆ ◆ ◆ ◆

We drove around Charleston, sticking to the east side, cruising East Bay Street.

"This is a fucking waste of time," Laramie said.

"Why is that?"

"Guys like Kenny Stone are nocturnal," he said. "They only come out at night."

"So, drop me at the Renaissance and go do something productive," I said.

"And have the captain up my ass?"

"Our little secret," I said. "You think I want to ride around with you all afternoon getting nothing done?"

Laramie Sims grinned. "You're okay, Youngblood."

We drove to the Renaissance drive-through, Laramie Sims stopped, and I got out.

"I'll be back here at six," he said.

◆ ◆ ◆ ◆

Back in my room, I emailed Gretchen to give her a schedule update, then sent another email to David Steele telling him about Kenny Stone. He would be surprised to find out that I was working with Charleston PD, given the general attitude of local law enforcement toward the FBI. Finally, I called Mary, hoping I might get her voice mail. No such luck.

"I'm not happy," she answered.

"Neither am I. But I need to stay and find a guy. The same guy Katt Kilgore saw Jessica Johnson with a few months back. A narcotics guy from Charleston PD is helping me, thanks to Big Bob."

"I'm horny, damn it," Mary said. "And I'm lonely. You'd better be back here tomorrow if you know what's good for you."

"Back tomorrow, guaranteed," I said, praying I was telling the truth.

◆ ◆ ◆ ◆

I picked up club sandwiches, chips, and two sixteen-ounce bottles of water from the restaurant and was waiting for Laramie Sims at six o'clock outside the Renaissance. Darkness had descended on Charleston, making the city even more inviting.

Laramie Sims was prompt. When I got in the car with the paper bag, he said, "What's that?"

"Food for two."

"Youngblood," he said, "I'm liking you more and more."

We drove up East Bay, then parked on the street across from a bar where Laramie said Kenny Stone was known to hang out.

"We'll wait and see if Kenny shows up," Laramie said. "While we wait, we eat."

We ate slowly and engaged in small talk. Kenny Stone was thoughtful enough not to show up and interrupt our nighttime snack.

"Is Laramie your given name?" I said.

"No," he said. "It's Guy."

We ate. I waited.

"You're a patient man, Youngblood. I like that. The answer to the question you haven't asked is that I was in the army before I became a cop. During basic training, my drill instructor decided he didn't want to call me Guy. Thought it might confuse the rest of the guys. You get the drift. He knew I was from Laramie, Wyoming, so he started calling me Laramie, and it stuck. I was never crazy about Guy, so I started using Laramie. I trust you can keep that secret."

"I can," I said.

We finished the sandwiches and chips and most of the water, and still no Kenny Stone.

"Want me to go in and have a look around, ask the bartender if he's seen him?"

"No," he said. "I don't want to alert Kenny we're looking for him. I'll go take a quick look. I go in there from time to time, so no one will pay too much attention. Hang tight."

Laramie Sims got out of the car and walked across the street. He was back in about ten minutes. He opened the driver's-side door and got in.

"No Kenny," he said.

"Now what?"

"We cruise," he said.

So we did. We cruised for an hour, watching the streets on both sides, visiting the corners where Kenny might be hanging out. Laramie drove up Meeting Street, then parked across the street from another bar.

"Something's up," he said. "Kenny must have gotten wind we're looking for him. Who else would know besides a few people in my department?"

I didn't want to mention the FBI or Katt Kilgore, so I backtracked. "I was here a couple of weekends ago trying to nail the blackmailer," I said. "Now, it looks like that could be Kenny."

I shared the Harold Keen story. He listened without interrupting.

When I finished, he said, "So, this Harry Keen was just a dope who got caught up in a blackmail scheme he knew nothing about?"

"Looks that way," I said.

"You never connected him to Kenny Stone?"

"At that time, I didn't even know who Kenny Stone was," I said. "But that doesn't mean Harry didn't tip him off."

Laramie was quiet for a while. His wheels were turning.

"Do you mind starting from the beginning and telling me all of it?" he said. "My word that it stays between us."

I didn't see any downside to telling him most of it, and I trusted he would keep his word, so I said, "It's a long story."

"We got time."

I told him most of it, substituting an unnamed prominent businessman for the congressman.

"You did good work to get this far," he said.

"I had some help."

"Like the FBI?"

I said nothing.

"It's okay," he said. "I did a little research before I picked you up tonight."

"I hate the Internet," I said.

"I know what you mean."

"How much did you learn?" I said.

"Enough to know you're a total badass."

"I do admit to a dark side."

"Glad you're one of the good guys," Laramie said.

I said nothing, and Laramie went quiet. Then he said, "We're going into that bar and restaurant over there and talk to a guy who seems to know everything going on in Charleston."

"Who's that?"

"A guy they call Jimmy the Ghost," he said. "Follow me."

We got out of the car, and I followed Laramie Sims across Meeting Street. He stopped at the bar's entrance and turned to me. "Be cool when you see Jimmy," he said. "He's different."

28

The clientele was mostly black. An unusual-looking man was sitting by himself in a booth at the back of the restaurant. As we approached, I wasn't exactly sure what I was looking at. Then it became apparent. Jimmy was not black. Jimmy the Ghost was an African-American albino. He looked up at us with eyes of a color I had not seen.

"Jimmy," Laramie said. "How's it going?"

"Hello, Laramie," he said. "Haven't seen you in a while." He was soft spoken but easily heard. He seemed calm and relaxed. He was a large man, and his unhurried demeanor made him even more intimidating, an aura I was so familiar with. "Gentlemen, please sit down. Let me buy you a drink."

He motioned for a waiter, and a black man hustled over and awaited instruction. "Sir?" the waiter said.

"Bring Laramie a club soda with a twist of lime, and bring Mr. Youngblood an AmberBock," he said. "And bring me a fresh one."

"Yes, sir."

I couldn't help smiling. Jimmy the Ghost had obviously known I was riding around with Laramie and had done some research.

"Since we all know who everyone is," Laramie said, "I'll dispense with the introductions. We'd like some information."

"Don't be in such a hurry, Laramie," Jimmy said. "I haven't seen you in a while. Enjoy your drink and chat a few minutes before we get down to business."

As soon as he said it, the waiter set our drinks on the table. Laramie took a drink. The waiter poured my AmberBock into a pilsner glass. I didn't see any reason for our drinks to be spiked, so I took a long pull. Laramie looked at me with envy.

Jimmy the Ghost turned to me. "Have you ever seen an albino Negro before, Mr. Youngblood?"

"Not that I recall," I said.

"We are extremely rare. Caused by a mutated gene. My eyes are sensitive to light, so I wear colored contacts to compensate. My people think I have magical powers and special insights. Therefore, I receive special treatment. They do my bidding and are afraid not to. Many bring me information as tribute. Some of that information proves to be valuable."

"Knowledge is power," I said. I took another long drink of AmberBock.

"Exactly," Jimmy said.

Laramie finished his club soda. We said nothing. We sat calmly and waited.

"I do like patient men," Jimmy the Ghost said. "How can I help you gentlemen?"

"We need to find Kenny Stone," Laramie said.

Jimmy touched his chin in a manner to indicate he was considering. "That's a hundred-dollar question."

From a roll of bills out of sight from Jimmy, I pulled a hundred and slid it across the tabletop. Jimmy smiled and accepted it.

"Kenny has left town, I'm afraid," he said. "You will not be seeing him anytime soon."

I slid another hundred across the table and said, "When?" I was hoping he hadn't left in the last twenty-four hours. That would mean Katt Kilgore had probably tipped him off.

"Soon after you confronted Harry Keen," Jimmy said.

Jimmy the Ghost really does know a lot, I thought. I looked at Laramie. He shrugged as if to say, *I told you so*.

"Where did he go?" I said, sliding another hundred.

"That's a free question. Buy two, get one free." He slid the hundred back. "Long distance information, give me . . . ," he sang in a pretty fair baritone.

"Memphis, Tennessee," I said. I could have sung it, but I didn't want to show off.

He pointed a finger at me.

"Have an address?"

He smiled. "I'm good, but not that good. I do not have an address."

"Was he with a woman?"

He waited. I proffered another hundred. This interview was getting expensive.

"Yes," he said, placing the hundred in his shirt pocket alongside the others. Jimmy was having a profitable night.

I paused for effect. Time to make him wait. Under the table, I peeled off another hundred for the big finish. "First name of the woman," I said, holding up the hundred.

He smiled. "You have paid enough for one night, Mr. Youngblood. Kenny was with one of the Johnson twins. The one that's still alive. Jessica, I think."

I put the hundred away and looked at Laramie. "We're done," I said. We stood.

"Nice doing business with you," Jimmy the Ghost said.

I nodded and turned to leave.

"Mr. Youngblood," Jimmy said, "I'll tell you this for free. Jessica Johnson is not in good shape. I hope you find her soon."

"So do I," I said.

Laramie and I walked out of the bar and back to the car.

"You were really fast and loose with those hundreds," he said.

"Hundreds are like pennies to the people I'm working for," I said.

He laughed, started the car, and drove me back to the Renaissance. He pulled in to let me off.

"Hey, thanks again for the snack," he said.

"My pleasure. Thanks for the help. I couldn't have done it without you."

"Are you headed back home?"

"Frist thing in the morning."

"Do me a favor and let me know how this all works out," he said, handing me a card. "My cell is on the back. Call me anytime."

"You can count on it," I said as I got out of his car.

29

We had been in bed for an hour or more, and I had given all I had. When our urgent coupling had begun, daylight was fading into twilight. Now, it was completely dark.

I had eaten breakfast in Charleston and then driven straight to Mountain Center with only one rest stop, arriving at the office in early afternoon. Rhonda was out on surveillance. Gretchen caught me up on the week, then left to meet Buckley Clarke, her main, and I guessed only, squeeze. I was left behind to mind the phones. I had left the office at five and high-tailed it to the condo. Mary had been upstairs waiting in bed, wearing a smile and nothing else.

"God, that was wonderful," Mary said. "I hate it when you're away, but I love it when you come home and we have catch-up sex. You have no idea how good it feels."

"Oh, I think I have a pretty good idea."

"You were gone two nights, and it felt like a week."

"Yesterday felt like a week," I said. "I started early and finished late."

She snuggled close, and I kissed her forehead.

"Are you hungry?" I said.

"Starved."

"Let's go to the club and eat a couple of steaks."

"Perfect," Mary said. "You really know how to treat a girl, Cowboy. Give me fifteen minutes."

♦ ♦ ♦ ♦

We sat at our usual table overlooking the eighteenth green. During the short, cold days of November, the diehards were still out there playing. I didn't get it, but I'm sure many of them didn't get skiing. We ordered drinks and a calamari appetizer.

"I want a precise, detailed report on what you did since you left me here alone," Mary said, trying hard to sound official.

"You make me sound like a deserter."

"Quit whining and tell me all," Mary said, taking a drink of wine.

I went through it step by step. The drinks and the appetizer arrived as I was about to interview Katt Kilgore. We finished the calamari and ordered a second round of drinks as I was about to have breakfast with Katt. We ordered steaks with Caesar salads and fries as I recounted my first visit to the Charleston FBI. I downplayed Katt's effect on the male population there. While we waited on the steaks, I told her about Richard James, identifying Kenny Stone, and my phone call to Big Bob. The steaks arrived, and I continued with my meeting with Hester Hall and Laramie Sims. Mary ate and listened. I ate and talked. We finished the main course as I completed the story of my encounter with Jimmy the Ghost.

Mary had questions and comments. "Jimmy the Ghost sounds like a real interesting character."

"Fascinating and unsettling at the same time," I said. "Calm, thoughtful, knowing, and intimidating."

"You could be describing Billy," Mary said.

"I could. I would love for those two to meet sometime."

We ordered after-dinner drinks.

"So, this Katt Kilgore was a looker and a flirt," she said.

"Yes and yes," I said. "And I think she had her sights set on the FBI sketch artist."

"I'm surprised she didn't come after you."

"I fended her off by showing her your bikini picture at Singer Island."

"You did not," Mary said sternly.

"I did. It's like shoving a cross in a vampire's face. Works every time."

"What did she say?"

"She said she thought she was losing her touch until she saw you. Then she understood."

"I cannot believe you did that," Mary said, her protest losing steam.

"Self-preservation," I said.

She smiled. "Well, that picture is pretty hot."

"Smokin'," I said.

◆ ◆ ◆ ◆

We were in bed reading later that night, but I couldn't concentrate on my book, a Harry Bosch novel by Michael Connelly. Mary noticed.

"What's wrong, Cowboy?"

"I can't forget the last words Jimmy the Ghost said to me about finding Jessica Johnson, that he heard she didn't look so good."

Mary closed her book. "I really hate to say this, but maybe you need to go to Memphis."

"You're right," I said. "I need to find her."

"Then do it," Mary said. "It's what you do best."

30

Ross Dean was a detective on the Memphis police force. An African-American and a savvy ex-football player, Ross had a reputation as an excellent investigator. I met Ross when I was working the Crane case and had liked him immediately. The last thing he had said to me when I left Memphis was that if I ever needed a favor, all I had to do was ask. There were special people I met on cases who I tried to stay in touch with, and Ross Dean was one of those. We emailed from time to time but rarely talked. I dialed his personal cell. I was hoping it was early enough that he was not knee deep in an investigation. His caller ID would let him know it was me.

"Youngblood," he said when he answered. "Long time, no talk."

"How are you doing, Ross?"

"SSDD," he said. "You know how it goes. I'm wrapping up a school shooting. Lots of wounded but nobody dead, thank God, except the shooter, who offed himself with his last bullet. Maybe you read about it."

"Seems to be one a day," I said. "I can't keep track. Guess I missed it."

"Cowards, every one of them," Ross said. "I hope they all burn in hell."

"Let God sort them out, Ross," I said. "You just keep protecting and serving."

He paused. "You're absolutely right, Youngblood. I'm losing my cool."

"I doubt it," I said. "Listen, Ross. This is more than a social call. I'm coming out there, and I need your help."

"What's going on?"

I told him about Kenny Stone, Jessica Johnson, the congressman, the Johnson family, the blackmail plot, Katt Kilgore, the Charleston FBI, Laramie Sims, and Jimmy the Ghost.

"Complicated," Ross said. "You got your hands full. When are you coming?"

"Tomorrow. I have some things here I need to do, but it's urgent I find Jessica Johnson as soon as possible. If a guy like Jimmy the Ghost is concerned, it can't be good."

"Must be urgent if you're coming on a Saturday. In the meantime," Ross said, "I'll run Kenny through my database and see what pops. I'll also contact some of my snitches and offer them a tidy sum for some info. You'll pay, of course."

"Of course."

"Don't worry. Money talks. If Kenny Stone and Jessica Johnson are in Memphis, I'll find them."

"I like your attitude," I said. "I'll call you when I hit town."

◆ ◆ ◆ ◆

Later that morning, I had a thought and called Congressman Gildersleeve. After I identified myself to the female who took the call, he came on the line.

"Mr. Youngblood, anything new to report?" he asked. "Did you find Jessica?"

"I'm narrowing in on her," I said. "The closer I get, the more I'm convinced she didn't have anything to do with the blackmail scheme."

"Well, that's good to hear," the congressman said. "Any idea who's behind it?"

"Yes, a small-time drug dealer who operates in Charleston. I think he's now in Memphis, and I'm headed there tomorrow. Jessica Johnson might be with him, or he might know where she is."

"What's this guy's name?"

"At this point, it's probably better you don't know," I said.

"You're right," he said. "What was I thinking? I withdraw the question."

"One other thing," I said. "Don't answer your office phone, especially after hours. And don't answer your cell phone unless you know who's calling. Make people leave messages."

"I rarely answer my office phone, and I never answer my cell unless it's someone in my directory," he said. "What are you thinking?"

"I'm hoping the blackmailer tries to sell the video to a supermarket rag. The only way those people would be interested was if they talked to you and felt you were dodging the issue. If you get a call, I want to know who it's from. Get the reporter's name and phone number. It could give me a lead." *Or it could give me a path straight to Kenny Stone.* I didn't share that thought.

"I understand," he said. "I'll let you know if I hear from anyone."

◆ ◆ ◆ ◆

That afternoon, I called Jim Doak. "Are you and your jet available tomorrow morning?"

"Are you aware tomorrow is Saturday?" he said.

"I am. And I'm also aware you would rather be flying than checking off items on a honey-do list."

"You got that right," he said. "When do we leave?"

"Eight o'clock."

"Where are we going?" Jim said.

"The land of the Delta blues," I said.

31

The next morning, I parked the Armada in the private hangar at Tri-Cities Airport not far from Fleet Industries jet number one. Jim was walking around surveying the undercarriage of the jet.

"We have another passenger," I said as Mary got out of the SUV.

"I can see that," Jim said. "How are you doing, Mary?"

"Just fine, Jim," Mary said. "Hope you don't mind my tagging along. I didn't want Don to have all the fun while I sat around by myself this weekend."

"The more the merrier," Jim said. "Welcome aboard."

We had decided the night before that there was no reason for Mary not to come with me. She would have to return home Sunday afternoon if I didn't find Jessica Johnson by then.

"Ready when you are," I said.

"Saddle up," Jim said.

We followed Jim up the stairs and into the jet, turning left toward our seats. I heard the whine of the motor that raised the stairs. We sat side by side with a narrow isle in between.

"Wheels up in a couple of minutes," Jim said over the intercom.

We started to move. We taxied out to our starting position and sat there a few seconds. Then I heard the twin engines rev, and we started forward, gathering speed as we went. I felt the tarmac fall away as we moved skyward. The jet made a long, sweeping bank, then leveled out, heading west.

We touched down on the Memphis airport tarmac ninety minutes later. Jim flew off into the wild blue yonder while I was renting an SUV from Hertz. He told me to call when I needed him back in Memphis. Mary and I drove into the heart of the city to the Peabody Hotel. We checked into a Romeo and Juliet suite complete with spiral staircase and fireplace.

I shooed the overly helpful bellhop away with a twenty-dollar bill. Mary disappeared up the spiral staircase and was back in a few minutes.

"If you're trying to impress me, you succeeded," she said. "Fabulous accommodations."

"Glad you like it."

"There's a king-sized bed up there."

"Really?"

"Really," Mary said. "But I know you have work to do."

"Hold that thought," I said. "I need to call Ross Dean."

◆ ◆ ◆ ◆

Ross answered on the second ring.

"I'm here," I said. "Me and my bodyguard."

"Bodyguard," Ross said, pausing to process. "Ah, your wife came with you."

"Quick as ever," I said.

"That's great," he said. "We'd love to meet her."

"We?"

Ross chuckled. It sounded like rolling thunder. "Someone you should know."

"You and Charlene Barry?"

"See there?" Ross said. "You're pretty quick yourself."

Charlene Barry was the widow of Thomas Barry, a Silver Star recipient and a U.S. Army Ranger who served on a special mission with a group that dubbed themselves the Southside Seven. Barry had been killed by an assassin I was chasing. Charlene had two young children. I remembered that Ross had been overly consoling when we interviewed her. I was not surprised he had followed up.

"You did seem pretty attentive during that interview," I said.

"I kept her informed of your progress, waited the appropriate amount of time, and then asked her out. One thing led to another, and I asked her to marry me. We're getting married, but Charlene is hesitant about setting the date. Whenever it is, I hope you can come. You're responsible."

"No, Ross," I said. "I may have set the wheels in motion, but you're responsible. Whenever it is, if at all possible, we'll be there."

"Yeah, you're right. I am responsible." He chuckled. "Anyway, I want you two to come to dinner tonight. I'm sure Charlene will be thrilled. After dinner, we'll work the street and see what we can find out. I've got some feelers out."

"All right," I said. "Give me the address and tell me what time."

He did.

I signed off and looked at Mary. "I'm free all afternoon."

"Then what are we waiting for?" she said, starting to undress.

◆ ◆ ◆

Hours later, we were still naked under the sheets.

"Ever hear of the Peabody ducks?" I said.

"The what?"

"Never mind," I said. "Get dressed. We have to be in the lobby before five. I have a surprise for you."

We dressed in jeans, turtlenecks, and leather jackets. My turtleneck was dark red and my jeans faded blue. Mary's turtleneck was black to match her jeans. Our jackets were dark brown, slightly different cuts, both with room enough to allow us to pack heat. At five o'clock, we went down to the lobby to see the Peabody Duck March, a tradition dating back before World War II. The ducks resided in luxury on the roof of the hotel and, under the guidance of the Duckmaster, came down to the lobby in an elevator at eleven o'clock every morning to make their red-carpet march to the lobby fountain. We were there for the return trip. We ordered drinks and waited.

Just before five, the Duckmaster, a tall, dark-haired, mid-forties man, appeared in a bright red coat and black pants and sporting a gold-headed cane, bringing to mind a circus ringmaster. The red carpet was rolled up against the fountain, and he made a big deal out of lining it up before he rolled it out to the elevator, maybe forty feet away. Then he came back and placed carpeted stairs against the fountain wall. The ducks, a male and four females, seemed attentive to what was happening. Then came the announcement introducing the ducks. The Duckmaster removed the block on the stairs inside the fountain and tapped the top of the stairs twice with his cane. The male duck led the females out and down the stairs to the red carpet and toward the elevator. I looked at Mary, who had a huge smile on her face, utterly amazed. The Duckmaster made a big deal of herding the ducks toward the elevator, which was open and waiting. The ducks entered, followed by the Duckmaster. The doors closed, and the duck walk was over. The whole thing took about three minutes.

"That was unreal," Mary said. "They do that every day?"

"I think so," I said.

"I want to be here tomorrow when they come back," Mary said.

"We'll see," I said. "We need to get rolling."

◆ ◆ ◆ ◆

I vaguely remembered where Charlene Barry lived but would not have found it without my GPS. Ross and Charlene came out of the house as we pulled into the driveway. Ross and I shook hands, and Charlene surprised me by giving me a big hug. I introduced Mary.

"Let's get inside," Ross said. "It's a little nippy out here."

We followed Ross inside. I noticed his firearm on a table in the entrance. I casually placed mine beside it. Mary's Glock was in her shoulder bag. He took our coats and led us to the living room.

"How 'bout a drink?" Ross said. "Beer or wine. No hard stuff."

"Whatever Charlene is drinking," Mary said. "I'm not particular."

Since when? I thought. "What are you drinking?" I asked Ross.

He grinned. "AmberBock okay?"

I smiled. "You have a good memory."

We talked for a while, the four of us. Charlene said her kids were spending the night with her sister. She looked at Ross as she said it. Ross grinned and changed the subject. It was unhurried, interesting conversation. Background stuff. Mary and I spent most of the time answering questions on subjects like how we met. That one went from Charlene to Mary.

"He saved my life," Mary said. "Three times, from the same guy. His reward was my marrying him."

"You have got to tell me more than that," Charlene Barry said.

So, Mary told her the whole episode involving Teddy Earl Elroy and his bank-robbing brothers. About the shootout where she killed one brother and was wounded herself. About meeting me and then my coming to her rescue in the hospital when Teddy Earl tried to kill her. About my whisking her off to Florida and putting her through my own personal rehab program. About slowly falling in love with me. About her moving in with me and taking a job on the Mountain Center police force. About Teddy Earl again trying to kill her. About Teddy Earl's capture and my finally killing him in the Mountain Center Police Station when he got his hands on a gun and once again tried to kill her.

"So, that's how we met," Mary said. "I was in love with him before we left Florida. Later, I had to propose to the big lug."

"I said yes immediately," I added.

"Wow!" Charlene said. "That's quite a story."

Later, Mary went to the kitchen with Charlene, leaving Ross and me alone. We heard muted conversation and laughter. I looked at Ross.

"They seem to be getting along," I said.

"They do."

"So, what's the plan?"

"We go out after dinner," he said. "My number-one snitch will be waiting in an alley downtown. We'll pick him up, drive him around, and see what he has to say. He'll procrastinate, negotiate, bargain, and whine, but in the end, he'll give up what he knows. You might have to flash some green to loosen his tongue all the way."

We had dinner half an hour later: Southern fried chicken, mashed potatoes with gravy, green beans, baked apples, and hot biscuits. Comfort food. I was in heaven. I turned the conversation toward Ross, and he steered it to Charlene, who shared some of her past and why she wanted to be a nurse.

"When I was young, I watched a TV show about a black nurse. I wasn't even born when it first came out. I watched it in reruns. *Julia*, it was called. Diahann Carroll played the lead, a black nurse. I had never seen a black nurse on TV. I thought it was so cool that this black woman was doing a job that was almost always a white woman's job. I must have been about six or seven at the time, and I thought, *That's what I'm going to be when I grow up.* I never wavered. I knew all along that I was going to be a nurse."

"That's absolutely awesome," Mary said.

"Thank you," Charlene said. "Did you always want to be in law enforcement, Mary?"

"Yes, I did," Mary said. She didn't elaborate.

"What about you, Don? Did you always want to be a private investigator?"

"No," I said. "That just kind of happened. Another long story."

"I'd like to hear it," Charlene said.

"Another time," Ross interrupted. "We need to roll."

I looked at Mary.

"I'll stay here," she said. "You guys do your thing. Try not to get shot."

32

Outside, I said, "Want to take the rental?"

"Hell no," Ross said. "It would stand out like a blonde in a brunette contest. Lowlifes see that thing coming, they run the other way." He pointed to a charcoal gray Crown Victoria. "We'll take my beater."

We got in and headed downtown. I didn't pay much attention to the direction we were going, figuring Ross knew his way. The Crown Vic had some age on it, but it was clean and smelled fresh. Darkness had fallen, and the nightlife was active. A lot of people were out. Ross drove into a neighborhood I can only describe as depressing, obviously at the bottom of the socioeconomic scale. It would be a hard road out for someone born there.

Ross turned down an alley and pulled up beside a dumpster. Out of the shadows a black man came. He opened the rear door behind me and got in the Crown Vic. Ross drove away in silence. After pulling into a side street and driving a few blocks, Ross said, "How you doing, Angle?"

"I'm doing," the man said. He was slender, about six feet tall, and looked like a university student.

"This is Nehemiah Dees," Ross said to me. "Angle is his street name, so acquired because he always has an angle. That right, Angle?"

"Always try to," Angle said.

"Angle gets in trouble from time to time, and I help him out," Ross said. "That right, Angle?"

"Right as rain," Angle said.

"Angle, this is my new partner," Ross said. "We call him Shooter."

"Nice to meet you," Angle said.

I said nothing.

"He likes to shoot people," Ross said. "Sometimes just for fun."

"Uh-huh," Angle muttered.

"What have you got for me about Kenny Stone from Charleston and a girl he's with?" Ross said. "You better have something, Angle."

"Since when Angle not had something?" Angle said. "I got something. I got a lot. Cost me, too. Risk my life to get this. Bad people be involved. I'm going to need some laying-low money."

I pulled out a hundred-dollar bill and handed it to him. His eyes widened and then went back to normal, like he didn't want to reveal that he was impressed.

"Lay low on this," I said.

He looked at the hundred and said, "It's a start."

I peeled off another and handed it to him. "The next thing I pull out will be my Beretta."

"Calm down, man," he said. "This is good."

"Spill it," Ross said.

"There's this new crack house been set up for a couple of weeks now," Angle said. "They took over the whole third floor of a run-down apartment building. It's full of addicts and whores. Run by mean, bad people. They'll shoot you over a dime bag."

"Location?" Ross interrupted.

Angle told him. It meant nothing to me.

"Go on," Ross said.

"Word has it that some white boy with connections brought in a good-looking white bitch as a gift to get in on the action. They say she's so strung out she has no idea what's going on. They going to charge a lot to get between her legs."

"What else?"

"They armed and dangerous, man," Angle said. "You-all be careful. I don't want to lose my protection. You can't just walk up and go in the front door."

"Your concern is touching," Ross said. "What do you suggest?"

"There some stairs in the back that lead down to a basement door," Angle said. "Door locked."

"So, if the door is locked, how do we get in?" Ross said.

I could see where this was leading.

"Might be a key hidden somewhere," Angle said.

"A hidden key," Ross repeated.

"Uh-huh."

"And how do you know about this key?" Ross said.

Angle grinned. "Hid it myself, at considerable risk."

I turned around and looked at Angle. "Tell you what. If the key is where you say it is, and if it gets us in, and if I find what I'm looking for, then you get a couple more C-notes. If not, you better hide from me."

"No problem, man," Angle said. "The key will be there. You got a deal."

He told us where to look.

Ross pulled over to the curb. "You watch your ass, Angle. I don't want to lose my best snitch."

"I hear you," Angle said as he got out. He kept the door open and leaned in. "One other thing. There's an elevator, but it don't work. There's stairs at either end of the building. There's also a couple of fire escapes. Just so you know. Good luck."

We watched him disappear into the night.

"Now what?" I said.

"Now I call my lieutenant," Ross said. "This could be big, Youngblood."

Ross turned his phone on speaker and called his lieutenant, Morgan Free.

"This better be good, Ross," Free said when he answered.

"Oh, it's good, all right," Ross said. "We're on speaker, Lieu."

"Who else is there?"

"Agent Youngblood, FBI," Ross said.

I guess "Agent Youngblood" sounded better than "Private Investigator Youngblood." I always carried my FBI creds, just in case.

"Agent Youngblood, welcome to Memphis," Morgan Free said. "How'd you get mixed up in this?" He sounded more sarcastic than welcoming.

"One of my cases led us to where we are now," I said.

"Okay," Morgan Free said. "Lay it out for me, Ross."

"Youngblood here is tracking a girl from Charleston who was apparently kidnapped and brought to Memphis and sold or traded, for what we do not know. Word from my snitch is that she's in this recently set-up crack house and not being treated so well, if you get my drift."

"How do you want to play it?" the lieutenant said.

"We'll probably need a SWAT team to surround the house," Ross said. "Youngblood and I have a way in. We'll go in and see if we can find the girl and the guy who kidnapped her. Probably going to flush out a few bad guys while we're doing that. SWAT team can round them up as they come out."

"Probably not going to come out with their hands up," Morgan Free said.

"Probably not," Ross said.

"Might look pretty good for you and me if we take down a crack house," the lieutenant said.

"No doubt," Ross said.

"What's the address?"

Ross told him.

"Where are you now?"

Ross told him that, too. The addresses didn't mean anything to me. I was in an unfamiliar part of Memphis I never wished to visit again.

"Sit tight," Morgan Free said. "I'll get back to you."

So we sat tight.

"I hate waiting," Ross said.

"So do I."

Ross looked at his watch. I thought about calling Mary, but she would just worry, so I trashed that idea. I texted her instead: **We may be a little late. We have a lead from one of Ross's snitches. I'll touch base later.**

Be careful, Mary texted back.

I sent her a thumbs-up.

A few minutes later, Ross said, "How do you like that Beretta? I haven't seen that model before." Nervous small talk.

"I like it," I said. "It's the 92X compact. A little smaller and lighter. Perfect for concealed carry."

"I don't worry too much about that," Ross said. "Everyone knows I'm carrying."

33

The SWAT team van was at our location in half an hour. No one got out. Ross's cell phone rang. He put it on speaker.

"Detective Dean," Ross answered. "Agent Youngblood is with me."

"SWAT team leader McDonald. How you doing, Ross?"

"Glad it's you, Jim," Ross said. "You made good time. I was getting antsy."

"Didn't want to be late to the party," McDonald said. "What do you need from us?"

"Backup," Ross said. Ross told him the location of the crack house. "We'll park a block from the site. Your team will wait at either end and take down whoever Youngblood and I flush out. Don't come in unless I call for you."

"Got it," McDonald said.

◆ ◆ ◆ ◆

We stayed in the shadows as we approached the apartment building on the opposite side of the street. From a distance, we could see a couple of guys out front. Security, no doubt. We crossed the street unseen and headed for the back, guns out. We knew the SWAT team would be approaching from either side. I let Ross lead. This was his show.

We found the key where Angle said it would be and slowly descended the stairs, eyes and ears on high alert. Ross slipped the key into the lock, and I heard it turn. We heard that creaking sound that comes when a door hasn't been opened in a while. We slipped into total darkness. I pushed the door closed behind us, and Ross locked it. We stood silently for a minute or so and listened. We heard nothing. Then Ross flicked on his flashlight, revealing a dusty room full of furniture, boxes, and all kinds of other junk. He continued scanning the room and found the stairs to the first floor.

Ross stopped at the bottom, and the flashlight beam tracked up the stairs to a door at the top.

"Doesn't look as if anyone has been down here in a while," he whispered. "Let's hope there's no one on the other side of that door."

We went silently up the stairs. At the top, we stopped and listened. We waited another minute or so. We heard nothing.

Ross handed me a pair of handcuffs. "You might need these," he said. "I have another pair."

Ross slowly opened the door and peeked out. Then he slipped through. The hallway was poorly lit but empty. The stairs to the upper floors were directly across from us. Ross nodded toward the stairwell. We slowly climbed to the first landing, paused, and then continued up to the second floor. We peeked down the hall, also empty. We heard what sounded like a TV playing. We stepped back into the stairwell and began climbing to the third floor. The only light in the poorly lit stairwell came from the second- and third-floor hallways. Ross stopped before he got to the next landing and peered around. He stepped back.

"Guard," he whispered. "He's got earbuds on. Probably couldn't hear a bomb go off."

We climbed the stairs as silently as we could, keeping as close to the wall as possible. A young black man sat in a chair with his back to us, head bobbing to music I couldn't hear. We tucked into a corner behind the door opening. Ross reached around and put the barrel of his Glock under the guard's right ear at the same time as he stepped around and clamped a hand over his mouth. I pulled off the guard's earbuds.

"One peep out of you and I put a bullet in your brain," Ross said quietly. "Understood?"

The guard nodded urgently.

"Stand up and back into the stairwell."

The guard did as he was told.

"Hands behind your back," Ross said.

Without being told to, I cuffed the guard.

"Sit down here in this corner and wait," Ross said. "If I hear you running, I'll shoot you. If I hear you yell, I'll shoot you. You understand me? This ain't worth dying for."

"Yes, sir," the young man said. "I won't run or yell."

I stepped across the opening to the other side of the door. The hallway was still empty. "Now what?" I whispered.

"Where's the white girl?" Ross said to the young guard. The guard said nothing. Ross removed a silencer from his jacket pocket and screwed it on the Glock. The guard's eyes went wide. "One last time. Where's the white girl?"

"All the way down the hall," the guard said quickly. "Last door on the right."

Then we heard someone holler, "Marvin! Hey, man, where are you?"

We heard him approaching. Ross unscrewed the silencer and slipped it back into his pocket. He leaned around the door, pointing his Glock, and loudly announced, "Police, drop you weapon!"

In an instant, the hall was filled with automatic weapon fire. Ross ducked back into the stairwell just in time to save his life. I saw blood on his shoulder. I slid down the wall as slugs pinged above me, wondering how I managed to go from the Peabody Duck March to a firefight in a crack house in a matter of hours. There was a pause in the gunfire, and I rolled out into the opening and fired three quick shots at the shooter. Red blooms grew instantly on his white wife-beater T-shirt, and he went down with a thud.

"Shooter's down," I said. "You okay?"

He was leaning against the wall in obvious pain. "Yeah," Ross said. "Just a scratch."

The amount of blood told me it was more than a scratch, but I said nothing. I looked down the poorly lit hallway and saw no movement. "Wait here," I said. "I'm going after Jessica Johnson."

"Not without me, you're not," Ross said.

We started down the hallway with our nine mils pointed and ready to shoot. A door opened near the end, and a large white man ran out, fired a couple of wild shots, and headed for the stairwell. We went down to our knees and returned fire, but we were too late. The man vanished down the stairs. I was pretty sure it was Kenny Stone.

"Watch my back," I said, and rushed down the hall to the door where the man had exited. With my Beretta leading the way, I slipped inside. The room was dimly lit and smoky. I heard gunfire from somewhere below me. An open door led to another room, a bedroom. I went in low, Beretta out front. The room was clear with the exception of a half-naked woman lying on the bed. The woman vaguely resembled Jessica Johnson.

◆ ◆ ◆

Ross had a patrol car pick up Mary and Charlene. A half-hour later, Mary was helping Jessica get dressed and Charlene was treating Ross's wound while giving him an earful for getting shot. I couldn't understand the words, but I had heard that unmistakable tone before, one I was likely to hear again before the night was over. Mary was doing most of the dressing with little assistance from Jessica, who was totally out of it. I doubted she knew where she was and what was going on. I looked out the window and down at the street. The scene below was a three-ring circus. A half-dozen patrol cars with light bars flashing lit up the night. A crowd was forming. A van full of suspects pulled away. Ross said they would sort them out later. An ambulance pulled out a few seconds after the van. Then the press arrived. The circus was growing. I walked into the hall and stood by Ross.

An older black man dressed in a good-looking suit appeared from the stairwell and walked down to us. "You okay, Dean?" he said.

"No, he's not okay," Charlene Barry said. "He's been shot."

"I'm all right, Lieu," Ross said.

"You did well," he said. "Now, get out of here and go to the hospital. Get some rest. Take some time off. All you need." He turned to me. "You Agent Youngblood?"

"I am."

"I'm Morgan Free," he said, extending his hand. We shook. "The dead guy in the hall is your work?"

I nodded.

"Heard you could shoot," he said. "I'll need your weapon."

"I'll give it to Ross later," I said. "I really don't want to be without it right now."

"It was a good shoot, Lieutenant," Ross said. "Let it go."

"Yeah, okay for now," he said, looking at me. "But we need to do this by the book, so give your firearm to Ross later, and we'll get it back to you as soon as we can."

I nodded. "Did you nab a big blond white guy in your roundup?"

"No," Morgan Free said. "Four black men, two of them wounded, one black woman, and one white woman."

"He may still be in the building. Can I have a couple of your guys to do a search?"

Two uniforms were at the other end of the hall, and the lieutenant called them down and told them to assist me in a search. They seemed less than enthusiastic.

"Good work, you two," he said to Ross and me. Then he turned and walked down the hall and disappeared into the stairwell.

I turned to Mary. "Get everyone back to Charlene's house. I'll find a ride. We're going to search for Kenny Stone."

◆ ◆ ◆ ◆

We started the search on the third floor.

"He's armed and dangerous," I said to the two uniforms. "Get those weapons out and pay attention."

That seemed to brighten their spirits a little. We searched the floor carefully. In each room, I announced, "Kenny Stone, we're the police. If you are in here, give yourself up now. If you point a gun at us, you're a dead man."

It took an hour to clear the floor. We didn't find Kenny Stone, or anyone else, for that matter. The floor was empty.

The second floor still had residents. Most were out in the hall observing the show.

"Any of you seen a big blond white guy in the last hour?" one of the uniforms asked.

Heads shook, accompanied by negative mumblings. We searched two empty apartments, to no avail.

The first floor was the same story. No one had seen a big blond white guy.

"Basement," I said, pointing to the door where Ross and I had entered the first floor.

We found a light switch at the top of the stairs and flipped it on. The basement, like everything else, was dimly lit. With my Beretta out front, we moved cautiously down the stairs. At the bottom, I looked toward the outer door. It stood half open.

"Game over," I said to the uniforms. "He's gone."

34

Charlene and Mary managed to bring Ross and Jessica Johnson to Charlene's house. Charlene was able to get some soup into Jessica and put her to bed. Then she gave Ross some pain meds and took him to the emergency room, leaving Mary to look after Jessica. Mary said that Ross didn't argue about going to the ER. In the meantime, the two uniforms gave me a ride to Charlene's house. When I finally made it back, Mary and Charlene were in the kitchen drinking wine.

"There's beer in the fridge," Mary said.

"How's Ross?"

"Asleep," Charlene said. "He was in and out of the ER pretty fast because he's a cop. The ER doc liked my work. He didn't mess with the wound. He did give Ross a script for an antibiotic. I had it filled at the hospital pharmacy. Ross is going to be sore for a week or so."

I grabbed a beer, sat down, twisted off the top, and took a long drink. "How's Jessica?"

"That girl's in bad shape," Charlene said. "Doesn't look as if anyone was feeding her. When she comes down off whatever she's on, I don't think it's going to be pretty. I didn't see any needle marks in the usual places, so they must have continued to give her something in her drinks."

I nodded and took another pull on my beer.

"What are you going to do, Don?" Mary said.

"Sleep on it."

"Speaking of which," Charlene said, "you two take the kids' room. You'll have to sleep on twins, but the mattresses are new and the sheets are clean. I put extra pillows on the beds. You'll find a couple of old XL T-shirts that will be comfortable to sleep in. New toothbrushes, toothpaste, and mouthwash are in the bathroom."

"Thank you, Charlene," Mary said. "That was so thoughtful. You seem to have thought of everything."

"Nurses are always prepared for the unexpected," Charlene said, "especially when they're dating a cop."

"Come on, Cowboy," Mary said. "You've had a long day."

In the kids' room, we undressed and took turns in the bathroom. One of the twin beds was tucked into a corner against the wall. I got in and moved as close to the wall as I could. Mary slipped in next to me, and I held her close.

After a few minutes of silence, Mary said, "Want to talk about it?"

"No," I said. "I'm beat. My brain is shutting down."

"Go to sleep. We'll talk in the morning."

I kissed her forehead and drifted off into a dreamless sleep.

◆ ◆ ◆ ◆

I didn't wake up until light was peeking through the drawn blinds on the only window in the room. Mary was not in my bed or the other bed or anywhere in the room. I was not fully awake and in no hurry to get up. I lay there thinking about last night. I wondered how I always managed to get myself in a position where I had to kill people. I felt justified because those deaths had always occurred when I was saving myself or somebody else from bad people. Still, I had taken lives, and I was losing count. Not a good thing. All those people were innocent children once. All had mothers, maybe some even had fathers who stayed around. At some point, they had all taken wrong turns and eventually died from a bullet from one of my guns.

Last night, Ross and I were lucky. The shooter had a huge advantage with an automatic weapon. Fortunately for us, he hadn't capitalized, and it cost him, making him another young man who had thrown his life away by being born in the wrong place at the wrong time and making wrong choices. *You did what you had to do*, I thought. *Forget about it.*

I moved on to my next problem: what to do with Jessica Johnson. She was in bad shape and, what was worse, probably didn't care whether she lived or died. I could call her mother and tell her to come get Jessica, but I had a feeling that wouldn't be a long-term solution. I had spent too much time looking for Jessica and didn't want her going down another black hole. I knew my best choice, which meant I needed to make a few phone calls as soon as I was awake enough to function.

I smelled coffee. I got up and put on my pants, socks, and shoes, then headed for the kitchen. Mary and Charlene sat at the kitchen table drinking coffee. They stopped talking and looked up at me.

"Want some coffee, Cowboy?" Mary said. "There's half-and-half."

"Sounds great," I said.

Mary fixed my coffee, and I took that first glorious, life-inducing drink and let out a long breath. "Ross still asleep?"

"He is," Charlene said. "I gave him some meds that should keep him out for a while. I'm going to take the day off and hang around here. You-all don't have to rush."

Charlene and Mary fixed breakfast, including the best biscuits and gravy I had ever eaten, along with sausage, scrambled eggs, and home-fried potatoes. I was in heaven again. After breakfast, we cleaned up and Mary went to the Peabody to pack our suitcases and bring everything back to Charlene's. One way or another, we would fly out before nightfall.

As I was finishing my coffee, Charlene said, "I have an office in the basement, if you'd like to use it."

"I would," I said. "Will a cell phone work down there?"

"Yes, it will," Charlene said.

She showed me the basement door and flipped on the lights. I went down into a family room with a couch, two recliners, a large-screen TV, lamps on tables, and bookshelves with books, DVDs, and video games. A Blu-ray player was hooked up to the TV, and there were a couple of video game controls. I was guessing the kids spent a lot to time down here. A door in the back led to a small office with a nice L-shaped desk that held filing trays, a couple of lamps, and a desktop computer that looked fairly new. I sat, took out my cell phone, and called Katie Johnson.

35

"Mr. Youngblood?" she answered.

"I found Jessica," I said. *No reason to beat around the bush*, I thought.

"Thank God. And thank you. Is she all right?"

"It's hard to say exactly how she is," I said. "She's sleeping now. I pulled her out of a crack house last night with some help from a Memphis police detective and six members of the SWAT team. Needless to say, she's not in great shape. I'll know more when she wakes up."

"Memphis?" she said, puzzled.

"It's a long story."

"I have time, if you do."

So, I hit the highlights of tracking Jessica to Memphis, along with the fact that she had probably been kidnapped by Kenny Stone. I left out the parts where Jessica might have been raped and where I had killed a young gangbanger to get to her.

"My God," she said. "Were you in danger?"

"We were all in danger, Mrs. Johnson. Detective Dean was wounded in the process."

"Is he going to be okay?"

"He should be fine," I said. "It's Jessica I'm worried about. She's going to need help to recover, both physically and mentally."

"She'll never listen to me," Katie Johnson said. "Do you have any ideas?"

"I do. I know a place that might be able to help her, but she has to go willingly. I can't just handcuff her and haul her off."

"Please try to convince her," she said.

"I'll do that," I said. "I'll be in touch, Mrs. Johnson."

◆ ◆ ◆

I called Jim Doak. "Where are you?"

"Who wants to know?" Jim said.

"Joseph Fleet," I said.

"In that case, I'm at Tri-Cities Airport overseeing maintenance on Fleet Industries jet number one."

"Good for you," I said. "When will jet number one be ready to fly?"

"Three or four hours. Ready to come home?"

"You bet," I said. "I've had all the excitement I can handle on this trip. We might need to make a side trip before we go home. Would that be a problem?"

"Where?"

"Hartford, Connecticut."

"That's a hell of a side trip," Jim said, "but doable. I'll get this wrapped up as soon as possible and head your way."

◆ ◆ ◆ ◆

I called the super nun of Silverthorn, Sister Sarah Agnes Woods, the *comandante* of the best and most expensive rehab center in the United States. Silverthorn treated all kinds of addictions and charged outrageous prices to the rich and famous. Occasionally, it treated a mere mortal at a reduced rate.

"Well, well," she said, "I haven't heard from you in a while. Are you completely recovered from Afghanistan?"

"Getting there," I said. "This is not a social call."

"Explain."

"I have a potential client for you," I said. "Do you have room?"

"For one of yours, always. A female, I'm guessing."

"You know me too well."

"You gravitate toward damsels in distress," she said. "What's her addiction?"

"She feels responsible for the death of her twin, which has led to some bad life choices," I said. "I'm not entirely sure of the extent of her dependencies, but she seems intent on slowly destroying herself."

"Okay, tell me everything you know."

So, I told her how a blackmail scheme had led me to Jessica Johnson's mother and finally to Jessica herself. I left out the part about the crack house shootout.

"Have you discussed Silverthorn with Jessica?"

"Not yet," I said. "I wanted to run it by you first."

"Well, then, if she agrees, bring her," Sarah Agnes said. "We'll see if we can help."

"If she says yes, Mary and I will be there with Jessica by dinnertime," I said. "I'll be in touch."

◆ ◆ ◆ ◆

A few minutes later, I heard the floor creaking above me and knew that Ross was up and moving. I made my way up the stairs and into the kitchen to find Ross sitting at the kitchen table while Charlene poured him a cup of coffee.

"How do you feel?" I said.

"Like I've been shot," he said. "Sore as hell."

"Ever been shot before?"

"No. That's what I get for hanging out with you. Thanks for saving my life, by the way."

"I was saving my own," I said. "You were just a beneficiary."

"Lucky me," Ross said. "I take it you didn't find Kenny Stone."

"Nope. Slick Kenny found his way to the basement and left by the same way we came in."

"You going to track him down?"

"Not now," I said. "I've got other things to do. Kenny will surface eventually, and when he does, I'll be there to take him down."

"I don't doubt that for a minute," Ross said, then moaned as he adjusted himself in his chair. "How many times have you been shot, Youngblood?"

"Four," I said. "Unless I'm forgetting one."

"Jesus," Ross said. "That must be some kind of record for a private cop."

"If it is, I don't wish to expand on it."

"How long did it take you to heal?"

"The lengths of time were different, depending on the wound," I said. "The next couple of days will be the worst, then the soreness will slowly start to go away, and one day you'll notice that you aren't sore anymore."

Our conversation was interrupted by a noise in the hall. We all turned toward the doorway that led into the kitchen. Jessica Johnson was leaning on the doorjamb looking as if she had just escaped from a prison camp.

"Where am I?" she said.

36

"Please sit down, honey," Charlene said. "Let me get you a cup of coffee and something to eat, and then Mr. Youngblood will tell you everything you need to know." Charlene poured coffee into a mug and handed it to Jessica. "Cream and sugar?"

"Black is fine," Jessica said softly. "Who are you?"

"I'm Charlene Barry." Charlene was low key and matter-of-fact, like she was giving directions to the local Walgreens. "I'm a nurse. You are in my home. The big, good-looking black man is Ross Dean. He's a cop. The white guy is a superhero disguised as a private investigator. His name is Donald Youngblood. How about scrambled eggs and toast?"

"That sounds nice," Jessica said.

Interesting choice of words, I thought. Maybe her world had been absent of *nice* since her sister died.

Jessica took a drink of coffee and looked at me. "What is going on?" she said, a quiet urgency in her voice. "I'm very confused."

"Eat breakfast and then we'll talk," I said.

Charlene was as fast as a short-order cook with the scrambled eggs and toast. They looked so good I could have eaten them myself.

"Ross, I think you should lie back down," Charlene said as she set the eggs and toast in front of Charlene. "Come on, I'll tuck you in."

Ross took the hint. "I think you're right. I am feeling rather tired." He stood and followed Charlene out of the kitchen. Seconds later, I heard them climbing the stairs to the second floor.

"What's wrong with him?" Jessica said. She had a fast start on the eggs.

"He was wounded last night," I said.

"Did it have anything to do with me?"

"Yes, but I need to start from the beginning," I said. "What's the last thing you remember?"

Her face went blank as she tried to come up with the answer. She continued to eat. I waited. She stared into space, looking confused. She drank some coffee. "My memory is a blur. I remember being at a bar having a drink with someone. I think I remember being in a car for a long time. I kind of remember a smoky room with people, but all that seems like a dream."

"Do you know that you're in Memphis?"

"What? Memphis? How?" Jessica was astounded. "Please tell me what's going on."

"Okay," I said. "I'll talk, you eat."

She nodded and went back to her breakfast.

I told her most of it—her mother hiring me, my going to Charleston, my conversation with Katt Kilgore, and my tracking her to Memphis. I left out the blackmail scheme. I didn't mention Kenny Stone by name. I'd get around to that later, when she was more lucid and couldn't fall back on not remembering. She listened in rapt astonishment as her breakfast disappeared. I finished with Ross and me pulling her out of the crack house after going through a firefight to get to her. I didn't mention she might have been raped. Maybe she wasn't. Snitches have been known to embellish their information. She was wide eyed and accepting.

"My God, Detective Dean was wounded saving me?"

"Yes. The guy you were with obviously had you on something that allowed you to be ambulatory but suppressed your memory. Some drugs out there can do that. Are you on anything? Crack, heroin, cocaine?"

"I don't do drugs," she said. "I prefer drinking myself into oblivion."

I believed her. I noticed that she was becoming more responsive. The fog was somewhat lifting. She seemed a bit more coherent.

"What happened to the guy I was with?" she said.

"He got away."

"Too, bad," she said. "I'd like to know who it was."

There was a long period of silence. She had a lot to process, an uphill battle in her condition. I wanted to ask her about the sex DVDs, but I knew it would have to wait.

"What happens now?" she said. "You taking me home to Mommy?"

"You're an adult," I said. "I'm not taking you anywhere you don't want to go. I do have a suggestion, however."

She took a minute. "What is it?"

"Why don't you stop trying to slowly kill yourself and start living for yourself and your sister?"

She gave me a questioning look but didn't say anything.

"I know your twin was killed. Maybe it was your fault and maybe it wasn't. But she is part of you, and as long as you're alive, she's alive. When you die, she dies. Live for yourself and live for her. Don't kill her twice."

There was maybe a thirty-second delay, and then the tears began. I guessed they were a long time coming. I waited. She sobbed painful sobs. It was not easy to watch.

Sometime later, Jessica said, "How do I get past this? I've tried. I just can't."

"If you're willing," I said, "I know someone who can help."

"I'm more than willing. I'm desperate. When can I meet this person?"

"Soon," I said. "Very soon."

• ◆ ◆ ◆

Jessica went back to bed, and I went downstairs to Charlene Barry's office. I had some time and wanted to make a couple of phone calls. I called David Steele, got his assistant, and left a message that things were "getting interesting." I knew that would tweak his curiosity. Then I made another call, one I hoped might net me Kenny Stone. I had already stored the name and number in my cell phone. I went to my contacts, found the name, and tapped the phone icon. I heard two rings and then a voice.

"Sims," he said.

"Laramie," I said, "it's Donald Youngblood."

"Youngblood, how are you?"

"Tired," I said. "I was up late."

"Doing what?"

"Shooting it out with a bunch of bad guys."
"Did you take anyone off the board?"
"One," I said. "He wounded a guy I was with."
"Shit," he said. "Wish I was there."
"Maybe not," I said. "The guy had an AK-47. We're lucky we're not dead."
"So how did you take him out?"
I told him.
"Gutsy," Laramie said.
"No choice," I said.
"Did you get the girl?"
"Yes."
"Alive?"
"More or less," I said. "Hard to tell at this point. She's asleep right now. I'm going to get her some help."
"How about Kenny Stone?"
"He slipped away," I said. "Which is the reason I'm calling. Let the Ghost know what happened and ask him to keep an eye out for Jimmy. Give him my number and ask him to call me if he hears anything pertaining to Kenny Stone. Tell him my credit is good."
"I'll do that," Laramie Sims said. "I've got to run. Keep me posted, Youngblood."

◆ ◆ ◆ ◆

Charlene had various pads on her desk, so I picked up a pen and made notes: thoughts, observations, things to do. I doodled. Kenny Stone was not getting away with blackmail and kidnapping. I was going to find him no matter how long it took. I wrote,

Kenny Stone will eventually return to Charleston.
Check in with Congressman Gildersleeve.
Reservations for the club pro tournament.

Touch base with T. Elbert. Call Billy.
Take Big Bob to breakfast.

These were all things I would have done anyway, but I felt a sense of accomplishment just writing them down.

My cell phone rang. David Steele. I answered by saying, "I found the girl."

"Is she okay?" David Steele said.

"She'll survive. She's probably worse off mentally than physically. She has agreed to get some help. I'm taking her someplace this afternoon."

"Are you still in Charleston?"

"Memphis," I said.

"Memphis?" David Steele said. "You'd better explain that."

I did.

"So, now Kenny Stone is not only a blackmailer, he's a kidnapper," he said.

"And not so good at either one," I said.

"Want me to open up an official Bureau complaint?"

"No," I said. "It's my case and my call. Neither the congressman nor the Johnsons want any record of this. When the time comes, I'll take care of Kenny Stone."

"Not going vigilante on me, are you?"

"No, but I wouldn't mourn his demise."

"I didn't hear that," David Steele said. "Don't get caught up in being judge, jury, and executioner, Youngblood."

Judge and jury, maybe, I thought. *The executioner part remains to be seen.* "I hear you, Dave. Get back to work. I'll be in touch."

♦ ♦ ♦ ♦

Sometime later, Mary returned. She texted me: **Where r u?**
I texted back: **In the basement. Come on down.**
I heard her on the stairs, and then she called, "Don?"

"Back here," I said.

She came into the office and sat down. "The house is quiet. Where is everyone?"

"Napping, I think. Let me tell you what I've been doing."

"Let me guess," she said. "You called Sarah Agnes, and you probably called David Steele."

"How did you know I called Sarah Agnes?"

"Because you want to fix all damsels in distress, and this one is going to need a lot of fixing. If anyone can get her back on track, it's Sarah Agnes."

"You're right," I said. "I did call the good sister, and I did call David Steele. And I also called Laramie Sims."

"And you told David you could handle it from here, and you told Sims to be on the lookout for Kenny Stone," Mary said. She seemed a little too pleased with herself.

"You got a tap on my phone?" I said, feigning annoyance.

"I know how you think. I know you want to keep this confidential, and I know you want to deal with Kenny Stone personally. I wouldn't mind getting a piece of him myself."

"You might just get your chance," I said. "Since you seem to know everything, do you know what time we're leaving?"

She smiled. "No, I don't know that."

"Later today. Jim Doak is coming to take us to Silverthorn. He should be in the air soon."

"I bought some clothes for Jessica and some makeup and other things she'll need," Mary said. "And I bought her a suitcase to put it all in."

"Very thoughtful of you. Why don't you go see if the clothes fit and get her moving so we can get out of here?"

"They'll fit," Mary said, standing up. "But I'll get her going. I'm ready to blow this town."

37

An hour later, Mary helped Jessica into the back of our rental and shut the door. Jessica looked just fine in her new jeans, long-sleeve T-shirt, boots, and leather jacket. Ross and Charlene waited beside the SUV.

"It's been real," Ross said. "Wounded in the line of duty. I'll get a lot of mileage out of that."

"Glad I could help," I said.

"You-all are crazy," Charlene said.

"False bravado," Mary said. "They know they were lucky."

Ross and I smiled and said nothing.

"Come see us," Mary said. "We would love to have you visit."

Nothing bonds like a crisis, I thought. We had made two new friends.

"We'll do that," Charlene said. "You have to come to our wedding, please. I won't take no for an answer."

"It's a date," Mary said, hugging Charlene. Then she hugged Ross. "Take care of yourself, Ross."

"Yes, ma'am," he said.

Charlene gave me a quick hug, and I shook hands with Ross.

"Thanks for everything," I said.

"Wouldn't have missed it," he said.

◆ ◆ ◆ ◆

The wheels of Fleet Industries jet number one lifted off the Memphis airport tarmac in the haze of early afternoon, and I said goodbye to Beale Street, the ducks at the Peabody Hotel, and the ghost of Elvis. I had every reason to believe we would return for Ross and Charlene's wedding. I was dozing in my chair by the time we leveled off at twenty-five thousand feet, but I picked up snatches of muted conversation between Mary and Jessica.

"I love the clothes you bought me," Jessica said. "You have a real sense of style."

"Thank you," Mary said. "They look great on you."

"What do I owe you?"

"A gift," Mary said. "A fresh start on a new life."

"You think that's really possible?"

"I do."

"I really hope so," Jessica said. "I need to start over."

That's the last thing I heard as I embarked on a three-hour nap. I was awakened by the thud of our landing.

"Rise and shine, Cowboy," Mary said. "We're in Hartford."

◆ ◆ ◆ ◆

An hour after we picked up a rental SUV, I pulled up in front of Silverthorn. Jessica headed with me toward Sister Sarah's office while Mary took charge of her suitcase. Sister Sarah was waiting for us in the lobby.

"Sister Sarah Agnes Woods, I would like you to meet Jessica Johnson," I said. "Jessica has a problem she has been dealing with and thinks you might be able to help."

"Walk with me and tell me about it," Sarah Agnes said.

"I'm going to check on Mary," I said.

I exited before anyone could object. At the front entrance, I found Mary talking to Regina Capelli. When Regina saw me, she ran and gave me a hug.

"So good to see you both," she said.

"You're still here," I said.

She smiled. "I am."

Regina Capelli was Carlo Vincente's granddaughter. Carlo was a New York mob boss I had crossed paths with on more than one occasion. Although we were on opposite ends of the legal system, we had an understanding. I had helped Regina with a gambling problem that led me to bring her to Silverthorn. Once she came to terms with her problem, she had started helping Sarah Agnes with the business end of her operation.

She had been at Silverthorn at least seven or eight years and was now an indispensable fixture.

"How is your grandfather?"

"Getting old but doing okay," she said. "I'll tell him you asked. It will please him. You and Mary are spending the night, I hope."

"Yes," I said.

"When I heard you were coming, I freshened up the guest suite. I'm sure you know where it is."

"I do," I said. "Thanks."

Regina's cell phone made a noise. "Jessica is ready to go to her room," she said, looking at Mary. "She wants you to go with us."

"Sure," Mary said.

We walked to Sister Sarah's office. Mary pulled Jessica's suitcase, rejecting my bid at being chivalrous.

Before leaving for her room, Jessica turned to me and said, "Will I see you in the morning?"

"Most likely," I said. "We're spending the night and aren't in a big hurry to leave. Given the opportunity, Mary likes to sleep late."

"And I intend on taking full advantage," Mary said. "No wakeup call, please."

"Can we have coffee in the morning?" Jessica said.

"Sure," I said. "I'm up early. I'll be in the cafeteria."

She nodded and walked away with Mary and Regina.

I went into the good sister's office. She looked up at me and nodded to a chair. I sat.

"What do you think?" I said.

"Too soon to think anything," she said. "We'll see."

"Did you have a good talk?"

"Yes," she said.

"Is there anything else you want to tell me?"

"No, but it sounds like there are some things you could tell me," Sarah Agnes said, arching an eyebrow. "What's this I hear about a shootout with one of your police friends getting wounded?"

"Oh, that," I said.

"Yes, that."

"It was part of the rescue mission. We closed down a crack house and took down some bad guys."

"Well, I hope you didn't have to kill anybody," she said.

I stared at her and said nothing.

"Oh, dear," she said.

"Self-defense," I said. "Am I going to hell?"

"Probably not," Sarah Agnes said. "I'll put in a good word. Want to talk about it?"

"Talk about what?" Mary said, appearing in the doorway.

"Talk about dinner," I said. "I'm starved."

"Let's go see what the chef can whip up," Sister Sarah said as she stood.

The chef whipped up some grilled salmon with a special sauce, wild rice, and crispy-fried Brussels sprouts. I'm not a big fan of Brussels sprouts, but I like almost anything that's crispy-fried. We began with Caesar salad with homemade dressing and fresh-baked bread. I felt like I was in a five-star restaurant until I remembered what the patrons were being charged to rehab at Silverthorn. They certainly would not go hungry. I'd stay simply for the food.

"This is sensational," Mary said. "Do you eat this way all the time?"

"When I want to," Sarah Agnes said. "It's why I kill myself in the workout center at six o'clock every morning."

I listened as Sarah Agnes and Mary talked. They discussed food and their workout routines. I could feel the tiredness washing over me, assisted by my third beer.

"I think it's time I put my husband to bed," Mary said.

"Past time, it would appear," Sarah Agnes said.

"Thank you so much for dinner," Mary said.

"You're most welcome. Don helps make all this possible, as I'm sure you know."

"Vaguely," Mary said. "I try to stay out of Don's business."

"She's more interested in guns than finance," I said.

"Among other things," Mary said. She was on her third glass of wine.

"Okay, you two," Sarah Agnes said. "Go!"

38

The cafeteria opened at six and served breakfast and lunch. The dining room served only dinner but had a fancy brunch every Sunday morning after a short church service. At seven o'clock the next morning, I was alone having coffee. The rich and famous were obviously in no hurry to get out of bed. I was reading the latest news headlines on my laptop. I didn't read anything I would consider encouraging. Near seven-thirty, Jessica walked in, saw me, went to get coffee, and walked over and sat down. She looked fragile. She smiled a weak smile and took her first sip of coffee in silence, tired and vulnerable.

"You'll be fine," I said.

She smiled. "Yes, I think I will. I already feel a sense of relief. There is something peaceful about being here. Does my mother know?"

"About your getting help, yes," I said. "Where you are, no. If you're not ready, I'll be glad to call her and tell her as much as you want her to know."

"I'm definitely not ready to talk with her," Jessica said. "I don't really know what I'd say. The last few months are a blur. I can't remember anything about the last week."

Not remembering was a good thing, as far as I was concerned. Some of those memories might be devastating.

She drank some more coffee. "Just call my mother and tell her I'm settled in, and I'll call her sometime in the next week or so, when I get my head on straight. Don't tell her where I am or she'll come looking."

"I'll call and point her in a different direction," I said.

She nodded. We were quiet for a while, then Jessica said softly, "I wanted to kill myself, but I didn't have the courage. I figured I could just self-destruct. Maybe drink myself to death. It might have worked if you hadn't come along."

I said nothing, just waited.

"I'm glad you did," she said. "You told me some things I needed to hear."

"Remember that if it hadn't been for your mother, I wouldn't have come along."

She nodded. "I haven't been much of a daughter to her lately. I have a lot of making up to do."

"Turning your life around will be enough for her, I promise."

Jessica finished her coffee. "By the way, Mary is awesome. She really knows how to take control. You're lucky to have each other."

"Well," I said, "I know I'm lucky to have her."

Before Jessica could say anything else, Regina walked over. "Hey, Jessica, ready to get started?" she said. "Sorry, Don, you're on your own."

Jessica stood. "Goodbye, and thanks for everything."

They walked to the other end of the cafeteria to get breakfast. Other guests were starting to file in. I got a second cup of coffee and went to find a quiet corner away from the gathering crowd.

There were a lot of nooks and alcoves with a chair or two around Silverthorn, and I had my favorite one, which Sarah Agnes had dubbed "Youngblood Corner." Whenever I disappeared, she knew she could find me there. I refreshed my coffee, packed up my laptop, and walked to my favorite spot. I sat and got comfortable, then dialed Katie Johnson's cell phone.

"Mr. Youngblood," she answered. "You have news?"

"Not too much at this point," I said. "Jessica is settled into an excellent West Coast rehab center. She asked me to call and tell you she's sorry for all the pain and suffering she has caused, and that she'll call when she feels it's time to talk with you." I was taking some editorial privilege with what Jessica said, but my message would certainly make Katie Johnson feel a little better.

"Thank you so much. I am in your debt."

"Not for long," I said. "You'll get a bill."

"I certainly hope so," she said.

"And when this is over, you'll get a bill from the rehab center."

"And I will happily pay both."

"You have my number if you need anything," I said.

"Thank you again, Mr. Youngblood," she said. "Goodbye."

◆ ◆ ◆

Five minutes later, Mary sat down with a lidded cup of coffee and took a sip.

"Hey, Doll," I said.

"Hey, Cowboy."

"How'd you find me?"

"You're not the only detective in the family," Mary said.

"True enough," I said. "How did you sleep?"

"Like a rock. You sure know how to relax a girl."

"We aim to please," I said.

"Who is we?"

"Well, you know."

"Mind of his own, huh?"

"Seems that way," I said.

Mary chortled. "Most certainly." She took a sip of her coffee. "What have you been up to this morning?"

"I had coffee, spent some time on my laptop, talked to Jessica, walked over here, and called Katie Johnson. That's it in detail."

"Tell me about the Katie Johnson conversation—unless, of course, it's confidential."

So, I told her practically word for word.

"West Coast?"

"In case she tries to track Jessica down," I said. "California alone has enough rehab centers to keep her busy for a year."

"Smart," Mary said.

We sat in silence and drank coffee.

"I'm ready to go home, Cowboy."

"Then let's pack 'em up and move 'em out," I said.

"Let's," Mary said.

39

Early the next day, I headed briskly up the walk toward T. Elbert's front porch carrying a Dunkin' Donuts bag filled with coffee and various goodies. Roy and T. Elbert were waiting comfortably under heat lamps that kept the cold at bay.

I was momentarily lost in the past. November in East Tennessee was known for some cold days, and this was one of them. I remembered one Thanksgiving when I was a kid maybe ten years old. I was eating my turkey dinner and marveling that the outside temperature was exactly zero. The lake was frozen. After gorging on the feast my mother had prepared, I went down to the dock to examine the ice. I stood there and breathed in the frigid air and marveled at how much I enjoyed the cold. The fact that it was a sunny, windless day made it relatively pleasant. A ten-mile-an-hour wind, not uncommon coming off the lake, would have made it brutal.

I handed the bag to Roy and sat down.

"It's been three and a half weeks since I last saw you," T. Elbert said as Roy distributed coffee and laid out the muffins, donuts, bagels, and such.

"But who's counting?" Roy said.

"And it's a lot longer than that since you've been in Little Switz," T. Elbert continued. "I hope you have a good story to tell."

"I do," I said, taking a sip of coffee. "But it doesn't have an ending yet." I chose a chocolate-glazed cake donut and took a healthy bite.

"So, let's hear it," T. Elbert said.

"I'm fine," I said. "How are you?"

"We're fine," T. Elbert said, feigning annoyance. "Now, get to it."

"In great detail," Roy added.

I told a version of the Jessica Johnson story, leaving out any mention of Congressman Gildersleeve. The theme was finding a daughter for a distraught mother. I didn't embellish or make things up, I just omitted anything to do with the blackmail scheme. The rescue of Jessica had them on the edge of their seats. As I described the shootout, even I thought it was exciting and a little scary. When I finally finished, we sat quietly and enjoyed the coffee and carbs.

"You could have been killed, Donald," T. Elbert said. "Then who would bring me coffee and donuts?"

"Roy," I said.

"Not me, Gumshoe," Roy said. "You need to be more careful. T. Elbert is counting on you."

"You guys are too much," I said. "Still, I have to admit, thinking back, it was scary as hell."

Nobody mentioned that I had sent another soul on its way somewhere. I shoved that thought into the dark closet I kept for such things and slammed the door.

◆ ◆ ◆ ◆

It seemed like forever since I was in the office. I had spent a long three days away from the friendly confines of Mountain Center. Gretchen went over a few things. She sensed my lack of interest and left, saying, "Your mind is somewhere else. We'll talk later."

I picked up the phone and called Jason Gildersleeve. I went through the usual screening, and then the congressman was on the phone.

"Mr. Youngblood," he said. "I take it you have more news."

"I do," I said. "I found Jessica Johnson."

"Well, that's good news. How is Jessica?"

"Fragile," I said. "She's getting some badly needed help."

"That's good. I'm glad to hear it. Anything else?"

I could tell he was in a hurry to get me off the phone.

"Call me if you hear any rumblings about that little movie I watched," I said. "I still have unfinished business with the agent."

"I understand completely," Jason Gildersleeve said. "Thanks for all your help, Mr. Youngblood."

"It might help if I had your personal cell-phone number," I said. "I won't share it with anyone."

"Of course," he said. "It's not highly classified." He gave it to me.

"Good luck with the campaign," I said.

"Thank you. Goodbye, Mr. Youngblood."

He didn't wait for my reply. He was gone. It wasn't exactly the bum's rush, but I could understand why Congressman Jason Gildersleeve wanted me in the rearview mirror. Somehow, I knew we would be talking again.

40

The following Monday, I was in the office early. I had been treading water since my return, trying to get Kenny Stone out of my mind, but it wasn't working. I didn't understand why I couldn't let it go. Kenny was a loose end, and I hated loose ends, but I was more obsessed than usual. I had to believe he would surface sooner or later. His kind always did. I needed to do something proactive.

I pulled up Sister Sarah's private number from my cell-phone address book and tapped the blue icon that initiated the call.

She answered on the second ring. "Donald, is that you?"

"It is I, calling from the hills of East Tennessee, where in the very near future there will be an extravagant Thanksgiving ball."

"I wouldn't miss it," she said. "Nice segue. Now, why did you really call?"

"How is Jessica?"

"She is progressing," Sister Sarah said. "You know I can't say too much, but the death of her sister caused catastrophic damage to her psyche. We are working through that. Her mantra has become, 'Live for two.' I don't know where you pulled that from, but it's perfect. Maybe you should have been a shrink."

"Stop trying to be funny," I said.

"Just saying."

"I'd like to pay Jessica a visit," I said. "Is that possible?"

"I'm okay with it," Sarah Agnes said. "Let me speak with Jessica, and I'll get back to you."

41

Two days later, I sat with Jessica in Silverthorn's cafeteria. We were drinking coffee, nibbling muffins, and exchanging small talk. I was waiting for what I thought was the right time to get down to business, but Jessica beat me to it.

"I'm sure you didn't come all this way to have coffee," she said. "What do you want to know?"

"Do you remember some sex videos you and your sister made when you were in college?"

She looked down at her coffee and shook her head. "Those fucking videos. Is that what this whole thing is about?"

"Kind of," I said. "Do you remember Kenny Stone?"

She didn't answer but stopped eating, her muffin half finished. Then she said, "You mean the biggest mistake of my life? Yeah, I remember Kenny Stone." *Kenny Stone* came out as a snarl, as if she was disgusted that she even had to say his name. "Was Kenny the one who took me to Memphis?"

"Yes," I said.

"The bastard."

"Did you and Kenny try to blackmail a U.S. congressman with one of those videos?"

"What?" she said, angry now. "You mean Jason Gildersleeve? No way."

She seemed genuinely surprised by the question. There was a shocked earnestness in her response, and I instantly believed she knew nothing about the blackmail scheme. I found myself relieved.

"How did you know Jason is a congressman?"

"I get this Princeton magazine, and he was featured in one of the issues."

"Well, Kenny tried to blackmail Jason," I said. "He sent him a DVD of a sex video starring you and your sister."

"That asshole. I knew he was bad news. I'd like to rip his heart out, if he has one."

"Do you still have all the DVDs?"

"There really weren't that many," she said. "But we still had some. Some we recorded over. Some we gave to the guys. Some we just lost. I smashed them to pieces after the accident. I must have missed one, or Kenny took it before the accident."

"Were the DVDs labeled?"

"No."

"How do you think Kenny knew about Jason?"

Jessica thought about that for a few moments, then started shaking her head. "My fault. I was pretty buzzed one day and was reading the article about Jason. Kenny was hanging out, and I made a comment that Jennifer and I once made a sex video with him. He seemed interested. Overly interested. He wanted to see it. I had no idea where it was, so I showed him another video of a guy who could have been Jason. All the guys kind of looked alike in our videos. Jennifer and I liked a certain type. Am I in trouble?"

"No," I said. "Jason figured out that it was not himself in the video and told Kenny to get lost. Kenny might think Jason is bluffing. I'm thinking he still might try to sell it to a supermarket rag or to TV. If he does, I'll be all over him. Any idea where he might be? He seems to have dropped off the grid."

"No idea," she said. "But if you find him, beat the shit out of the conniving bastard."

"Glad to," I said. *Hell hath no fury . . .*

◆ ◆ ◆ ◆

On my way out, I stopped to see Sister Sarah Agnes. She was hard at work shuffling papers. I poked my head in her office and said, "I thought Regina did all the paperwork."

"She does, but she took a week off to go see her family. Until she gets back, I have to muddle through. How did it go with Jessica?"

"She couldn't help me much, but I'm convinced she didn't do anything criminal. She may have some other things to share with you since my visit."

"Thanks for letting me know," she said. "On another note, I'm thinking about building another wing on to Silverthorn, devoted to teens and preteens."

"There's a demand?" I said.

"You'd be surprised. Can I afford it?"

I had, from the beginning, handled the investments for Silverthorn and hired a CPA to file the taxes. Silverthorn was flush.

"How much?"

"Five million," she said.

"Not a problem," I said. "Build away."

"Hot damn!" Sarah Agnes exclaimed.

"Such language for a nun."

"I guess I'm a little out of the habit of being a nun," she said with a wry smile.

I was laughing. I couldn't help myself.

42

Two days later, I was alone in the Mountain Center Diner with a mug of coffee and the paper, catching up on local football news. The Tennessee Vols had still not found their way out of football hell. Doris was quick to point out how long it had been since I was in.

"I've missed you, too, Doris," I said.

She scurried away, and I returned to the sports section. Mountain Center was having another strong season, with only one close loss to the number-one team in their division. They were in the semifinals of the state playoffs. A rematch was possible.

I heard Big Bob enter the diner. Well, I didn't actually hear him. What I heard was the usual noise level drop when he walked in. It returned to normal when he reached my table. He tossed his cowboy hat on a vacant chair and sat. It was weeks since I had seen him.

"Hello, stranger," he said.

"I've been busy," I said. "Why don't you start coming in the back door?"

"Why would I do that?"

"So you won't interrupt everyone's breakfast with your presence."

"Only the guilty give pause," he said. "Got to keep them on their toes."

"Well, I think you're succeeding," I said. "What's new?"

"What's new is all these stories of excessive force by police around the country."

I could tell he was agitated. "How is that affecting you?"

"I'm giving mini-seminars reminding my guys of what they can and cannot do, and for how long they can do it," he said. "It's necessary but time consuming. I have to take guys off the street to do it."

"Law enforcement walks a fine line," I said. "And it's under a microscope, with almost everyone carrying a camera in their pocket."

"Well, sometimes they can point out a bad cop, but they don't always tell the full story. Look, I know there are some bad cops out there. I'm just trying to make sure none of them are on my police force."

"Hard to tell sometimes."

"It is," Big Bob said. "But if you pay attention, the signs will be there."

"You're being proactive. Stop stressing about it."

"Easy for you to say. You never worry about anything. Never have."

I wish, I thought. I said nothing.

Doris arrived, and we ordered.

"Let's talk about something else," he said. "How is your case going?"

I told him everything that had happened since we last met, and that Kenny Stone was still in the wind.

"So, you had to take another bad guy off the board," he said.

"He was a kid."

"A kid with an automatic weapon," Big Bob said. "You're lucky to be here."

I started to say I had no choice, then decided against it. I had never killed anyone that young, and no matter what the circumstances, it was bothering me.

"So, your case is pretty much over," Big Bob said.

"Unless Kenny tries to sell the video. I kind of hope he does. I'd like to nail his ass."

"Because he's a slimeball."

"Couldn't have said it better myself."

Doris arrived with our breakfast, and our serious conversation ended. Our attention turned to more important things, like Mountain Center football and East Tennessee football and Tennessee football and football in general. Not a bad way to start the day.

◆ ◆ ◆ ◆

Later that morning, I called Joseph Fleet on his cell phone.

"Donald," he said when he answered. "Good to hear from you. How have you been? Is everything okay?"

"Fine, sir. Everything is fine."

"I do wish you'd stop with the sir," he said.

"It's what I'm comfortable with. I tried for months to get Oscar to call me Don and finally gave up. He just couldn't do it. It's a show of respect."

"Very well," Joseph Fleet said. "I appreciate the sentiment. Let's move on. I'm guessing you called for a reason."

"I did. I wanted to know if it would be okay to ask two more people to the Thanksgiving feast."

"Certainly," he said. "Just let Roy know, so he can add them to the list."

"I'll do that," I said. "How is your health?"

"Fine. I'll tell you more about it when we have our traditional after-dinner drink."

"I'll see you then," I said.

43

The following Wednesday, Mary and I stood on the observation deck at Tri-Cities Airport watching a tiny dot get bigger as it came toward us. We had spent a quiet weekend at the lake house. I watched Tennessee win a football game. We ate well and loved well and enjoyed the peace and quiet of the beautiful late-fall days. I had taken Monday and Tuesday off and done odd jobs inside and out around the newly built lake house. We were getting it the way we wanted, room by room, piece by piece.

"Think that's it?" Mary said.

"Should be," I said.

We watched as the tiny dot became a Delta passenger jet from Atlanta. It seemed to hang in midair before it finally dropped safely onto the tarmac and taxied toward the main terminal.

"Let's go," I said.

We walked to security to meet our arrivals. Far down the terminal, we could see passengers disembarking from the flight. The good-looking couple heading our way were the first passengers off the jet. They spotted us, and the woman waved excitedly while her male counterpart tried to remain unflappable, as always. A slight smile crossed Henry Cole's face in spite of himself.

Rosa Cole hurried ahead and hugged Mary fiercely. "So good to see you," Rosa said in beautifully Spanish-accented English.

"We're so glad you could come," Mary said.

Rosa gave me a quick hug as Henry greeted Mary. Henry and I shook hands and gave each other manly *abrazos* like the two comrades we were. We had recently been through hell together while on a mission in Afghanistan for the president of the United States, a mission both of us would just as soon forget. We had spent time in an army hospital nursing our wounds, giving thanks that we were alive, and getting to know one another. Henry Cole was a complex man who had led an extraordinary life working for the CIA.

"Good to see you, Henry," I said.
"Good to see you, too, Don."
"How was your trip?"
"Uneventful."
"Best kind," I said. "Let's go get your luggage."
"Let's hope it made it," Henry Cole said.

44

The next morning, I sat on the lower deck drinking coffee from an insulated Yeti mug and enjoying a crisp, windless November morning in the mid-fifties. November was that way in East Tennessee: some occasional warm days scattered among below-freezing ones. This particular November had been kind.

We had shared an early dinner with Rosa and Henry. Then Henry and I went to the den to watch football, leaving Mary and Rosa in the dining room with a freshly opened bottle of wine. Football was none too exciting, so I had headed for bed at halftime. I was vaguely aware of Mary joining me around midnight. I knew she would be sleeping late.

I heard the back door open, and Henry came down the stairs carrying another Yeti I has set out by the Keurig. He sat across from me. We were dressed alike in turtlenecks and sweaters, slacks and sneakers—not exactly twins, but close enough.

"Must feel cold to you, considering where you just flew in from," I said.

"A little, but I'll adjust. I kind of like it." He took a drink from his Yeti. "Good coffee."

"We aim to please," I said. "How did you sleep?"

"Like a rock. That's a great guest suite you have. I could get used to it."

"Stay as long as you like," I said.

"Three nights with you, then down to Gatlinburg for three nights, if I can borrow one of your rides. Rosa wants to hike the Smokies. Then back with you for one night. Does that sound okay?"

"Sounds like a plan," I said. "You can take the Armada. You should be safe from old enemies. It's been upgraded—reinforced steel and bulletproof glass."

"You're kidding."

"Nope. I had the same package on my Pathfinder and it saved my life once. It saved Billy, too. I lost the Pathfinder in the fire, so I made the same upgrades for the Armada."

"I didn't realize a PI's life was so dangerous."

"Only mine, it seems," I said. "I attract the worst of the worst."

We drank coffee and stared at the lake.

"This is a really nice place," Henry said. "Love the view from here. You been here long?"

"I grew up here."

"Really?" Henry said. "It looks brand new."

"It is. It burned to the ground in last year's wildfires. The dogs and I got trapped and almost didn't make it out. The barge saved us." I proceeded to tell Henry the story of the wildfires and my escape. "There were a few moments when I was sure I wasn't going to make it out."

"I've had a few of those myself," Henry said.

"I'll bet you have."

He didn't elaborate, and I didn't push. We drank more coffee.

"What have you been up to?" he said. "Anything exciting?"

"I spent some time healing and helping Mary set up the new house. I sponsored the local pro in the Tennessee PGA golf tournament. I was part of the security team at the tournament. I was mostly there for show. The worst that happened was some golf clubs getting stolen. Lacy was caddying for our pro, and it was the only way I could walk along with them." I told him a little about the tournament, Tony's story about the Dobbs brothers, and then T. Elbert's coming to the rescue with Tony's backup clubs.

"You think the other brother had something to do with the stolen clubs?" Henry said.

"I did for about a minute or two after I heard Tony's story. Then I decided it was just a random case of bad luck. The other brother is in the wind."

"Are you always in the middle of something . . . ?" He searched for a word.

"Strange, weird, unusual, unbelievable?" I said. "Yeah. Pick one. About the time my life is getting boring, it's not."

"How'd your guy do?"

"He finished fourth and qualified for the national club pro championship," I said. "It's in March."

"What happened after the golf tournament?"

"I caught a case I could sink my teeth into." I told him about an elite family hiring me to find their daughter and the problems I encountered trying to run down Kenny Stone. I told him about the albino, tracking Kenny to Memphis, Ross and Charlene, and the rescue of the damsel in distress. I didn't mention the congressman or the Johnsons by name. "I had to kill this young kid, maybe nineteen or twenty, during the shootout, and it's nagging me," I said.

"Sounds like you didn't have a choice."

"I didn't. I've killed bad guys before, even killed a woman once, so why is this one bothering me?"

"Don't know," Henry Cole said. "All I can tell you is you have to absolve yourself and move on."

"I'm getting there," I said.

Henry deftly changed the subject. "So, no sign of Kenny Stone?"

"Nope, he's off the grid," I said. "But I want him bad. Why is that, Henry?"

Henry was silent for a minute, and then he had an epiphany. "I think you blame Kenny Stone for the kid's death, and you want to make him pay. Once you find Kenny, you can move on from shooting the kid."

"Jesus, Henry. I never thought about that. You should have been a shrink."

"Not likely," Henry Cole said.

◆ ◆ ◆ ◆

Later that evening, the Joseph Fleet Thanksgiving bash was in full swing. The gourmet buffet was nothing if not spectacular, featuring lamb riblets, salmon in a pastry shell, beef bourguignon, and, of course, turkey. Tables were set up for six people with place cards identifying everyone's seats. I noticed a table for four with a quartet of younger men in dark suits—Fleet security, no doubt. I wondered why they were there. A perk, maybe. Each table was numbered. When your table number was called, you proceeded to the buffet. If you wanted seconds, you didn't wait to be called, you just went. The table for four got the first call. Mary and I were at a table with Henry, Rosa, Billy, and Maggie. It was the first time Henry had met Billy, although I had told him a lot about Billy and Billy a lot about him. They seemed cautious around each other.

When dinner ended, I was already planning a ten-mile run to burn the calories I had consumed. As was my custom, I stood in a quiet area away from the crowd and observed the guests: who was talking to whom, how they were reacting to each other. I stood there in my Armani tux holding a glass of champagne, mostly as a prop. A beer would have been gauche. I remembered the first time I had met Joseph Fleet, years ago. He had sent Roy, who at the time was his chauffeur, to fetch me. Saying no to the invitation had not been an option. Fleet had hired me to find his missing daughter. It was my first big case. It did not end well, but justice was served. The following year, Roy and I had organized the first Thanksgiving meal at the mansion, for maybe a dozen people. Lacy was a freshman in high school. Over the years, the event had grown into an extravaganza.

As I scanned the crowd, I thought I might have known half. Many were Fleet Industries midlevel employees. A few regulars were missing. Bruiser Bracken and Wanda Jones were down in the Caribbean enjoying the sand, sun, and each other. Lacy and Biker had stayed in Arizona to be with friends. Lacy promised we would see them at Christmas.

As the night wore on, I worked the crowd, talking to people I didn't see often and making new acquaintances. When the dancing began, I grabbed Mary. My gorgeous blond wife was always popular at these events. The banquet hall was full of upper-middle-class to upper-class people dressed to the nines. It certainly did not represent the real world. As we took a turn around the dance floor, I noticed Roy dancing with Sarah Agnes. They looked quite chummy.

Later, a member of the Fleet security staff approached me and said quietly, "Mr. Youngblood, Mr. Fleet would like you to join him in his study."

"Thank you," I said. "I know the way." I wanted to be clear that I didn't need an escort.

"Very good, sir," he said.

I casually made my way out of the giant hall and through a door that led to a hall that, after a few lefts and rights, eventually led to Joseph Fleet's study. He was waiting.

"Well," he said when I walked in, "I'm still here."

"As in, you made it to another Thanksgiving."

"Precisely," he said, handing me a goblet filled with Baileys Irish Cream and ice.

"Never doubted it," I said. "How do you feel?"

"Better than this time last year. The doctors are using a very precise method of delivering a pinpoint dose of radiation once a week. The brain tumor is cooperating by shrinking, and I haven't had any side effects. The cancer seems to be in remission."

"Good to hear," I said, taking a drink. "How's business?"

"Couldn't be better. Did Roy tell you about the latest contract he landed?"

"No," I said. "In case you haven't noticed, Roy is extremely tight lipped."

He laughed. "Yeah, I have noticed. Anyway, you'll get the details at the board meeting. Roy is doing a hell of a job. I'm surprised and not surprised at the same time."

"Roy's a lot smarter than we knew," I said. "And he has good instincts."

"Indeed he does."

"Does the contract have anything to do with the security team being here?"

"Yes," he said. "They're part of the contract. Their salaries are built in. They rotate twenty-four/seven in the plant, looking for who knows what. Since they are on the government's tab, I figured I'd treat them to dinner as a little perk. As you can see, they take the job seriously."

"Well, there are certain branches of our government that have always been a little paranoid."

"Very true," Joseph Fleet said.

We sat on a large couch in front of the fire and drank in silence.

After a while, Joseph Fleet said, "I don't need to know any of the details, but were you able to help Jason Gildersleeve with his problem?"

"Yes," I said. "There may be a few loose ends to tie up, but I now think it's a non-problem."

"Good to know. I really want him in the Senate. The country needs good young men like Jason."

"He'll have my vote," I said. "He seemed honest and direct during the time I worked for him. He asked me to be on his staff."

"And you said no, of course."

"Politics is one area I'd like to avoid."

"Smart decision," Joseph Fleet said. "I enjoyed meeting the Coles. Henry is an interesting fellow. When I asked what he did before he retired, he said, 'Government work,' and didn't elaborate. CIA?"

"Could be," I said.

He laughed. "Roy's not the only one who's tight lipped."

"I have to be. I know too many secrets, even a few of yours."

"Well put," he said. "I'll quit being nosy."

We sipped our drinks.

"You going to be around for Christmas?" I said.

"No. I'm leaving soon for Amelia Island. I'll be there for the winter. I no longer enjoy long stints of cold weather."

"Alone?"

He smiled.

"Aha!" I said.

He said nothing, but the smile remained. We were quiet for a time, enjoying our drinks and watching the fire. Then a voice from the doorway broke the silence: "I knew I would find you in here."

I turned and saw my gorgeous wife standing in the doorway. Joseph Fleet and I stood.

"Mary," Joseph Fleet said. "You are looking spectacular, as always."

"Thank you, Joseph. A woman can always use a good compliment. Your fabulous party is breaking up, and I need to steal my husband so he can take me home."

"Of course," Joseph Fleet said. "I didn't realize it was so late. I need to say goodbye to my guests. It was great seeing you-all. We must get together before next Thanksgiving. Maybe dinner at the club one night."

"Sounds good," I said.

"Please excuse me," he said. "Drive safe."

"We will," I said as he left the study like a man who had missed a meeting. "Ready?" I said to Mary.

"More than ready. This was great, but I'm partied out."

"Too bad," I said.

"I'm never that partied out, Cowboy."

45

Again, on Friday morning, Henry joined me for coffee on the lower deck. The day was a duplicate of the previous one, mild for November and with no wind. I had been there maybe ten minutes when he sat down. We both had a Yeti to keep our coffee warm.

"One hell of a party," Henry said.

"Always is," I said. "It's grown over the years."

"Joseph Fleet is an interesting fellow."

"He said the same thing about you. He thinks you were probably with the CIA."

"What did you say?" he said.

"I was vague."

We drank coffee and stared at the lake.

"Your partner is impressive," Henry Cole said. "I'd want him on my side no matter what I was doing."

"Billy is exceptional," I said. "He's connected to the universe in a way that others aren't. He sees the past and senses the future. He has always had my back, and he's a mother hen."

A few boats were on the lake. Most were bobbing in place, fishing. Running around the lake on a mid-fifties day could feel like the low forties, if you were going fast enough.

"Roy is also impressive," Henry said. "I wouldn't want to mess with him either."

"Nor would I," I said. "Roy came up the hard way. He doesn't talk much about it, and I don't ask. He was real fortunate to find a mentor like Joseph Fleet."

We sat awhile longer, and then Henry said, "I'd better roust Rosa so we can pack and get out of here. I'd like to do a little hiking this afternoon. It's a perfect day for it."

He walked up the stairs to the upper deck and through the door that led to our kitchen.

46

Monday morning, Mary and I stood in the exact same place on the observation deck at Tri-Cities as we had the past Wednesday when Henry and Rosa arrived. After the Fleet Thanksgiving bash, the Coles had spent one more night with us, then three days and two nights in Gatlinburg, which they described as glorious, then a final night with us. We drove them to the airport, the Armada still intact, since no one had taken a shot at Henry or tried to blow him up. Maybe he really was retired.

We watched their jet taxi out and maneuver into position for takeoff, then heard the big engines engage as the plane moved down the tarmac, gaining speed and then lifting ever so slowly skyward before it disappeared into the distant clouds.

"I'll miss them," Mary said.

"Yeah, me, too."

"Promise me we'll go see them."

"I promise."

"Good," Mary said. "Now, buy me breakfast. I'm starved."

47

On a clear Sunday morning right after New Year's, I sat on the lower deck with my customary coffee-filled Yeti, trying to wrap my mind around another year. The holidays had been busy, full of family and the Christmas spirit. Bruiser Bracken and Wanda Jones had been back in town. Lacy and Biker had flown in from Arizona. Mary's daughter, Susan, flew in from California, and her son, Jimmy, and his family drove in from Nashville. We had kids and grandkids. For the first time in my life, I felt like a patriarch.

Between the condo and the lake house, we were able to accommodate all the family. Christmas was a three-day party that started on the twenty-third and finally broke up on the morning of the twenty-sixth. We had all been together for Christmas dinner, including T. Elbert, Billy, Maggie, and Little D, and my mind had been far away from the disquieting events of the previous eleven months. After those three days, Mary and I were ready for an empty house, and I was now enjoying the peace and quiet.

Peace and quiet made a quick exit as I picked up my Yeti and stood up with the intent of getting a refill. The Yeti exploded in my hand and was driven hard into my chest. While I was trying to register the fact that someone was shooting at me, another bullet, as silent as the first, glanced off the metal umbrella post and ripped into my side. I instinctively grabbed the edge of the umbrella and pulled it over with the table, shielding myself from the assault, which was no doubt coming from the lake. Another bullet slammed into the underside of the table but could not penetrate it. My side was killing me, and my chest hurt. I reached for my phone on the floor of the deck as I heard an engine roar to life. The roar slowly faded as I peeked around to observe a boat speeding away. I called Mary.

"Don?" Sleep was in her voice.

"I'm on the lower deck. I've been shot." I was talking through clenched teeth. "The shooter is on a boat. He's moving away." I was straining to get the words out through the pain. "I need something to stop the bleeding."

"How bad?"

"I'll live," I said.

"On my way," Mary said.

I called Jimmy Durham, friend and county sheriff, on his personal cell phone.

"Blood?" he answered. "Everything okay?"

"Jimmy, listen. I was just shot by a sniper from the lake. He was in a bass boat. Try to track this guy down. Be careful."

"Got a description of the boat?"

"No," I said. "I was busy trying not to get killed. Just look for one moving fast."

"I'm on it," he said. "Are you okay?"

"I'll live," I said as I heard the back door slam. "Mary is taking me to the hospital. Call me later."

Mary came running down the stairs with a towel. By the time she got to me, I was sitting up, leaning against the deck railing, and holding my side.

"Jesus," Mary said. "Let me look at that."

When I took my hand away, the blood poured. Mary quickly pressed the towel over the wound.

"Can you make it to the truck?" She was standing there barefoot in jeans and a T-shirt.

"With your help."

She pulled me to my feet, and we went up the stairs to the upper deck and back through the house to the front door.

"Put on your sneakers and get a coat," I said. "I'll be right here."

"Thirty seconds," Mary said as she bounded up the stairs toward our bedroom.

A minute later, we were in the truck, up the driveway, and out on the main road. Mary activated her Bluetooth and called the Mountain Center Police Department.

The dispatcher answered.

"This is Mary Youngblood. Who's in?"

"Mary, what's wrong?"

"Don's been shot. I'm on my way to the hospital, and I'm in a hurry. Tell whoever's in charge and get me an escort."

"Stay on the line," the female voice said.

The next voice we heard was that of Sean Wilson, Big Bob's brother.

"Mary, is Don okay?"

"He'll live. Get me some help."

"What's your route?"

She told him. I was listening to everything through a fog of wooziness.

"We'll pick you up at the main road."

And that's what they did. Two cruisers were waiting for us with lights flashing and traffic stopped. We got behind them on the four-lane into Mountain Center, sirens blaring. I dared not look at the speedometer. Let's just say nobody has ever gone to the hospital faster than we did.

"You okay, Cowboy?" Mary said.

"Just dandy, ma'am."

"Hang on."

Mary called our doctor, Evan Smith, and ordered him to meet us at the emergency-room entrance. He didn't argue.

◆ ◆ ◆ ◆

In the emergency room, they cut off my sweater and turtleneck while setting up a morphine drip. The morphine drove the pain away. Evan Smith examined my wound.

A nurse poked her head into the room and said, "The chief of police is here and wants to talk to Mr. Youngblood."

"He'll have to wait," Evan Smith said.

"I'll deal with him," Mary said. She left the room.

"How bad?" I said.

"Nice bruise on your chest and a bullet wound in your side. Looks like a rib deflected the bullet from doing too much damage, although there seems to be a few fragments in the wound. The rib is broken. I've seen worse. You'll be okay in a few weeks. I'm going to give you something to make you sleep. I'm going to keep you overnight."

"No more morphine, okay?" I said.

He smiled. "Okay, tough guy. I forgot how you like to embrace the pain."

I lay back and relaxed and let the morphine take over. I floated away and then I was gone.

I woke up in time for dinner. Billy sat in a chair next to my bed. He was reading the local paper.

"Anything interesting?"

Billy looked up and smiled. "Not a thing. How do you feel?"

"Like I've been shot," I said.

"Who is trying to kill you, Blood?"

"I wish I knew. I thought I had been a good boy lately. Maybe it was a case of mistaken Identity."

"Not likely," Billy said.

"I'll have to give it some thought. Right now, I'm not very focused."

Mary came in and looked at me, then Billy.

Billy stood and put his hand on my shoulder, concern on his face. "We need to get to the bottom of this before the shooter tries again. I'll leave you two alone." He nodded at Mary as he walked from the room. "If you need anything, call me." He closed the door, leaving us alone.

"Jimmy Durham called while you were asleep and said they found the boat. It was stolen early this morning. I've been thinking. Someone must have been watching you and knew your routine of going out on the deck for coffee in the morning. This was carefully planned. I told Jimmy to check rentals for the last couple of weeks and see if anyone rented more than once."

"Good thinking," I said.

"This couldn't have been Kenny Stone, could it?" Mary said.

"I seriously doubt it," I said. "I'll think about it later. Right now, I'm tired and hungry and I need to use the bathroom."

◆ ◆ ◆ ◆

The morphine was wearing off. I made a painful trip to the bathroom, then sent Mary out for dinner. I polished off a ten-ounce burger and a large order of fries from the Mountain Center Diner, assisted by a sixteen-ounce can of Yuengling lager Mary had picked up at the condo and smuggled in. Cops! The staff stayed away and let us eat in peace.

An hour after we finished, Evan Smith came in. He spied the remnants of our meal and smiled. "How was dinner?"

"Just fine," I said. "My appetite is intact."

He looked at the monitors. "Everything looks good. How is the pain?"

"Tolerable."

"I'll prescribe something later to help you sleep, if you're not too tough to take it."

"He'll take it," Mary said.

"I'll see you-all in the morning," he said. "Get some rest." Evan Smith smiled, nodded at Mary, and left the room.

"I want to hear your account of what happened," Mary said. "Spare no detail."

"I stood up to go get a coffee refill, and suddenly my Yeti was slammed against my chest. It took a second to realize someone was shooting at me from the lake. Then another bullet ricocheted off the umbrella post. You know where that bullet went. I grabbed the edge of the umbrella and pulled it over. The table came with it, giving me something to hide behind. I heard another bullet slam into the bottom of the table. I didn't hear any shots, so the rifle must have been silenced. Then I heard the boat motor rev, and I peeked around the edge of the table and saw a bass boat pulling away in a hurry. Then I called you, and then Jimmy Durham. Then you came down the stairs looking sexy as hell in jeans and a T-shirt and barefoot."

"Men," Mary said. "Is that all you think about?"

"Pretty much," I said. "That and cold beer."

Mary shook her head and laughed. "You're impossible. And you're lucky to be alive. I mean, saved by a Yeti? Unbelievable."

"Don't forget the umbrella post."

"My God, Don. You could be dead."

"But I'm not."

"We've got to find this shooter."

"Yes, we do," I said.

The nurse came into the room with a pill in a paper cup. "When you're ready to go to sleep, take this," she said.

"I'll be sure he does," Mary said. "I'll be staying the night. Please let the other staff know that if they see anyone on the floor who doesn't belong to let me know immediately."

"I'll do that," the nurse said, looking a little uneasy as she said it. She made a quick exit. Mary's badge and Glock were fully visible.

Mary and I talked awhile longer, and then she said, "Take this. You'll need all the rest you can get. You're going to hurt like hell in the morning."

I took the pill and within minutes was fading away, fighting to keep my eyes open and losing. If I dreamed, I do not remember.

48

I'm not sure you can ever get a really good night's sleep in a hospital, meds or no meds. There always seems to be some background noise: a monitor beeping, an ambulance siren, a door opening, someone in the room, voices from the hall. I came out of it around seven o'clock Monday morning, remembering bits and pieces of the night like leaves blowing in a strong wind. Night and day were battling for the morning time slot. Night was winning, but not for long. I could see faint daylight approaching, slow and steady. A new day was coming and with it the painful reminder of why I was where I was.

I looked around the room: empty. I knew Mary was not far away. I tried to sit up. The pain knocked me back down. I needed to go to the bathroom, but the rails were up on my bed. I buzzed the nurse. She was in the room in twenty seconds.

"Want those rails down?" she said.

"You guessed it."

"I'll bet you're sore."

"Right again," I said.

"Grab my arm and I'll help you get to a sitting position."

I grabbed her arm, and she pulled me up as I swung around, legs dangling from the side of the bed.

"Bathroom?"

I nodded.

"Go ahead and get to your feet," she said. "I want to make sure you're steady enough to make it on your own."

I slid off the edge of the bed. My feet hit the floor, and I took a few steps. I was in pain but steady enough, and I really had a mission. "I'm fine," I said.

"I'll leave you to it," she said. "Buzz if you need anything."

◆ ◆ ◆ ◆

As I came out of the bathroom, Mary entered my room with Dunkin' Donuts coffee and blueberry muffins.

"My hero," I said.

"How do you feel?"

"Better by the minute. When can we blow this joint?"

"As soon as Evan releases you," Mary said.

"Well, he better hurry or I'm going to bolt."

"What you're going to do is follow orders," Mary said. "Now, get back in bed and I'll give you coffee and muffins."

"Blackmailer," I said, working my way painfully whence I came. Using the bed's control console, I made myself as comfortable as possible as Mary served me. "Have you told Lacy?"

"No. She can't do anything about it, and she would worry needlessly. I might tell her when it's over."

"Sounds right," I said. "Have you told anyone?"

"No," she said. "We're keeping the lid on."

Good luck with that in a small town, I thought. I ate in silence, making a few appreciative sounds along the way. "Why do coffee and a blueberry muffin always taste so good after I've been shot?" I said.

Mary laughed. "You're impossible."

"Just wondering."

◆ ◆ ◆ ◆

Evan Smith finally released me that afternoon, but not before carting me off to the x-ray room to check for chest and rib damage. The results were one fractured rib and deep bruising near the breast plate.

"You're going to be sore for a while, and your chest is going to go from black to purple to yellow as you heal," Evan Smith said. "The rib will work its way back in place and heal on its own. You know all about that. Nothing to do about it except give it time."

"Thanks, Doc," I said.

"I called in some pain meds and sleep meds to your pharmacy. Use them. Don't try to be so tough. Come see me at the office in a week," he said, looking at me and then Mary.

"He'll be there," Mary said. "And I'll be sure he takes his meds."

"And Don, find another line of work," he said. "You're beginning to look like Frankenstein's monster."

◆ ◆ ◆ ◆

I wasn't up for a trip to the lake house, so after stopping by the pharmacy, Mary took me to our Mountain Center condo. I tried to sit in my chair in my office, where I had a desktop computer, but I couldn't get comfortable. I actually felt best standing up. The kitchen bar wasn't too bad if I alternated standing and sitting.

"Are you hungry?" Mary said.

"Yes."

"What sounds good?"

"Anything," I said. "You pick."

"Chinese?"

"Perfect."

"Want a drink?"

"As soon as possible," I said.

Mary opened a bottle of a perfectly chilled Chardonnay and poured two glasses half full. "To being alive," she said as we touched glasses.

"You're being awfully calm about this," I said.

"Only on the outside. On the inside, I'm going crazy trying to figure out who would do this."

"We'll figure it out," I said. "And when we do, there will be hell to pay."

49

Tuesday morning, I hurt like hell but got up anyway and moved around to see if the pain would go away. It didn't. I took a pain med and slowly maneuvered my way down to the kitchen. The place was quiet. Mary had left a note on the counter:

Sorry, but I have to go to work. Call if you need anything. Love you!

I was able to make coffee and stir in cream and sugar. I managed my way to a barstool, got semi-comfortable, and sipped the hot elixir, hoping the miracle of caffeine would make things better. My cell phone was lying on the bar, and I saw I had a text message from Peggy Ann Romeo, a local TV reporter who, on more than one occasion, had helped out on my cases with timely stories. It read, **Don, can you call me please?** So much for keeping the lid on.

Peggy Ann made me think about the press. Should I try to keep this quiet or get it out in the open? I decided out in the open was better. The attempt on my life was going to find its way to daylight anyway. Maybe I could put some heat on whoever was trying to kill me. I called Peggy Ann Romeo.

"WMCT, how can I direct your call?" a pleasant female voice said.

"Peggy Ann Romeo," I said.

"May I tell her who's calling, please?"

"Don Youngblood."

"Please hold, Mr. Youngblood."

"Don," Peggy Ann said. "Are you okay? I heard you had an accident, but everyone is being so buttoned up, I thought there might be more to it."

"You're a good newshound, Peggy Ann," I said. "You can sniff out a story a mile away."

"Ha!" Peggy Ann said. "You must want something."

"What I want is to give you the rest of the story. Get Gail Fields and come to my condo this afternoon."

"What time?"

"Two o'clock. And stop by Dunkin' Donuts and get some coffee and muffins. Cream and sugar for me. Charge it to my account."

"You have an account at Dunkin' Donuts?"

"I do," I said.

"See you at two," she said.

I was still hurting, but I had to make another call. I called her private cell.

"Hello there," she said. "Haven't heard from you in a while."

"Just thought I'd check in. Did Jessica Johnson go home?"

"Yes," Sarah Agnes said. "She's doing fine, mostly thanks to you."

"I'm flattered."

"No, you're not," Sarah Agnes said. "Flattery is not something you crave or accept. You are all about results."

"Looks who's talking," I said.

"Touché. Anything else? I don't have a lot of time to chat."

"Before you might possibly hear it in the news, someone took a shot at me."

"Are you okay?"

I gave her the specifics.

"Mercy," she said. "I keep telling you to find another line of work. Who would do this?"

"Don't know yet," I said. "But I will."

"I don't want to know any more," she said. "I'll pray for you."

"Appreciated," I said.

◆ ◆ ◆ ◆

A few minutes past two o'clock, I sat at the kitchen bar drinking coffee with Peggy Ann and Gail Fields, a reporter for the *Mountain Center Press*.

"Spill it," Peggy Ann said.

"And not the coffee," Gail said.

"Same deal as before," I said. "Peggy Ann waits until eleven to use it, and you, Gail, run it in tomorrow's paper."

"Agreed," they said almost simultaneously.

"Somebody tried to kill me Sunday and damn near succeeded."

"What?" they said at the same time.

I told them all of it. They asked a few questions, and I answered as best I could.

"Somewhere in your story, say to contact the Mountain Center police with any pertinent information," I said. "I'm particularly interested in anyone who thinks they might have seen the boat at the lake."

They nodded. They were pros. They would know how to spin it.

That night when the eleven o'clock news came on, I was sound asleep. Mary told me later that Peggy Ann did a fine job. Gail Fields did equally well in the next morning's edition of the *Mountain Center Press*.

50

Tuesday, I walked around the condo parking lot just to get some exercise, but it was slow going and did little to alleviate the soreness in my chest and side. Wednesday morning, I went to the office. I was going stir crazy. When I got up Thursday, I could feel some improvement. Mary dropped me off in front of my building so I could take the elevator and not have to climb the back stairs.

"Stay alert," she said. "I've put the word out to every cop on the force to be on the lookout for anyone suspicious. Stay away from your window, just to be safe. Call me when you're ready to go back to the condo, and I'll pick you up."

"Thanks, Doll," I said in my best Bogie.

Mary laughed. "Get out of my truck."

Inside the building, Sam, the security guard, said, "You're moving kind of slow, Don. I read what happened in the paper. You okay?"

"Getting there, Sam," I said as I pressed the elevator button. "Keep an eye out for anything suspicious, especially packages."

"Will do," Sam said.

The elevator doors opened, and I got on and pressed the button for the second floor. Seconds later, the doors opened and I stepped into the hall with my hand on my Beretta. The hall was clear. *Better paranoid than dead*, I thought. I made it down the hall to the Cherokee Investigations entrance. Rhonda and Gretchen were already in. A morning paper lay on the conference table. They smiled at me—"poor Don" smiles, if I had ever seen them.

"Relax," I said. "I'm alive and healing. No fussing allowed. Rhonda, go do what you need to do."

"Yes, boss. Good to have you back." Rhonda turned and went back into her office.

"Gretchen, get me all the major case files."

"On your desk," Gretchen said.

"You're thinking what I'm thinking."

"I think if the answer is in one of those files, you'll find it. And I have a gut feeling it just might be."

"Let's hope it is," I said.

I walked into my office, sat at my desk, and looked out the window. From where I sat, there was no way anyone could get a direct shot at me, so I left the blinds up. I moved around in my chair, got as comfortable as possible, and opened the *Henry Cole/Afghanistan* file. I started my list of possible shooters with **Unknown terrorist group?** A long shot for sure, but I had to start someplace. The *Three Daggers* file had numerous possibilities. I wrote, **Colonel Hayes?** I had taken down Hayes, supposed leader of the Midnight Riders, a homegrown terrorist group. Where Hayes was now was unknown to me. Whether the group was completely dead or not was also unknown. The last time I saw Hayes, he was alive, and he had at one time sent an assassin to the lake house to kill me. I got lucky that time, too. The assassin, not so much. I wrote, **Midnight Riders?** I had no doubt Hayes would like to see me dead. I put away the *Three Daggers* file, took a pain pill, and moved on. As I opened the *Ricky Carter/Clown* file, my intercom buzzed.

"Can I get you some coffee?" Gretchen said.

"Mind reader," I said.

"Dunkin' Donuts?"

"You bet. For you and Rhonda, too. Get whatever you want and charge it."

"Something to eat?"

"Blueberry muffin, toasted, with butter," I said.

Ten minutes later, I was back at it with my coffee and muffin to spur me on. Nothing in the *Ricky Carter/Clown* file. The major players were dead. I opened the *Three Dragons* file and went through it. Nothing popped out. The one major player was dead from cancer. On to the *Jessica Crane/Southside Seven* file. Nothing. Nobody left alive who would be after me. The *Three Devils* file also netted no leads. The *Tracy Malone* file reminded me that Victor Vargas could still have friends who would like to see me dead, but the word from Vegas was that I had killed Victor in a fair fight and that no retribution would be sought.

Finally, I looked at the *Sarah Ann Fleet Fairchild* file. It was during that time I had met Mary. The memories came flooding back. It was also during that time I had killed Teddy Earl Elroy—with no regrets, since he was trying to kill Mary. I wrote down, **Friends/family of Teddy Earl Elroy?** Another long shot, since it had been years ago. For good measure, I added **Kenny Stone?** to the list. Unlikely, but you never know.

The blueberry muffin was long gone and the coffee dwindling as I drifted back into my past, trying to dredge up any other potential suspects. *Confrontations*, I thought. I sat for a while and finally came up with one name and another person, name unknown. The first was Roger Allen, serial killer. He certainly would like to kill me, since I had ultimately led to his capture. Where was Roger now? I wrote, **Roger Allen?** The second was a stretch. Mary had killed Teddy Earl Elroy's brother during an attempted bank robbery and had been seriously wounded during the shootout. There were four robbers. Two were killed at the scene. Teddy Earl and another unidentified robber initially escaped. I later killed Teddy Earl, with an assist from Billy, but as far as I knew, the fourth man, or possibly woman, got away clean. I wrote down, **Fourth man, Elroy gang?**

I looked at the list. They all seemed like long shots to me, but somebody was certainly trying to kill me.

Just as I was finishing my coffee, my cell phone rang. David Steele.

"Must be a slow day if you have time to call me," I said.

"I never have slow days," David Steele said. "I heard you were shot."

"How did you hear that?"

"Sources," he said.

I thought for a moment and said, "Yeah, I get it. Gretchen told Buckley. Buckley called you."

"Confidential," David Steele said. "Anyway, how are you?"

"Healing. My doctor is recommending another line of work. Says I'm beginning to look like Frankenstein's monster."

"You've had your fair share of mishaps," he said. "Anything I can do?"

"Actually, there is. I made a list of potential suspects who might like to see me dead. Remember Colonel Hayes?"

"I do. You want me to find out where he is?"

"That would be nice."

"I'll get back to you on that," he said. "Anything else?"

"Yes. I'd like to use John Banks to do some computer tracking. You okay with that?"

"Damn right I'm okay with it," David Steele said. "I'm going to open an official file on this. Someone tried to kill one of my special agents. The more I think about it, the more pissed off I get. I'm going to put Buckley on it. If your snooping around leads to anything, let him know."

"Thanks, Dave," I said. "Nice to know you have my back."

"I've got your back," he said, "but you need to watch your ass. Whoever tried to kill you may try again."

After my call from David Steele, I studied the list and put a check mark by Colonel Hayes. I got up from my desk and walked around the office, hoping I could shake some of the soreness. If I did, it was minimal. I sat back down, got comfortable, and started to doze off. The pain meds, no doubt.

I snapped myself out of it and called Scott Glass, SAC of the FBI's Salt Lake City office, on his private cell phone.

"I was going to call you," he said. "I heard what happened."

"News travels fast in the FBI."

"Especially bad news," Scott said. "How are you?"

"I'm on the mend. I need John Banks to do a few things for me. Steely Dave gave me his blessing. He doesn't like his consultants being shot."

"Sure," he said. "Let me transfer you. Take care of yourself, Blood. Come out and ski before all the snow melts."

"On my list," I said.

John Banks came on the line, and I had to go through the same routine: "How are you? How are you doing?"

Then John got down to business. "What can I do?"

I told him about Roger Allen and Kenny Stone. "There will be files in the system on both," I said. "I need you to dig deeper. Find out where Roger Allen is, and dig into Kenny Stone's past."

"I'm on it," John Banks said.

◆ ◆ ◆ ◆

A little past noon, I called Liam McSwain, Mary's former boss and chief of police in Knoxville, Tennessee.

"Donald Youngblood," he said in that fine Irish brogue. "Long time, no talk. How the hell are you? How is the lovely Mary Youngblood?"

"Mary is still lovely, but I've been better," I said. I told him someone was trying to kill me and had almost succeeded. I told him I was tracking down all possible suspects, no matter how far back. "The robbery that took place when Mary was shot. One man got away. Was it ever established who that fourth man was?"

"Let me pull the file and call you back," Liam said.

◆ ◆ ◆ ◆

Early in the afternoon, I was hurting from sitting so long. I called Mary. "I've had enough for the day. I'm walking back to the condo."

"No, you're not. Somebody out there is trying to kill you."

"Oh, yeah," I said. "I almost forgot. Whoever it is, they're probably long gone by now."

"We are not taking any chances. If you feel a need to walk, walk down the hall and back."

"Not much of a walk," I said. "Anyway, I'll tough it out here until you get off."

◆ ◆ ◆ ◆

Later that afternoon, my boredom and self-pity were interrupted by a phone call from Jimmy Durham. "How're you feelin', Blood?" he said.

"Like I've been shot, Bull. I'm sore and cranky. But I'm better today than yesterday. What's up?"

"Just wanted to tell you we've checked all the rentals at the different docks on the lake, and the few multiple renters all check out. Doesn't look like your guy rented a boat. We'll be patrolling around your place until you catch this bastard, though I doubt he'd be dumb enough to try again from the lake."

"I doubt it, too," I said. "Thanks for watching the back door."

"Anytime," Jimmy said. "Take care of yourself. Watch your six."

◆ ◆ ◆ ◆

David Steele called late that afternoon.

"What have you got?" I said.

"According to Homeland Security, Hayes is dead," David Steele said. "Although if you have another source, you might want to confirm that."

"Don't trust the HS boys?"

"Not a damn bit. It felt like it was easier to say he was dead than to go into details. I'd try to verify his demise if I were you."

"I might be able to do that," I said. "Thanks, Dave."

◆ ◆ ◆ ◆

I played bridge on my computer for half an hour, then called Mary. "I've had it. Either come get me or I'm walking."

"Five minutes, out back," Mary said. "I'll come down the alley. Don't come out until I pull up to the door."

"Yes, ma'am."

I took my time closing down my computer and straightening my paperwork. I said goodbye to Gretchen, left the office, and walked slowly down the back stairs. There was a small window in the door at the bottom.

I looked out just as Mary pulled up. Perfect timing. I went out the door and into the passenger seat of her truck in a few seconds.

"Tomorrow, I'm driving myself," I said.

"We'll see," Mary said.

◆ ◆ ◆ ◆

That night while having drinks at the bar, I showed Mary the list. She studied it for a few minutes.

"Roger Allen?"

"The guy who beat up Sandy Smith," I said.

"Oh, yeah."

Sandy Smith was an ex-girlfriend who had left me for a job in Marietta, Georgia, when I could not commit to a long-term relationship. She was beaten by a stalker and ended up marrying Jim Murphy, the cop investigating the assault. Mary and I had gone to the wedding.

"A lot of these are old case connections," Mary said. "It's got to be connected to the Midnight Riders. You brought down a lot of people there."

"I don't know," I said. "I think most of them were glad it was over."

Mary kept staring at the list and drinking wine. She poured a second glass. She squinted like her brain was in overdrive. Then she looked up at me. "You forgot a prime suspect."

"Who?"

"Remember the sniper who tried to kill you from the woods at the lake house?"

How could I have forgotten him? I thought. "You could be on to something," I said. "I'll look into it tomorrow."

"I think I deserve a reward."

"What do you have in mind?"

"Use your imagination, Cowboy."

"Give me twenty-four hours," I said. "I can imagine a lot in twenty-four hours."

51

The next day, I drove myself to the office, but not before I had to negotiate my keys from Mary, who had hidden them in hopes I would agree to her conditions for their return. I reminded her that my SUV had bulletproof glass and reinforced steel. She made me agree to wear my bulletproof vest, which I could take off once I was at my desk. I was still sore but discovered it was easier to find a comfortable position.

After I settled in, I called David Steele on his private line. "Mary had an excellent thought last night."

"Go on," David Steele said.

"Mary thinks the present sniper has to be connected to the Midnight Riders. I'm starting to think she's right. Remember the sniper I killed in the woods near my lake house?"

"I remember."

"Was he ever identified?"

"That, I don't remember," he said. "But I see where Mary is coming from. If the sniper had siblings or a close friend, you might be a target for revenge. The Midnight Riders is a new-enough case where it makes sense. It could be connected. I'll see what we have and get back to you."

◆ ◆ ◆ ◆

In midmorning, the phone rang. Most of the time, I would wait for my intercom to buzz, and it never did. This time, my intercom buzzed.

Gretchen announced, "Liam McSwain on line one."

"Liam," I said, receiver to my ear. I was so used to my cell phone that the office phone felt weird.

"I tried your cell phone but didn't get an answer," he said.

I looked at my cell phone lying on my desk. I picked it up, and it was nonresponsive. I was famous for letting it run out of charge. "I think I left it in my SUV," I said. "What's up?"

"The fourth man in that robbery was never identified. My detectives thought it was probably Eddie Lee Elroy, a first cousin of Teddy Earl. That was never confirmed, but the rumor was Eddie Lee lit out for California right after the robbery."

I wrote **Eddie Lee Elroy** on my list of suspects on my notepad. "Know what happened to him?"

"I don't," he said.

"Thanks for looking into it, Liam."

"No problem," he said. "Watch your back, and tell Mary hello from me."

"I will," I said. "Thanks again."

◆ ◆ ◆ ◆

That afternoon, my cell phone, now fully charged, rang. Well, it didn't actually ring; it played a nice little tune I had picked out from an extensive list of choices. Caller ID read, "Private caller." I had a good idea who it was.

"Very Special Agent Youngblood," I answered.

"Funny," David Steele said. "I'm glad you haven't lost your sense of humor. That sniper you killed was a ghost. A note in the file indicated that, based on dental work, he was probably native to Russia or a bordering country. He is not in any known database, including Interpol."

"You've got prints and DNA?"

"We do," David Steele said.

"A facial of the corpse?"

"That, too."

"Can you send me a copy of the file?"

"Sure can," he said. "I'll overnight it."

"What happened to the body?"

"It was held for a while. Then it was cremated."

"Okay, thanks."

"Keep me in the loop on this, Youngblood," David Steele said. "Identifying this guy may be the key."

◆ ◆ ◆ ◆

Late in the day, the office phone rang again, and again my intercom buzzed. "Buckley Clarke, special agent in charge of the Knoxville office of the FBI, on line one," Gretchen said.

"Is this the same Buckley Clarke my junior partner is shacking up with?"

"Sounds like him," Gretchen said.

I picked up the phone. "Hey, Buckley. How's it going?"

"Excellent," he said. "But I hear you have a problem and I'm supposed to help. Want to fill me in?"

"Well, you know a lot of it already, but I'll walk you through it step by step."

And that's what I did. Buckley listened without interruption. I could envision him taking notes.

"Scares me just hearing about it," Buckley said. "How are you holding up?"

"I'm trying not to think about it. He had his chance, and I got lucky. If he's still here, it's going to be a lot harder for him to make another run at me. MCPD and the county sheriff's office have BOLOs out for military-looking types who don't fit in. I'm hoping to zero in on this guy in a day or two. I have a lot of people working on this."

"What can I do?"

"You can check airlines and rental car agencies for anyone who looks ex-military and speaks with a European accent. I'm guessing he drove here from a distance, but who knows? Mary thinks it's tied to the Midnight Riders, and I'm beginning to agree."

"Makes sense," Buckley said. "I'll cover Tri-Cities and the Knoxville and Asheville airports."

"At this point, just make some calls. Tomorrow, I'll be getting a face shot of the sniper I killed. If you hear anything promising, you can take my sniper photo and show it around. If the dead sniper and my shooter are related, then they may look alike."

"Good thought," Buckley said. "Anything else?"

My eyes fell on my list of suspects. "There is. See if you can track down Eddie Lee Elroy. Probably born in East Tennessee. Cousin to Teddy Earl Elroy, who I had to kill. Age should be somewhere in his forties. Should have held a Tennessee driver's license. He's on my suspect list but a long shot."

"Will do," Buckley said. "Be careful out there, Don."

◆ ◆ ◆ ◆

My last call of the day was to Colonel Bradley Culpepper at the Pentagon. I had met the colonel, a lieutenant colonel at the time, while I was working the Crane case. He had been most helpful, and we had developed a friendship of sorts. Bradley Culpepper was a no-nonsense straight shooter, military through and through. I liked him immensely.

"General Culpepper's office, Sergeant Taft speaking," a male voice said.

A general now, I thought. I regrouped. "Donald Youngblood for the general," I said.

"One minute, sir," the sergeant said.

In about fifteen seconds, Bradley Culpepper said, "Donald Youngblood. It has been awhile. How are you?"

"I'm fine, General," I said. "It seems like every time I call, you've been promoted. Congratulations."

"Thanks," he said. "Maybe you should call more often. I'm just a lowly one-star, a brigadier. I sure would like that second star, although I doubt that will ever happen. Anyway, what can I do for you?"

I told him the sniper-on-the-lake story.

"This got anything to do with your adventures in Afghanistan?"

"I doubt it," I said. "How did you know about that?"

"The military grapevine reaches far and wide. I hear you put on a shooting exhibition that is fast becoming legendary."

"Mostly luck," I said.

"I doubt that. I've seen a photo of the target. So, what do you need from me?"

"Remember the Midnight Riders case you helped me out with?"

"Sure. Colonel Hayes and his gang of malcontents. What about it?"

"Hayes was supposedly taken by Homeland Security, who recently told the FBI he was dead," I said. "The FBI is not quite sure that's true. I was wondering if you had any connections to HS, and if you could find out anything about Hayes."

"Someone I know might be able to tell me if Hayes is still alive," the general said. "If HS got him, they probably locked him up at Gitmo and threw the key away. Let me make a call. I'll get back to you as soon as I can."

◆ ◆ ◆ ◆

Mary picked up an Italian sausage pizza on the way to our downtown condo, and I made my locally renowned Caesar salad. We sat at the bar, ate pizza and salad, drank beer, and talked about the events of the day. Mary went first.

"I can't believe how many dumbasses are out there," she said. "If they worked as hard at getting a job as they do at stealing, they would do fine. Do you ever read the police blotter in the paper?"

"I have at times," I said. "Some of it is pretty funny. You can't make that stuff up."

"It's sad." Mary opened her second beer and got another one for me.

"That, too."

"Forget my day. Tell me about yours."

"I spent most of it on the phone." I recounted my phone calls.

"So, at this point, you haven't ruled anyone out," Mary said.

"Not yet."

We were quiet for a while. Mary had another beer. She was a wine drinker who liked beer with pizza.

"How are you feeling?"

"Fine," I said, hoping I knew where this was going.

"Sore?"

"A little."

"I'm craving some closeness," Mary said.

"Really, not much soreness at all. I'll do the hard part if you'll do the rest."

Mary laughed. "You've got a deal, Cowboy."

52

The next day, I was in the office early. The unknown sniper's file was attached to an email from David Steele. I looked at it briefly, forwarded it to Buckley, and then saved it to my desktop.

I was anticipating some early calls, and I was not disappointed. The first was from General Bradley Culpepper on my cell phone.

"Youngblood," I answered.

"Culpepper here," he said.

"Good morning, General. What can you tell me?"

"For what's it worth, I think Hayes is probably still alive. I couldn't get a straight answer, but I think Hayes is locked up at Gitmo for the rest of his life. He could be dead, but I don't think so. I know one thing. You are never going to talk to him. I doubt he had anything to do with the sniper. If he's alive, he's too isolated."

"Thanks, General. That helps."

"You're welcome. Now tell me, what was that Afghanistan thing about? You and Henry Cole."

"We were part of a plan that deceived even us," I said. "We were almost killed and later found out we were not playing the parts we thought we were. Neither of us was any too happy. Both of us were wounded."

"Was the overall goal accomplished?"

"I'm told that it was."

"So, whatever part you played wasn't in vain," he said.

"No, it wasn't."

"You took one for the red, white, and blue. You'll have to be content with that."

"Yes, sir," I said. "We took one or two for the team."

"And you know the most important thing, Youngblood?"

"Sir?"

"You and Cole came back alive."

"Excellent point."

"Call me when this is over and fill me in, Youngblood," General Culpepper said. "Your life is always a hell of a lot more interesting than mine."

"That's a promise, General," I said. "Always a pleasure."

General Culpepper hung up, and I crossed Colonel Hayes off my list.

◆ ◆ ◆ ◆

Later that morning, Buckley called my cell. I didn't ask why he hadn't called the office. Maybe to avoid unwarranted questions. FBI business was FBI business.

"Agent Clarke," I said. "What have you got?"

"I hate caller ID," he said.

"Welcome to the club."

"Anyway, I ran down Eddie Lee Elroy," Buckley said. "He's in California."

"You're sure?"

"Positive."

"Where?"

"San Quentin. Death row."

"For what?"

"Killing a police officer while committing a bank robbery," Buckley said.

"History repeating itself," I said.

"Looks like."

"I'm surprised California has the death penalty," I said.

"Well, they haven't executed anyone since 2006. I looked it up. The information is rather confusing. San Quentin doesn't have any execution facilities at the present time, but they still have a death row."

"Sounds political," I said.

"Most likely. Anything else I can do?"

"Not right now," I said. "I'll be in touch."

I disconnected from Buckley and crossed Eddie Lee Elroy off the list. *The process of elimination: a detective's best friend*, I thought.

◆ ◆ ◆ ◆

I had just finished homemade chicken and rice soup from the Mountain Center Diner when the office phone rang. I waited.

"Agent John Banks on line one," Gretchen said over the intercom.

I picked up. "John," I said, "what have you got?"

"The alias Roger Allen—and they're still not sure who he really is—resides in a maximum-security prison in Colorado. He has a lifetime lease on a ten-by-ten cell, which he occupies twenty-three hours a day. He's not your guy. No contact with the outside world in quite a while."

"That's good," I said. "I'm narrowing down the list pretty fast."

"Kenny Stone, on the other hand, is an extremely interesting story," John said.

"I don't like this already."

"No record of him anywhere in the system. No prints. He does have a South Carolina driver's license, plus a Social Security number. Kenny has never reported income. I'm guessing maybe he got into the drug business."

"Good guess," I said. "So, what you're telling me is ten years ago he ditched his old identify and created a new one."

"Looks like it, but here's the thing. The Social Security number is an older number issued in the late forties or early fifties. I think that somehow he got hold of the number from a dead guy named Kenny Stone and made it his. Or maybe he killed this guy, got rid of his body, and took over his identity, so no one knows that guy is really dead."

"Wouldn't someone miss the guy if he was killed?"

"Maybe not," John said. "If your guy is as smart as you think he is, he picked a guy who wouldn't be missed."

"You're making my head hurt," I said. "I'll have to think about this. Anyway, I doubt he's the shooter. Thanks, John. I'll put in a good word with your boss."

"Like that will matter," John said.

"How about an extra treat in your Christmas stocking?"

"Now you're talking, Youngblood," John Banks said.

I crossed Roger Allen off the list and put another question mark beside Kenny Stone. It was beginning to look more and more like Mary was right. The attempt on my life was somehow connected to the Midnight Riders case. I needed to focus on the sniper I killed.

◆ ◆ ◆ ◆

By midafternoon, I was starting to hurt. I walked around and stretched, but the pain persisted. I gave in and took a pain med. In fifteen minutes, I was feeling better, so I asked Gretchen for the Midnight Riders file again. I was going through it slowly when an email caught my eye. I had passed over it the first time because it hadn't meant anything to me. Now it did. It was from Steve Dobbs, the helicopter pilot for the Midnight Riders, who had been most helpful with information about the facility housing the group. He owed me a favor, and I was about to collect. His cell-phone number was in the email. I called it. Instead of Steve Dobbs, I got his voice mail: "You have reached the cell phone of Steve Dobbs, U.S. Forestry Service. Leave your name and number, and I'll call you back."

I left a message: "Dobbs, this is Donald Youngblood. You said to call if I ever needed anything. I need to pick your brain about the Midnight Riders. Call me as soon as you can. Congratulations on the job."

I disconnected. I was counting on Dobbs to know something about the sniper who tried to kill me. He might be my last hope.

◆ ◆ ◆ ◆

I stayed in the office later than normal, hoping Steve Dobbs would call me back. Night falls early in January, and Gretchen and Rhonda had long since left the building. Dobbs didn't call. I put on my bulletproof vest and descended the back stairs. Under cover of darkness, I went quickly to the Armada and slipped in. No one took a shot at me.

On my way to the condo, I called Mary. "I'm on my way," I said.

"I'll meet you in the parking garage," she said.

Minutes later, I pulled into my reserved space. I did not immediately see Mary, so I stayed put. Then she came out of the shadows, and I got out.

"All clear," she said.

Extra-cautious, I thought. *Not a bad thing.*

We took the elevator and soon were safely inside our condo.

"I have a bottle of Cabernet opened and breathing," Mary said. "I want to hear about you day. Mine was boring as hell."

"Great," I said. "A glass of red sounds really good."

I shrugged out of the vest and settled in at the kitchen bar. I had to move around on the barstool to get comfortable.

"You're hurting," Mary said.

"A little. You know, end of the day."

She poured the wine, and we raised our glasses.

"To being alive," Mary said.

"For a long, long time."

We touched glasses and had that first drink of the day.

"Not bad," I said.

"Glad you like it. Now, tell me."

I recounted my conversations with General Culpepper, Buckley, and John Banks. Mary liked details, so I strung it out as long as possible.

"So, the general wasn't too sympathetic about Afghanistan," Mary said.

"Not so much, but not surprising. The general is a real patriot. As far as he's concerned, I took two bullets for God and country."

"Easy for him to say," Mary said. She drank more wine. "You've really narrowed down the list."

"I have. And I'm waiting for a call from Steve Dobbs, who was the Midnight Riders' helicopter pilot. I'm hoping he can give me some background on the sniper I killed."

"He owes you one, as I recall," Mary said.

"He does."

Mary finished her first glass of wine and poured another. My glass looked as if it had barely been touched. *Sipping is all.*

"Stay put," Mary said. "I'll get dinner ready."

◆ ◆ ◆ ◆

An hour later, I was still in the same position. I had managed to eat dinner and finish my first glass of wine and start on a second. The bottle was empty. Mary had prepared angel hair pasta with Bolognese sauce, Caesar salad, and garlic cheese toast. I had taken another pain med and was really chilling out.

"That was awesome," I said.

"Glad you liked it."

"I think I'm buzzed."

"Why don't you go to bed?" Mary said. "I'll be up soon."

"Good idea," I said, but I didn't move. I had no desire to leave my spot at the kitchen bar. I thought I just might stay there forever. Then my cell phone rang, and I snapped back to reality.

"Youngblood, it's Steve Dobbs. Sorry I didn't call sooner, but I just got off work. I'm in California. Three-hour time difference from you. How can I help you?"

"You work for the U.S. Forestry Service?" I said.

"I do," Dobbs said. "I'm one of their helicopter pilots. Right now, I'm fighting wildfires, dropping fire-suppressing chemicals."

"Sounds dangerous."

"Well, at least no one is shooting at me." Steve Dobbs had flown helicopters in Afghanistan. Dangerous business. "What's up?" he said.

"When I was working on the Midnight Riders case, Hayes sent a sniper to either kill me or scare me off, I never knew which. The sniper took a shot at me from a fairly long distance from a wooded area near my lake house. He missed by maybe an inch. Whether he was really good or I was really lucky, I'll never know."

"I'm guessing he meant to kill you," Dobbs said. "What happened to him?"

"I caught him coming out of the woods. I wanted him alive, but he was having none of that. He went for his weapon, and I killed him."

"Sweet Jesus," Dobbs said. "That guy was dangerous. He scared the hell out of us."

"What can you tell me about him?"

"Not much," Dobbs said. "He mostly kept to himself. Occasionally, I saw him with Hayes. Some of the guys called him 'Hayes's pit bull.' He was Hayes's enforcer. Sometimes, he went with me to pick up supplies. He didn't talk much, but his English was good. A little Eastern European accent. Russian, maybe."

"Any other snipers at the compound?"

"Not that I was aware of," Dobbs said. "If there were, I think I would have heard about it. News traveled fast in that place."

"Okay, thanks. How is your lady friend from the compound?"

"We're married and have a kid," Dobbs said. "A little boy. He's two."

"That's great. Glad it worked out."

"Thanks to you, Youngblood. I still owe you. Why are you interested in the sniper?"

I chose not to tell him someone was trying to kill me. The fewer people who knew, the better. "We never did identify him," I said. "The FBI is now interested in who he was. He has become a loose end."

"Let me know if you're ever out this way," Dobbs said. "I'll take you up for a ride. It's spectacular out here."

"Thanks, Dobbs," I said. "Take care of yourself." I disconnected.

"Anything?" Mary said.

"Nothing that's going to help," I said.

53

Even though it was Saturday, I was in the office early, trying to figure out how to find a ghost. Then it dawned on me. Who better to find a ghost than an ex-spook?

I called Henry Cole. "How is life on the beach?"

"Youngblood!" Henry exclaimed. "It's good to hear from you. Life on the beach is great. Low humidity, temp in the seventies, gentle breezes. What's not to like?"

"Sounds inviting. We may have to come for a visit."

"And we would love to have you. When can you come?"

"Not right away, Henry. I have a pressing matter I need to attend to."

He must have heard the tone of my voice change. He turned serious and said, "You think I can help. That's why you called."

"I'm hoping you can," I said. "I'm sending you a file of a man I killed a few years ago. He's a ghost. We cannot identify him. He's not in any of our databases. We think he's of Eastern European descent, possibly Russian."

"Why do you want to identify a dead man?" he said.

"It's complicated. A long story."

"Tell me," Henry Cole said. "I have all the time in the world."

"When we were laid up in that army hospital in Afghanistan, did I tell you about the Midnight Riders case and the sniper they sent to kill me?"

"I don't think so. My mind is a little fuzzy when it comes to that hospital stay."

So, I told him all of it.

"And now you think someone has come back for revenge?"

"Maybe," I said. "I keep narrowing the suspect list, and it comes down to the Midnight Riders. I need to find out who this guy was."

"I have a couple of off-the-grid databases I can check. I also have a friend in Russia who can get into their secret databases. If this guy was a trained assassin, he has to be in a database somewhere. If I find him, and I think I will, I'll do a check on close friends or relatives to see if there is a candidate who would want to avenge his death."

"One thing bothers me, Henry."

"Let's hear it."

"Only a few people knew I killed this sniper," I said. "The FBI swooped in, took the body, and covered it up like it never happened. If revenge is the reason I'm being targeted, how did the shooter find out it was me?"

"Simple," he said. "If there's a file, and if a person has connections, and if a person digs deep enough, a person can find out almost anything. The file was probably not top secret and by itself looked rather harmless. Whoever leaked it was probably well paid and didn't think they were doing any harm. Your name may not have even been in the file. But I'll bet a lot of people at the FBI knew you took down the sniper. It would have been juicy office gossip."

"Well, that's comforting," I said.

"Did the press get hold of the recent attempt on your life?"

"Yes," I said. "We were trying to put some heat on the sniper, make him hole up somewhere while we looked for him, or make him run and get spotted."

"My guess is he got out of there right away, especially if he saw you go down. He would have had an exit plan. If he tries again, it will be much later. That gives us time. I'll find this guy," Henry said. "I'm sure of it."

"Thanks, Henry. I don't want to spend the rest of my life looking over my shoulder."

"Give me a few days," he said. "And don't worry, I guarantee he's long gone."

◆ ◆ ◆ ◆

That night, I met Mary at the lake house. While sharing a bottle of wine, I told her about my conversation with Henry Cole. I had to admit I felt somewhat better about my chances of not getting shot after talking with Henry.

"I trust Henry like I trust Billy," Mary said. "Henry won't let it rest until we resolve this."

"You know I'm not good at waiting," I said.

"This time, you have no choice. It's out of your hands. I've let it be known to a few of my snitches that there's a big reward for good information about any suspicious foreigners. If anyone is out there, I'll hear about it. Money motivates these guys. They'll be digging, I'm certain of it."

"If you turn up anything, I'll give you a big reward."

Mary smiled that smile I knew so well. "Can I collect in advance?" she said, moving closer to me.

54

A few days passed without anything from Henry Cole. On Sunday, Mary and I had gone skiing at Sugar Mountain. The weather was cold, and they had made lots of snow during the week. The mountain was completely open, every trail with good snow cover. We got there early, skied until the lift lines got long, and went in the lodge for a late breakfast.

Monday, Mary went to work and I stayed at the lake house and worked on some things from my to-do list. At dusk, I loaded the dogs and returned to our Mountain Center condo. I wasn't too worried about the sniper anymore, but it never hurts to vary your routine if someone might be gunning for you. Mary insisted I keep wearing the vest. It was easier to wear it than to fight about wearing it.

On an uncommonly cold Tuesday morning, I went to the office early and then to the diner to have breakfast with Big Bob. I wasted no time as I walked down the back alley and slipped through the diner's back door to my table.

"Anything to report?" Big Bob said a few minutes later as he settled in across from me.

"Nothing," I said. "You?"

"No. All my guys have their eyes and ears open, but not one thing of interest so far. I think your shooter is long gone."

"That seems to be the general opinion."

"What about this Henry Cole you told me about?"

"Ex-CIA," I said. "Lots of connections. I think he's my best bet. I'm waiting to hear from him."

We ordered and ate in relative silence.

"Keep me informed," Big Bob said on his way out.

◆ ◆ ◆ ◆

Henry Cole called my cell phone later that morning. He got right to it. "I have identified your man. A Lithuanian. His name was Emile Wirkus. He was a gun for hire—sniper, self-trained, never in the military. Word is, he went off the grid with his girlfriend and hasn't been heard from in a few years. I'm guessing he joined the Midnight Riders. It makes you wonder if maybe the girlfriend was also part of the Midnight Riders."

"Worth checking out," I said. "Anything else?"

"I still have contacts digging for more background," Henry said. "As soon as I know anything important, I'll let you know. Maybe he has a brother."

"Maybe. I'm going to check out the girlfriend angle. I'll let you know if I find anything useful. Thanks for all of this, Henry."

"No thanks needed, Youngblood. You'd do the same for me. Don't worry. We'll find this guy."

Well, he was right about one thing: I would do the same for him. Henry and I had become close friends in a short time. Nothing makes for a close friendship like almost dying together.

◆ ◆ ◆ ◆

I called Steve Dobbs. With the time difference, I was hoping to catch him before he went to work. I did.

"Dobbs," he answered.

"It's Youngblood," I said. "Quick question. Do you know if our shooter had a girlfriend at the compound?"

"Sorry, but I just don't know. I was gone a lot and spent most of my free time with my wife, Gina. Of course, we weren't married yet."

"Okay," I said. "Ask Gina if she remembers anyone. If she does, get back to me."

"I'll do it," he said. "Good luck, Youngblood."

I went back to the Midnight Riders file, looking for a name. It didn't take me long to find it: Lisa Troutman, alias "Trout," Colonel Hayes's ex-girlfriend. Her cell-phone number was in the file. I hoped it was current.

I called it. It rang five times and then, "This is Lisa. Leave a message." Short and to the point. I expected no less from a woman who had spent years in the military.

I left a message. "Lisa, this is Don Youngblood. I'm sure you remember me. Anyway, you are not in any trouble. I just need to ask you a few questions about the sniper Hayes sent to kill me. If you're screening your calls, call me back right away. If not, call me ASAP. Thanks. I hope things are going well for you."

A minute later, my cell phone rang.

"This is Lisa," she said. "Make it fast. I have to get to work." So much for idle chit-chat.

"Did the sniper have a girlfriend?"

"Yes," she said. "Her name was Elsa. She didn't speak very good English and therefore kept to herself. Why are you asking?"

I ignored her question. "Do you know the sniper's name?"

"They called him Adams," she said. "But I don't think that was his real name because Jeff called him Work. I asked why one time and Jeff said, 'Because he's a piece of work.' I think he was lying about that. I believe it was short for his last name, like Workman, maybe."

"Good guess," I said. "His last name was Wirkus." I spelled it for her.

"Anything else? I have to run."

"No," I said. "Thanks for calling me back, Lisa. Take care of yourself."

◆ ◆ ◆ ◆

I took a coffee break and then called David Steele's private cell. It was still early, and he answered. "How is the investigation going, Youngblood?"

"Good morning to you, too," I said, deflecting his question. I didn't want to share the name Emile Wirkus with anyone else just yet. If the shooter was tied to Emile, I didn't want him to know that I knew. One way or another, he must have gotten that information from the FBI file. My killing the sniper was never news; only a few people knew. If David Steele started sniffing around, trying to find a leak, it might do more harm than good.

"I hope it is," he said. "I have a budget meeting in five minutes. I'd rather do an overnight stakeout. What do you need?"

"I need to know what happened to the women who were rounded up when we took down the Midnight Riders. I'll need pictures of all the women and their whereabouts, if that's possible."

"Okay," he said. "I'll make some calls. It will probably be tomorrow before I can get back to you."

"The sooner the better," I said.

"Yeah, I hear you," David Steele said. "By the way, if you identify your shooter, we're going to put him on our Ten Most Wanted list. If you can get a picture, we'll program it into our airport security software. If he comes back to the U.S., or if he's still here and tries to fly out, we'll catch him."

"I'm touched," I said.

"Don't be. I don't want to have to deal with Mary if anything happens to you."

I wouldn't either, I thought.

◆ ◆ ◆ ◆

That evening, I was in the condo before Mary got off work. I changed into jeans, a long-sleeve T-shirt, and a pair of beat-up sneakers. I was at the kitchen counter when she came in. I immediately opened a bottle of chilled Chardonnay and poured a couple of stemless goblets half full. Mary walked over, kissed me lightly on the lips, and picked up one of the goblets.

"My hero," she said, then took a healthy drink.

"How was your day?"

"Fine. Nothing exciting. How about you?"

"Let's go sit by the fire and I'll tell you about it."

I took the bottle, and we went into the living room. Our penthouse condo was a multi-split-level with two gas-log fireplaces, one in the den on the lower level and one in the living room. We sat on a couch in front of the fireplace. I started my recap with the call from Henry Cole. Then I moved on to the phone calls with Steve Dobbs and Lisa Troutman. I finished with

David Steele's call. Mary didn't interrupt with questions. She drank Chardonnay and listened. When I finished, her glass was empty. I poured her a second round.

"That's about it," I said. "Now, I wait for David Steele to get back to me. Henry will call if he finds out anything new."

"So, you're going to try to track down this Elsa," Mary said.

"It's the only lead I have right now."

"I'm betting Henry will come up with something."

"That would probably be a good bet. I hope you're right."

Mary drank more wine, and I sipped. We stared at the fire. It had a hypnotizing effect. I could feel my whole body relax.

"How are you holding up?"

"Better," I said. "As each day passes, I think the likelihood of again being shot at diminishes. I try not to think about it."

"Best to find this guy and put an end to it," Mary said, staring into the flames. "I would gladly do the honors."

It was a statement that didn't require a response, so I gave none. We watched the flames dance on the gas logs and finished the Chardonnay. Much later, we had dinner. Later still, Mary seduced me. She was urgent and spectacular. I wondered what was driving her libido.

55

The next day, I was at my desk early when David Steele called. I guessed it was probably him and decided to have some fun.

"Cherokee Investigations, Donald Youngblood speaking. How can I help you?"

"Jesus," David Steele said. "Do you recite that spiel every time you answer the phone?"

"I usually don't answer the phone. That was a test. How was I?"

He was silent for a moment. "You're messing with me. You must be feeling pretty good."

"Improving daily. What have you got?"

"All of the Midnight Riders women spent a short time in a minimum-security prison and were then cut loose. They got a high-powered lawyer to defend them as a group, claiming they were held against their will. They cut a deal and served their time, and now they're all out."

"Do you have a list of names?"

"Yes," he said. "I figured you'd want it. I'll email it to you as soon as we finish. Are you going to try to track down all of them?"

"At this point, only one," I said. "But send the list anyway."

"Anything you care to share?"

"Is an Elsa on the list?"

"Hang on," David Steele said. "Yes, Elsa Kakoff. Want her file?"

"I do. But don't let anyone know it's coming to me."

"Getting paranoid, are we?"

"You bet."

"Welcome to the FBI," David Steele said.

◆ ◆ ◆ ◆

Elsa Kakoff was Russian. Her file contained a not-so-flattering picture of a woman with blond hair, blue eyes, and a tight smile, as if she was amused by something. Elsa was listed as five foot eight inches tall and 150 pounds. All I had to look at was a head shot, but I was betting she was in shape. She had been in the country legally until she overstayed her visa and went off the grid. When she was released from prison, she was put on a flight back to Russia. It was anybody's guess where she was now.

I called Henry Cole's cell phone and got his voice mail. "It's Don," I said. "I have another piece of information. Call me back."

I went online and looked at ski resort snow reports in Utah. As usual, Brighton and Solitude were leading the pack in total inches to date. I was hoping to get out in March. Before that could happen, I had to track down the sniper and find Kenny Stone. Tony Price's next golf tournament with Lacy caddying was only weeks away in Florida. I was hoping to fit that in, too. I was wondering how I was going to make all of that happen when the phone rang. I looked at caller ID: a string of unrecognizable numbers. Maybe Henry, maybe not.

"Yes," I answered.

"Relax," Henry Cole said. "I'm on a burner. Didn't want a record of all our calls back and forth. Do you have a burner?"

"Got a couple of brand-new ones," I said. "Part of the private investigator's startup kit."

Henry laughed. "Call me back," he said. Then he was gone.

On an earlier recommendation from David Steele, I had one fully charged burner phone and one still in the packaging. I looked at my cell-phone log, keyed in the number Henry had called from, then erased his call from my log. I pressed the send button on the burner phone.

"That was quick," Henry said.

"Speedy Gonzales at your service. Where are you?"

"Need to know only," Henry said. "What have you got?"

"The girlfriend of our dead sniper was Elsa Kakoff. I'll email her file."

"Sooner the better."

"On the way. Be careful, Henry. I don't want you getting hurt or worse on my account."

"I'm doing what I do best," Henry Cole said. "You may not hear from me for a while, but don't worry. I'll call when I have news."

Then he was gone again.

◆ ◆ ◆ ◆ ◆

That afternoon, my spirits lifted. Light snow floated down on Mountain Center. There was a dusting on Main Street that left tire tracks from the occasional passing vehicle. I had been ignoring the weather, with everything else going on. A quick look at my weather app told me the current temperature was thirty degrees. The night's low was forecast to be twenty-five. Snow accumulation was forecast at one to three inches, with more in the mountains.

I called Mary. "It's snowing."

"I can see that. Does it make your heart go pitter-patter?"

"The only thing that makes my heart go pitter-patter is you."

"Sweet talker."

"Want to go to the club for dinner?"

"Excellent idea," Mary said. "I'll see you back at the condo after work. Stay sharp, Cowboy."

◆ ◆ ◆ ◆

We sat at my favorite table overlooking the eighteenth green, which was completely hidden by darkness and snow. The snow was coming down in earnest, and I was enjoying a glass of superior Cabernet Sauvignon with my beautiful wife. I couldn't have been happier. I shared with Mary my conversations with David Steele and Henry Cole.

"I think Henry may be in Europe," I said.

"He is," Mary said.

"And you know this how?" I said, fully knowing she had been talking to Rosa.

"Sources," Mary said.

"Well, I hope he's careful."

"He will be."

I looked out the window at the snow falling. The outdoor lights made it look heavier that it probably was. For the first time in a long while, I felt a sense of peace. "I hope it snows a foot," I said.

"Speaking of snow, I talked to Lacy today, and she has a four-day weekend coming up and wonders if we'll fly out and meet her and Biker somewhere and go skiing."

"Can you get off?"

"Already arranged," Mary said.

"Sounds like a done deal."

"Pretty much. We decided that since you'll be paying for everything, you get to pick where we go."

"Sounds fair."

"Good daddy," Mary said.

"When do we leave?"

"Tomorrow. You better get busy on transportation and lodging."

"Guess I better," I said.

56

The Fleet jet was free, and Jim Doak was only too happy to check another airport off his bucket list. So, the next day, Mary and I flew into La Plata County Airport near Durango, Colorado. Our final destination was Purgatory Ski Resort, twenty-something miles north of Durango. I had reserved a two-bedroom condo at Peregrine Point within walking distance of a base mountain lift. We picked up two hours en route and landed at two in the afternoon local time. Gretchen had rented a Suburban for us. She said we'd need all the room we could get.

When we exited the jet, the rental car agent standing by the SUV walked over. "Mr. Youngblood? Here are your keys and your contract," he said, handing them to me. His nametag said he was Justin.

"Great service, Justin," I said, handing him a twenty.

"Thank you very much, sir," he said. "Can I help you with your gear?"

"Sure," I said.

Jim Doak opened the cargo hold, and we went to work transferring suitcases, ski bags, and boot bags to the Suburban.

"We have to meet another couple coming in from Phoenix," I said to Justin. "Where can I leave the SUV?"

"It will be fine here," he said. "There's an elevator near baggage claim. When you have their luggage, take the elevator down and come out that door." He pointed to the door he was talking about. "Once you're loaded, drive through that gate." He pointed again. "I gave the guard a heads-up, so he'll open up and let you right out. After that, just follow the signs out of the airport. When you return, tell the guard you're flying private and leave the Suburban right here with the keys in it. Got any questions?"

"No," I said. "You've been very helpful."

"You've got good snow, and more on the way," he said. "The skiing is going to be great."

An hour later, with Lacy and Biker in the backseat and the Suburban loaded to the gills, we headed for the mountain.

◆ ◆ ◆ ◆

That night, we had dinner at a nearby restaurant. Biker and I mostly listened while Mary and Lacy did the talking.

At one point, Mary, reading my mind, said, "You two look great. What's your secret?"

I saw eye contact and a subdued smile pass between Lacy and Biker. I didn't dwell on it.

"We've been doing a lot of rock climbing and mountain biking," Lacy said.

Biker said nothing.

"How are your classes?" I said, just to contribute.

"They're fine," Lacy said. "Biker and I have the same schedule, since we're both criminology majors. That makes it easy. We can study together and hold each other accountable."

"That work for you?" I asked Biker.

"It does," he said. "Lacy is a slave driver. Our grades are excellent."

The conversation was casual and relaxed through dinner and dessert. We got back to the condo around nine and went our separate ways. Our bedrooms were at opposite ends.

When we were in bed, I said, "What do you think they're doing back there?"

"The same thing we're about to do," Mary said as she rolled toward me. "Be quiet, Cowboy. Very quiet."

57

For the next four days, we skied like crazy. Mary and I usually quit in midafternoon, but Lacy and Biker skied until the lifts closed. Sunday, we went into Durango and walked around the town. Mary and Lacy shopped while Biker and I watched and got bored. Biker bought a cowboy hat that looked really good on him.

"You can't wear that on campus," Lacy said when she saw it.

"Why not?" Biker said.

"Because she'd have to spend all her time shooing the coeds away," Mary said.

Later, we found a good steakhouse and pigged out. After all, we had a lot of calories to replace.

That night, Biker went to bed early, and so did Mary. Lacy and I sat by the fire.

At one point, Lacy said, "Don, why do you have two cell phones?"

I had absentmindedly left both of them on the kitchen counter. I mentally kicked myself in the butt.

"I'm working something with Henry, and it's off the books, so to speak. The fewer people who know about it, including you, the better. We don't want any record of calls."

"It must be dangerous," Lacy said.

"Maybe," I said. "But that's nothing new."

"Why don't you retire?"

"Same reason Mary doesn't retire."

"Yeah, I know," Lacy said. "It's who you are."

Smart girl.

◆ ◆ ◆ ◆

Tuesday morning, we drove to the airport, checked luggage for Lacy and Biker, and walked with them to security.

"We had a great time," Lacy said, tears in her eyes.

"We certainly did," Biker said. "Thanks for everything."

"Wouldn't have missed it," I said.

Mary and Lacy hugged, Mary hugged Biker, and I hugged Lacy. Biker and I bro-hugged with hearty pats on the back.

"Love you two," Lacy said.

"We love you," Mary said. "Have a safe flight."

Lacy looked at me, and I was close to losing it. She hugged me again and whispered in my ear, "You be careful. We could never survive losing you."

"Go," I said.

She smiled and looked at Biker, who was wearing the hat he bought in Durango. "Let's go, Cowboy," she said.

They turned and went through security and never looked back.

Mary looked at me with tears in her eyes. "I miss her already."

"Me, too," I said.

58

Wednesday morning, I was in the office early and alone. Henry Cole called on the office phone before I had a chance to make coffee. What was he thinking?

"You must be back in Mexico," I said. "You called my office on your personal cell."

"Friends keeping in touch," Henry said. "Makes sense after all we went through in Afghanistan. I don't like using burners any more than I have to."

"I assume you have something," I said.

"Emile Wirkus had an older brother. His name is Elijah. Acquaintances call him Eli. The Wirkus family is a sniper family. The father was a decorated shooter in the Russian army. Eli was also in the Russian army. I guess the Russian army will take Lithuanians. There was no mention in the file that Emile was ever in any army, but he had the skills. According to the file, the father taught both sons the art of sniping at an early age."

"How did you get this file?"

"Spread some cash around," Henry said.

"What do I owe you?"

"We'll talk about it later. It wasn't a lot. Times are tough."

"Is there a picture in the file?"

"Yes," he said. "I'll email the file to you after we complete this call."

"Do you know where he is?"

"Somewhere in Europe. Eli is an experienced woodsman. The consensus is that he's hiding out in a remote area of forest somewhere, maybe in the Alps. Somewhere he's not known. He won't be easy to find."

"So, what now?"

"I know a very good hitman I could contract to end this thing," Henry said. "If you want me to take him out, it will cost ten grand, if we can locate him. For you, a bargain. I have a few people looking for him. If they find him, I'll hear about it."

"Doing it myself is one thing. Paying to have it done is something else entirely. That just doesn't feel right."

"The guy tried to assassinate you, Don," Henry said, raising his voice a little. "He might try again."

"Think he will?"

"Maybe not," Henry said. "According to some contacts I talked to at the U.S. embassy in Lithuania, it's unlikely. These contacts have informants around the country. They reached out with that question to a couple of their most trusted. It took me a few days to get the answer. Apparently, there is some sort of Lithuanian code the Wirkus clan abides by that says you have to try to avenge the killing of a family member. But if you try and fail, you're absolved of making another attempt, as long as the effort was sincere. If the target survives, then it's a sign that the killing of the family member was deserved."

"I hope Eli Wirkus believes that."

"I'll say it again. He tried to kill you," Henry said. "If we find him, we should take him out."

"Find him first, and then we'll talk about it," I said. "It would be hard for Eli Wirkus to make another attempt at me. When I tell David Steele who he is, he's going on the FBI's Ten Most Wanted list, with all the perks thereof."

"That's a start," Henry said.

"Remember, Henry, we're still not one hundred percent sure he's our guy."

"Has to be him," Henry said. "Too many coincidences."

◆ ◆ ◆ ◆

I made coffee. By the time I returned to my desk, I had the file from Henry. I opened it and looked at the photo of Eli Wirkus. He looked very much like his brother, a face I'd never forget. I closed the file and called David Steele. I skipped the niceties and got right to it.

"The shooter's name is Eli Wirkus," I said when he answered.

"You're sure?"

"Ninety-nine percent."

"Tell me what you learned," he said.

I told him everything Henry Cole had told me.

"Where did you get this from?"

"The CIA," I said. Not exactly the truth, but close enough. I wanted to keep Henry's name out of this.

"You do get around," David Steele said. "Do you have a file to send me?"

"Yes."

"Picture?"

"Yes."

"So, your source doesn't think he's going to make another run at you?"

"No. But to be safe, my source has offered to take him off the board."

"I didn't hear that," he said.

"I don't much like the idea either."

"Send me that file and I'll make it extremely difficult for Eli Wirkus to get back into the country," David Steele said.

"The file is on the way," I said. "I'll be in touch."

◆ ◆ ◆ ◆

Nothing much happened the rest of the day. Gretchen and Rhonda came and went, leaving me alone with my thoughts. I watched a cold wind blow snow flurries outside my window. The well-spaced flakes danced to and fro, finding it difficult to reach the ground. Those that did skidded along the street and sidewalk, seeking a resting place.

I felt less and less concerned that Eli Wirkus would make another attempt on my life. I knew the smart thing to do would be to take him out, but I couldn't quite make myself order the assassination of another human being, even if he had tried to kill me. Bringing myself down to his level was not the answer. What I wanted was a showdown, and that was highly unlikely. I had to put Eli Wirkus out of my mind and return to finding Kenny Stone. Even Kenny Stone could wait. Right then, all I wanted to do was go home and have a drink with my lovely wife.

My phone rang. Mary. *ESP!*

"World's greatest private investigator," I said.

"Ha! World's horniest private investigator is more like it."

"Guilty," I said.

"Get home, Cowboy. I have a bottle of red wine breathing on the kitchen bar that's getting impatient."

"On my way," I said.

◆ ◆ ◆ ◆

We sat drinking wine and nibbling cheese and crackers. Actually, Mary was nibbling. I was doing serious damage. It was the exact opposite of the way we drank wine. Mary drank wine; I sipped.

"Henry called," I said.

"Did he find who he was looking for?"

"He did."

"Tell me all of it," Mary said.

I told her, leaving out the part where Henry wanted to send a hitman to dispose of Eli Wirkus. Mary drank and stared at me over the top of her glass. I paused and looked out at the blowing snow, illuminated by our parking-lot street lamp. The snow was heavier than before.

"There's something you're not telling me," Mary said.

I couldn't discount the fact that Mary may have talked to Rosa. I doubted Henry kept much from Rosa. Mary might already know about the proposed hit.

"Henry wants to put a hit on him," I said. "Says he has a guy who will do it for ten grand."

Mary said nothing. She drained her glass and poured a second. She stared at me and took a drink from her refill. "And you don't want to," she said. "It would offend your sense of fair play. You'd rather have an Old West shootout in the street."

She was getting agitated. I said nothing. A smart remark at this point might get me a faceful of red wine.

"What would you do if it was me?" Mary continued. "What if a sniper tried to kill me and you had someone willing to get rid of him? What would you do?"

I took a sip of my wine. Anything I said would be wrong.

Mary glared at me. "Say something."

"What's for dinner?" I said.

Mary's face was getting redder by the second.

"Okay, okay," I said. "If it was you, I'd give Henry my blessing. But it's not you, it's me. And I'm not one hundred percent sure Eli is our guy. That, plus the fact that he's now on the FBI's Ten Most Wanted list, and I just can't justify paying someone to kill him. If it came to that, I'd take Henry and go looking for him myself."

"Fine," Mary said. "You are who you are, and I can't change that. I love you for it, but it scares me. I'll have to trust you on this. Don't get yourself killed, Cowboy."

"Not going to happen," I said.

"Better not," Mary said.

59

I was in early the next day when my office phone rang. Caller ID showed a series of numbers that led me to believe the call was coming from outside the USA. I have received a lot of unusual calls during my time as a private investigator, but this one was the weirdest.

"Cherokee Investigations," I said. "Donald Youngblood speaking."

"You can stop looking for me," a voice with an Eastern European accent said. "I will not come for you again."

"Is that you, Eli?" I pushed the record button on my office phone console.

"Yes, Mr. Youngblood."

"Why should I believe you?"

"Because is the truth. Family honor dictates that I try to kill you, but when you survive, I know the angel, he protect you. Maybe more than one angel. I never miss. There is no other explanation. That tells me my brother deserved that you kill him. Could you tell me please circumstances that led to your killing him?"

His English was precise and methodical, but his sentence structure left something to be desired. He sounded sincere, but then again, so did the snake in the Garden of Eden, I'd bet. Though there was no way to trace the call, engaging him in conversation might reveal something useful, so I indulged him.

"He took a shot at me as I was going out the back door of my lake house," I said. "You know the one. I was able to get between him and his escape route. I gave him a chance to give up, but he pulled a gun on me, and I shot him in the head. He was dead before he hit the ground."

"I don't understand," Eli Wirkus said. "Why would he want to kill you?"

"He was working for the Midnight Riders, a domestic terrorist group. I was getting too close to finding them and shutting them down. Their leader sent him to kill me. I really wanted to talk with your brother, but he wasn't interested."

"Emile was always arrogant and impulsive. He probably thought he could take you. Big mistake on his part. I thank you for telling me, and now that I know the reason Emile is dead, I am glad the angels protect you."

I didn't really believe the angels thing, but if he did, maybe that benefited me.

"Tell me." He said. "How did you survive two bullets from my rifle?"

I told him about the Yeti and the umbrella post. "If it makes you feel any better, the second bullet did some damage when it ricocheted off the post. I spent a night in the hospital."

"You were fortunate," Eli said. "I am now glad that you survive. I must go now. Believe me when I tell you that you have nothing to fear from me."

"That's nice to hear. I do hope I can believe that."

"My word of honor. Have a long and prosperous life, Donald Youngblood."

"One question, Eli," I said. "Tell me how you knew I killed your brother?"

"Everything has a price. Even an FBI file."

"I don't suppose you would give me a name."

"I could not do that," he said. "I have reputation to uphold."

"Would it be available for a price?"

"Possibly," he said. "Let me think about that."

"One other thing. I did not send anyone looking for you."

Well, that was technically true. Henry did, and without my knowledge.

"Interesting," he said. "Well, I have many enemies, but I will be hard to find and even harder to kill. Thank you for sharing that, Donald Youngblood. It was a pleasure speaking with you. *Dasvidaniya*."

Eli Wirkus was gone.

◆ ◆ ◆ ◆

I sat at my desk and thought about the phone call from Eli Wirkus. I wondered how often the hunter talked to the hunted. Rarely, if ever. This could be one for Ripley's Believe It or Not! I wanted to believe Eli. I could understand wanting to avenge his brother's death. I could also understand family honor and religious superstition. But guardian angels? That might be going too far. Still, I liked the possibility. What I really needed to know was whether or not Eli Wirkus was sincere.

I called Henry Cole's cell phone using my own cell. "I just got confirmation that it was Eli Wirkus who tried to kill me."

"How did you manage that?" Henry said.

"Eli called and told me so."

There was a moment of silence. Henry was probably making sure he heard right. "You're kidding."

"Nope."

"Well, that's interesting. Tell me about it."

"I can do better than that. I can play you a recording of the entire conversation."

Henry laughed. "Are you sure you aren't in the CIA?"

"Scout's honor," I said.

"Play it, Youngblood."

I hit the play button on my console and put my cell phone near the speaker. When it was over, I hit the stop button.

"He speaks pretty good English," Henry said. "A bit of an accent, but not bad."

"Do you believe him?" I said.

"Yes, I think so, but I cannot be one hundred percent sure. Would I still take him out if I could find him? Yes, I would."

"At this point, I would prefer you leave him alone," I said. "Call your guys off."

"As you wish," Henry said. "Mary told Rosa that beneath that tough, pragmatic exterior of yours lies a hopeless romantic. I'm beginning to believe it. I hope it doesn't get you killed."

"Nobody really knows what lies beneath anyone's exterior," I said.

"That is very true," Henry said.

◆ ◆ ◆ ◆

"I've got a little recording for your listening pleasure," I said to Mary that night. "I think you'll find it very interesting."

"I'm all ears."

We had just settled in with glasses of a very fine Cabernet Sauvignon and an assortment of cheeses and crackers. I pushed the play button on my mini-recorder. Mary listened to my conversation with Eli Wirkus in disbelief.

"How weird was that?" she said when it finished.

"Pretty weird. Do you believe him?"

"Maybe," Mary said. "He didn't have to call you. You need to play this for Henry."

"Already did."

"And?"

I told her what Henry said.

"A hard and practical man, that Henry," Mary said.

"He is that," I said.

60

Days turned into weeks, and nothing much happened. Nobody took a shot at me, and no one saw or heard from Kenny Stone. The PGA Professional Championship was a few days away, and Lacy was excited and nervous.

"What if I make a mistake?" she said one night when she called us. "It would be so embarrassing."

"You won't," I said. "You're cool under pressure. Stay in the moment, concentrate, don't get distracted, and you'll be fine."

"I hope."

"You'll be *fine*," I said with emphasis.

The tournament was being played on the PGA National Champion course in Palm Beach Gardens, Florida, which was maybe a twenty-minute drive, depending on traffic, from my Singer Island condo. So, on a Monday in mid-February, Tony Price and I flew Fleet Industries jet number one into Palm Beach International Airport three days before the tournament. We would go to the course the next day for a practice round. I wanted to see the head of security for special creds that would allow me to walk with Tony and Lacy.

We landed and wheeled our luggage to a shuttle bus that took us to Hertz. I rented a Lincoln Navigator and returned to the airport to wait on Lacy, who was flying in from Phoenix.

Lacy came through security wheeling her luggage, all business. She gave me a hug and looked at Tony. "You ready?"

"You bet," he said. "You?"

"Absolutely," Lacy said. "We're going to qualify for the PGA."

"We certainly are."

I wasn't sure either of them believed it, but it was a great effort at being positive.

"Well," I said, "let's lay in supplies and rest up for tomorrow."

◆ ◆ ◆ ◆

We sat on the balcony after dinner. I was finishing up a beer. Tony and Lacy were drinking club soda with lime. The ocean was a great sea of ink with an occasional whitecap visible in the light of a half-moon. We faced east into the darkness, high above the muted sound of the surf far below us. Although it had been a warm day, the wind was cool, and we each wore a long-sleeve T-shirt to keep our arms warm.

"A little spooky up here," Tony said. "I don't think I've ever been this high up."

"You get used to it," I said. "I had an office in Manhattan once that was thirty-five floors up. I noticed it for maybe a week, and then one day I didn't."

"I love it up here," Lacy said. "I think I'll turn in. I'm pretty tired."

"Tell Biker hello," I said, "in case you happen to call him."

"Right," Lacy said. "And tell Mom hello, in case you happen to call her."

"I will. Sweet dreams."

She patted my shoulder, went through the sliding glass door into the living room, and disappeared into the hall that led to her bedroom.

"You have quite a daughter," Tony said.

"I do. We were lucky."

"You-all have done a great job raising her."

"Thanks, but I think Mary gets most of the credit."

"I'm pretty sure it was a team effort," Tony said.

I finished my beer and set the glass on the table. "You ready for tomorrow?"

"More than ready," Tony said.

"Ever play in this tournament before?"

"Never."

"Nervous?"

He thought about that. "Anxious," he said. "I wish I could tee off right now. I want to get started."

"How many players are in the field?"

"Three hundred and twelve. There will be a cut after the first two rounds; the top seventy and ties move on. Seventy-seven players made the cut last year. We'll be playing on two different courses, the Palmer and the Champion. Half of us will be on one course one day and the other course the next, so first-day standings don't mean a lot. The last two days will be on the Champion course. That's where they play the Honda Classic. The course was redesigned by Jack Nicklaus in 2014. It's a real challenge, especially the Bear Trap."

"What's the Bear Trap?"

"Three very tough holes on the back nine: fifteen, sixteen, and seventeen," Tony said. "Play those holes well and you're likely going to have a good day."

"Better you than me," I said. "What time do we have to be there tomorrow?"

"I'm supposed to arrive at eleven, check in, and go to the practice tee with Lacy at eleven forty-five. We have to report to the first tee of the

Champion course at twelve-thirty for a practice round. I tee off at twelve forty-five. I'm in the next-to-last group. We have an assigned parking spot. Everything is super-organized. Tuesday, I have an earlier tee time on the Palmer course for another practice round. Wednesday, I'm taking the day off. Thursday, it's for real."

"You two are going to have a long week."

"Exactly why I'm turning in now," Tony said as he stood.

He left me alone. I called Mary. "I'm on the balcony staring out at a mostly dark ocean. I can see lights from a cruise ship, but that's about all," I said.

"Wish I was there," she said. "Are they ready for this?"

"Seem to be. They're talking the talk. We'll soon find out if they can walk the walk."

61

Tuesday morning, we had breakfast at Johnny Longboats. Lacy and Tony seemed relaxed, but you never know what's going on inside. After breakfast, we drove out to PGA National, and I dropped Lacy and Tony and went to park the SUV. Then I went looking for security. I found it under a large tent near the main clubhouse. At the entrance was a guy wearing a light blue polo shirt with a tasteful **Miami-Dade Security** logo in gray on the heart side. I walked up to him and flashed my FBI creds. "Who's in charge?" I said.

"FBI," he said. "Is there going to be trouble?"

"Not that I know of. Can I speak to the boss, please?"

"Sure," he said. "Follow me."

I followed. Once inside, the security guy stopped and turned to another security guy and said, "Frank, watch the entrance." Frank disappeared outside.

I continued to follow the security guy to the back, where we stopped near another security guy giving orders to other security guys. No doubt, he was the man in charge.

"Claude," the first security guy said, "this guy asked to see you. He's FBI."

"I'll take it from here, Fred," Claude said.

Fred went back toward the entrance.

"Can I see your credentials, please?" Claude said.

"Sure." I gave him a good look.

"Donald Youngblood, special consultant," he said. "Your name sounds familiar."

People in law enforcement and the security business are a close-knit group. They share information. Some of my exploits were bound to have made the rounds. I was not surprised.

"Unfortunately, I've made the news a couple of times," I said.

"Sometimes, it can't be helped," he said. "I'm Claude Akers." We shook hands. "Is there a problem?"

"No," I said. "A favor."

"Name it."

"My daughter is caddying for one of the players. I'd like to follow them around. I'd be available if there was trouble. I did the same thing at the Tennessee PGA, if you want to check."

"No need to," Claude said. "Glad to have another body, especially FBI. Let me get you a badge. And some shirts. XL, I'd say. They run a little small."

Claude went to another part of the tent, and I took time to observe all the activity. Tables were set up with laptops monitoring course cameras. Meetings with three or four people were being held at different tables. I was glad to see that some of the security people were women. They were all carrying sidearms.

Claude interrupted my observations with a badge and four shirts, all different colors. They were marked for Thursday, Friday, Saturday, and Sunday.

"They're not new. We do laundry," he said. "Turn them in when the tournament is over. Wear khaki pants if you've got them. Are you packing?"

"I can be if you want me to," I said. "Glock Nine."

"I'd like that. In this day and age, you never know. We want to show we mean business."

"Expecting trouble?"

"Best to expect it and not get it," Claude said.

"Not a bad philosophy in the security business," I said. "How big is Miami-Dade Security?"

"Big," he said. "Around five hundred employees. Lots of work in Miami—concerts, ball games, parties, golf tournaments, political events. You get the idea."

I nodded and said nothing.

"Good luck to your player," Claude said.

"Thanks."

We shook hands again, and I left the tent.

Outside, I texted Lacy: **Call me**. I knew she and Tony were on the practice tee, and I didn't want to disturb them with a phone call.

Less than a minute later, she called. "Make it quick."

"I've got my creds," I said. "I'm not sticking around. Call me when you're ready to leave, and I'll pick you up. Have fun out there."

"We will," Lacy said.

◆ ◆ ◆

That night, we picked up two calzones from Romana's, and I tossed a Caesar salad. They talked little and went straight to their respective showers. Clean and refreshed, they joined me at the kitchen bar. The calzones disappeared. Lacy and Tony ate like field hands. They drank bottled water. I drank beer.

"Tell me all about your day," I said. "I want the details."

"We learned a lot," Tony said. "Lacy did great. Practice rounds aren't for keeping score. You're out there taking shots from different places, putting from different places, getting a close-up look at the course."

"The course was beautiful," Lacy said. "Tony hit the ball well. I got a lot of good yardage information. I took some pictures on my phone."

"I think this is the best calzone I've ever had," Tony said.

"You're just hungry," I said.

"No, really, this is exceptional."

"It is," Lacy said.

"What time tomorrow?" I said.

"We need to be there at seven," Tony said. "We tee off at eight-fifteen. I want to spend some time on the practice tee."

"I'll be ready," I said.

"I'm turning in," Lacy said.

"Me, too," Tony said.

62

The next morning, I dropped Lacy and Tony near the practice tee and headed with my laptop to the Paradise Café for breakfast. I spent an hour online while slowly consuming ample portions of scrambled eggs, bacon, and biscuits with gravy. The coffee was flavorful and served with raw sugar and real cream. I mentally gave the place five stars. I sent a long email to T. Elbert.

Back at the condo, I changed into swim trunks, a T-shirt, and sandals. I grabbed my beach bag, took the elevator down to ground level, and headed to the beach.

Ray, the young beach attendant, waved happily when he spotted me. He knew a good tip was in his future. He jogged my way. "Good to see you, Mr. Youngblood," he said. "How long are you here?"

"The rest of the week. Don't know how often I'll get out. My daughter is caddying in the PGA Professional Championship this week."

"Cool," Ray said.

A row of wooden lounges stretched north and south. The south end was closer to where we stood. There must have been forty or so double lounges with a small table between each pair, constructed as a single unit. About half the lounges were occupied, mostly by people older than me—snowbirds from the North, many from Canada. It was, after all, the high season in South Florida.

"Set me up on the south corner, and give me a little space," I said.

"Sure thing," he said. "Take the corner lounge down there. I'll make sure no one is beside you. Do you want full shade?"

"Thanks, Ray. Full shade sounds good."

I took my beach bag to the corner lounge. Ray adjusted the umbrella, moving and twisting the pole deeper into the sand so a gust of wind couldn't carry it away.

"Let me know if you need anything," he said.

"I'll catch you later," I said.

He knew what that meant and went away happily.

I put the pad on the lounge and then my beach towel on the pad. I removed a can of suntan spray from the beach bag and gave myself a good spray. I put on my wraparound shades and removed my sandals. I programmed my watch for a walk and headed for the shoreline. At the water's edge, I turned north. I was carrying my T-shirt. I didn't want to get burned my first day out. I walked leisurely. I saw some very fine bodies sporting some very nice bikinis and wished Mary were with me. My watch let me know when I had gone a mile. I put on my T-shirt, headed back, settled in under the umbrella, and called Gretchen.

"Is that surf I hear in the background?" she said.

"It is. I could FaceTime you and give you a good look."

"Don't you dare. I'm jealous enough already."

"Need anything from me?"

"Nothing," Gretchen said. "At the first sighting of a serial killer, I'll call."

I adjusted the back of the lounge to suit me and leaned back. *Perfect.* I pulled a John Grisham novel out of my bag and started reading. I didn't get far before the surf and the warm, gentle breeze caused me to drift off. I woke up, read some more, and drifted off again. After repeating that process for a third time, I gave up, put the book away, and watched the bikini babes go up and down the beach. That kept me awake. An hour or so later, I went in, fixed a Diet Coke, and booted up my laptop. I spent an hour looking at news, sports, and the market. Then I stripped down and took a shower.

Lacy called in midafternoon. "Come get us," she said. "We've had enough golf for one day."

"On my way," I said.

♦ ♦ ♦

We picked up dinner from Johnny Longboats. Tony and I had fish and chips, and Lacy had fried shrimp. I put off asking about their day, and they put off telling me about it. They seemed relaxed and positive, so I guessed it had been good.

Finally, I said, "Well?"

Lacy smiled. "Awesome day. The course was beautiful. We went around with a club pro from California."

"Yeah," Tony said. "He had a good-looking young caddie who paid more attention to Lacy than his pro."

"He asked me out," Lacy said.

I waited and said nothing.

"I told him I was spoken for," she said.

"Good for you," I said. "How did your pro do today?"

"He did very well. He's having a little trouble with the speed of the greens."

"I'm right here," Tony said.

I looked at Tony. "Fast?"

"Lightning," he said.

When we finished dinner, Tony retired to his bedroom to check his email and call home. Lacy stayed at the table with me.

"So, how did you do out there?"

"Fine," she said. "I'm glad I had these practice rounds. I'm feeling really comfortable about it. I think we have a chance to make it to the big tournament."

"Then you might not feel so comfortable."

"True," Lacy said. "But I sure would like the chance to find out."

63

The crowd around the first tee of the Champion course was light, even though there was no charge for admission. I could tell Tony and Lacy were totally focused on the job at hand. The weather was cooperating, with mild temperatures and no wind. I stood watching at the back of the tee. The first introduction was for a club pro from Texas, the second for a club pro from Florida. They both found the fairway with their tee shots. Then came the final announcement: "Ladies and gentlemen, now on the tee, from Mountain Center Country Club in Mountain Center, Tennessee, club pro Tony Price."

There was light applause as Tony bent down and teed up his ball. He checked his line, stepped back, and made a couple of practice swings. He addressed the ball and wasted little time drilling his tee shot down the middle of the fairway past the other two pros.

"Nice," Lacy said, taking the driver from Tony.

Tony began his trek down the first fairway to his ball. Lacy was a few steps behind, effortlessly carrying his golf bag. I was almost beside her, within talking distance. She said nothing, and neither did I.

Tony's second shot found the green, and he two-putted for a par. It went like that for most of the day. He missed the green on the seventh hole, a 226-yard par-three, and made bogey. He immediately made up for it on the par-four eighth by sinking a twenty-five-foot birdie putt. A par on the par-four ninth gave him even par on the front side. Lacy was calm and confident as they discussed distances, club selection, position, and yardage. On the greens, she helped Tony read putts. I was more nervous for her than I was for Tony, who looked relaxed and focused.

Tony was still at even par when they arrived at the Bear Trap. He found the green on the 176-yard par-three and just missed a twenty-foot birdie putt. He tapped in for par. He missed the fairway on the tough par-four sixteenth and made bogey. A par at seventeen left him one over for the day. He ripped a 300-yard tee shot on the 556-yard par-five eighteenth. I heard the following conversation when they arrived at the ball.

"Too risky," Lacy said.

"I can make it," Tony said.

"Not worth it. Lay it up. Hit a wedge close, and make the birdie putt."

"Well, that sounds easy," Tony said.

"You don't gamble on the first day," Lacy said.

"You're right," Tony said. "I'll lay up."

And that's what he did. His second shot rolled to a stop about a hundred yards from the flag. Tony then hit a wedge to within ten feet of the pin and rolled the putt in for a birdie.

After the handshakes, they walked over to me, and Tony said, "She was right. Always listen to your caddie." He headed for the scorer's table.

"Good thing he made that birdie putt," I said.

"A really good thing," Lacy said.

◆ ◆ ◆ ◆

That night, we had an early dinner at Bonefish Grill. We shared a couple of orders of Bang Bang Shrimp.

"Were you satisfied with today's round?" I said to Tony.

"Very. Even par is a pretty good score on the Champion course. If I can shoot even for the whole tournament, I'll probably make the top twenty. Even par last year tied for eighth. I just have to keep playing one hole at a time and be smart. It's a long way to the finish line."

"To one hole at a time," I said, raising my glass.

"Copy that," they said in unison.

64

Early the next day, we were on the Palmer course, designed by and named for the man who, while playing on the senior tour, set the Champion course record of sixty-three. The Palmer was supposed to be easier that the Champion, but Mother Nature had other ideas. A stiff wind greeted the participants at the first tee.

Tony seemed unfazed as he drove his tee shot in the center of the first fairway. He finished the front side at even par, with two bogeys and two birdies. On the back, he started with six straight pars before bogeying the tough par-four sixteenth. He bounced back immediately with a chip-in birdie on seventeen and then birdied the 601-yard par-five eighteenth with a third-shot wedge and a twelve-foot birdie putt. Tony and Lacy shook hands with their competitors, then walked over to where I was waiting.

"Good job out there," I said. "I think that was a lot harder than you made it look."

"Thanks," Tony said. "Lacy really keeps me focused. I'll bet there won't be a dozen rounds under par on that course today."

We learned later that only a total of 21 out of 312 players on both courses had been under par. The wind had picked up even more for the afternoon players. Luck of the draw.

Finishing the round early meant we had the afternoon free. Tony elected not to go to the practice tee or the putting green. "I'm exactly where I want to be," he said. "I don't want to mess anything up."

Conditions were even windier at the beach. From our balcony, we watched wind-assisted, ankle-stinging sand skittering in sheets along the beach. Very few lounges were occupied, and no umbrellas were up.

"Let's go to the pool," Lacy said. "It won't be that windy."

"You hope," I said.

"Don't be a wuss."

"Okay," I said. "I'm game."

"Tony?" Lacy said.

"I'm going to shower, and then I'd like to borrow the SUV and go back out to the club for a while, if that's okay. I've got some club-pro friends I haven't seen in a while."

"Sure," I said. "Keys are hanging in the kitchen. We'll see you for dinner."

"I'll be glad to pick up something on the way back," he said. "I'll call when I leave the club."

Tony headed for his room, and I turned to Lacy. "How long?"

"Give me ten minutes," she said.

It was less windy at the pool. Lacy lay in the sun for a while, then went in the water. I stayed in the sun for about ten minutes reading my Grisham novel, then found some shade. I tired of reading after a while, so I sat and thought about Eli Wirkus and Kenny Stone.

I was ninety-nine percent sure Eli would not make another attempt to take me out. If he intended to, he would not have called me. Maybe I was naïve, but for some reason, I believed what he said. Still, there was that one percent.

Kenny Stone was a different story. Obviously, that was not his real name. He must have been running from something, but what? Attempted blackmail? I thought for a while and came up with nothing.

"Ready to go up?" Lacy said, bringing me back to the here and now.

The sun was sinking fast in the west, leaving the pool area in complete shade.

"Sure," I said.

I gathered my belongings, and we headed to the elevator.

◆ ◆ ◆

Tony wanted a calzone again, so we split a large one from Romana's. Lacy opted for Italian sausage pizza. I prepared my Caesar salad. We sat at the dining-area table, not far from the kitchen bar and near the sliding glass door to the balcony. We had a good view of the ocean. Daylight was slowly receding. Charter boats were coming in from an afternoon of fishing. A cruise ship was heading out past the twelve-mile limit. From our lofty perch, the ocean looked calm and peaceful.

"Did you see anyone you knew?" Lacy said to Tony.

"Yes, I did," Tony said. "Harley Dobbs and Bobby Wilkins."

"The Bobby Wilkins from the story you told me?" I said.

"That's the one. He was on the tour my first year and then took a club-pro job in Texas."

"Did they make the cut?" Lacy asked.

"They did," Tony said. "I'm not sure where they stand, but they're not in the top twenty."

We were silent for a moment, staring at Tony, who was playing it cool.

"Well?" Lacy said.

She had been patient in asking, and I suspected the news was good, since Tony seemed to be in an upbeat mood.

"Tied for fifteenth," he said.

"Yes!" Lacy exclaimed. She high-fived Tony.

"We're in the sixth-to-last group," Tony said. "We tee off at twelve-ten. It looks like it's going to be windy again."

"Good," Lacy said. "You play well in the wind. I think it will give you an edge."

"One shot at a time," Tony said.

"Copy that," Lacy said. "I'm turning in." She looked at me. "Call Mom. You didn't call her last night."

"I texted," I said.

"Not the same."

"Go call Biker and leave me alone," I said.

She smiled. "Call Mom."

I nodded. She went to her bedroom.

"I need to call home myself," Tony said. "See you in the morning."

Alone at the table, looking out into the night, I called Mary.

"Hey, Cowboy," she answered.

"Hey, Doll."

An hour later, I went to bed.

65

The next day, I stood at the back of the first tee as Tony and two golfers I had never heard of were introduced. Tony was right in his preview of things to come. The wind was stiff. He bogeyed the first two holes and struggled to finished two over on the front nine. He had an early birdie on the back nine, then got in trouble at the Bear Trap and finished the day with a two-over seventy-four.

After the customary handshakes, we left the eighteenth green. Tony went to the scorer's tent, and Lacy went to check the leader board. I kept watch over Tony's clubs. Lacy and Tony arrived back at the same time. I could see the tiredness in Tony's face and in his stride. Lacy seemed no worse for wear, despite carrying a fully loaded pro golf bag for eighteen holes. *The young!*

"Want to go to the practice tee?" Lacy said.

"Too tired," Tony said. "You can get into some bad habits on the practice tee when you're tired."

"I'll remember that," Lacy said. She picked up his bag, and we headed to the SUV. "Forget the score," she said as we approached our ride. "You played pretty good today."

"Where do we stand?" Tony said.

"Tied for fourteenth. You gained one position. You were solid. We're off at twelve-twenty tomorrow."

◆ ◆ ◆ ◆

After long, hot showers, we walked to a local restaurant called Two Drunken Goats. I ordered a fried grouper sandwich, fries, and slaw, and Lacy said, "Make that two."

"Sounds good to me," Tony said. "Make it three."

Our dinner conversation was casual and did not include the tournament. I mostly listened. Lacy talked about Biker and college. Tony talked about his family and told funny stories about golfers at the Mountain Center Country Club without naming names. One of the stories went this way:

"So, we had this member-guest tournament one year, and we made the mistake of having a Bloody Mary breakfast. It was a shotgun start, playing best ball, and the leaders were a father-in-law/son-in-law team. Unfortunately, the father-in-law had one too many Bloody Marys at breakfast. They started on the par-three seventeenth. The father-in-law teed up his ball, addressed it, took a big swing, and whiffed. He quickly said, 'Practice swing,' took another cut at it, and hit into a green-side bunker. The son-in-law hit his tee shot seven feet from the pin. He didn't have any Bloody Marys for breakfast."

"I'm guessing there's more," I said.

"You're right," Tony said. "So, the father-in-law couldn't get out of the sand trap. He took five or six swings, moved the ball a few inches, and finally gave up. He picked up his ball. The son-in-law made the birdie putt, so it didn't matter. The father-in-law got in their golf cart and stayed there the rest of the day. He was relatively sober by the time they finished."

"Did they win?" Lacy said.

"They did. The son-in-law had one of his best rounds ever. Talk about coming through under pressure."

◆ ◆ ◆ ◆

Later that night, in the sanctity of my bedroom, I called Mary. "I think Tony may make the big dance," I said. "He has a seventy-one, a seventy-two, and a seventy-four. He's tied for fourteenth."

"And the top twenty advance," Mary said.

"Correct."

"How is Lacy doing?"

"She's a pro. You would be so proud. She may have found a new career."

"You must be tired," Mary said. "All of you."

"And then some. I don't know how pro golfers do it week in and week out. They would have to love it."

"Well, go get some rest," Mary said. "You'll need it when you get home. I've really, really missed you."

"Signing off now," I said. "Love you, Doll."

"Love you, too, Cowboy."

66

The next day was sunny and warm, with a brisk wind that wasn't as bad as the day before but still made play tricky. Tony and Lacy stood to the side of the first tee in muted conversation.

"Par will be a good score today," Lacy said quietly.

"I think you're right," Tony said. "Don't let me do anything stupid."

"One shot at a time."

"Copy that," Tony said, smiling.

On the first tee, Tony hit a low draw into a crosswind and found the middle of the fairway. His playing partners found the rough. I followed Lacy and Tony at a discreet distance down the fairway to where the ball had come to rest. After much discussion with Lacy, Tony hit his approach fifteen feet from the pin. He turned to Lacy, and I heard him say, "You were right."

Lacy smiled, handed Tony his putter, and picked up his bag. I followed them to the first green, where I watched as Tony rolled in the putt for a birdie three.

They were methodical. Tony played at a pace that was neither rushed nor lingering. They would arrive at his ball for the next shot and, after a short discussion, Tony would hit. I followed them around, sometimes glancing from side to side for trouble, my Glock on my hip like a warning that I meant business. The crowd was light, and I saw no threats.

Tony kept ringing up easy pars and finally made another birdie on the par-four ninth. He had other birdie opportunities that resulted in tap-in pars. Tony was solid, and Lacy was calmly encouraging. The Bear Trap almost got him on sixteen, but a marvelous chip and putt netted a par. He finished the round with a birdie on the par-five eighteenth for a three-under sixty-nine. I had no doubt Tony was headed to the PGA Championship. He hugged Lacy, waved at me, and headed to the scorer's tent.

"I have something I need to do," I said to Lacy. "I'll see you two at the Navigator."

"We'll be there. I'm going to see where Tony finished. I'm pretty sure we're going to the big one."

At the Navigator, I stored my Glock and changed shirts. I stuffed the dirty shirt in a plastic grocery bag with the others and headed to the security tent.

Claude Akers spotted me as I came in carrying the bag and pointed to a large laundry cart close by. I tossed in the dirty shirts.

"Thanks for your courtesy," I said. "I owe you one."

"No way," Claude said. "Word gets around that we know the FBI and business will be even better than it already is. How'd your guy do?"

"Three under today," I said. "Tied for fourteenth going in, so I'm sure he made the final cut."

"Good for him," Claude said. "If you ever want to join us for any golf tournament we're part of, you're always welcome."

"I'll keep that in mind. I like it when I don't have to shoot anyone."

"I heard that," he said.

"Do you know who is doing security at the big event?"

"Sure do," Claude said. "I can call him and get you on the team, if you like. I'm sure he'd love to have you."

"Do that," I said. I handed him a business card. "Let me know what he says."

"Sure thing," Claude said.

◆ ◆ ◆ ◆

Back at the condo, after everyone showered, I popped the cork on a half-split of champagne and proposed a toast. I looked from Tony to Lacy. "May your drives be straight, your bag be light, and the wind be always at your back. Well done." We touched glasses and drank.

Tony had finished in a tie for sixth and secured a place in the big one. Not only that, but he had won over twenty thousand dollars in prize money, ten percent of which would go to Lacy.

"I can pay you back, Don," Tony said. "Then I can pay Lacy and still have about ten grand to put in the bank. Not bad for a week's work."

"You don't have to pay me," Lacy said. "I had a great week."

"We've had this discussion before. You're getting what you deserve, young lady," Tony said. "You were a big part of where we finished. These checks officially make you a professional caddie. Besides, I want you on my bag at Pinehurst. You okay with that?"

Lacy smiled broadly. "Wouldn't miss it."

67

The next morning, we got up early and cleaned the condo. Everyone was responsible for their own bedroom and bathroom. When that was done, we all pitched in and cleaned up the kitchen and common areas. I must admit that it looked pretty good when we left. We drove to the airport.

"Just drop me," Lacy said. "No need to see me to the gate. There'll be a wait at security."

We got to passenger drop-off. Tony said goodbye to Lacy and stayed in the Navigator. I got out and retrieved her luggage from the cargo area. She hugged me fiercely. "Loved every minute," she said. "Thank you."

"It was fun," I said.

She started for the entrance and over her shoulder shouted, "Love you!" She didn't wait for a reply. Sneaky.

I got out my cell phone and texted her, **Love you, too!**

We dropped the Navigator and got a ride back to the private hangars. We found Jim Doak waiting by the stairs to the jet.

"Good work," he said to Tony as we boarded. "You made the headlines in the *Mountain Center Press*. Two copies of the paper are on the table."

"Thanks," Tony said.

We got on board and buckled in. Tony ignored the newspapers. I picked one up and stared at the front page. A big, bold headline proclaimed,

LOCAL PRO QUALIFIES FOR PGA CHAMPIONSHIP

"I may need your autograph," I said, flipping the paper around so he could see the headline.

"I'm not very comfortable with this celebrity stuff," Tony said.

"Welcome to the club," I said.

◆ ◆ ◆ ◆

We landed early in the afternoon at Tri-Cities Airport. We had both left our rides in the Fleet Industries hangar. We loaded our luggage in our respective vehicles and shook hands.

"Couldn't have done it without you, Don," Tony said. "Thanks."

"It was a bargain. I now have a lot of respect for professional golfers that I didn't have before. Actually, I never gave it much thought. These last four days were an eye opener. Plus, I got to spend some quality time with Lacy. That was a bonus."

"I'll send you a check," Tony said.

"No hurry."

Tony got in his SUV, gave me a brief wave, and drove away.

As I departed the airport, I called Mary. I tried to think of something clever to say, but I was too tired. "I'm back. Meet me at the condo as soon as you can."

"No," Mary said. "The lake house. I don't want anyone anywhere near us. I can't wait to get my hands on you."

"On my way," I said. "When can I expect you?"

"Before dark. I'll come as soon as I can. Jake and Junior are there. I'm sure they'll be thrilled to see you. Turn them out."

"Will do," I said. "See you soon."

◆ ◆ ◆ ◆

We were sitting at the bistro table in front of the fireplace eating ribs Mary had picked up on her way home. Baked potatoes and barbecue beans came with the ribs. We had worked up an appetite, making up for lost time. A week away from Mary seemed like a year.

She smiled at me. "You seemed pretty needy, Cowboy."

"Look who's talking."

"I'm so glad you're home. I hate it when you're gone."

"That makes two of us. I wish you could have been there. They made quite a team."

"No doubt," Mary said, "based on the results."

The ribs were disappearing, along with the beer and wine. Outside the picture window, light snow danced in the floodlights. I felt my tiredness wash over me like a puff of warm mist.

"What were you thinking?" Mary said. "You were gone for a minute."

"I'm too tired to think. I may have been asleep with my eyes open."

"It's time for me to put you to bed," Mary said.

68

I was in the office early, thankful that I didn't have to walk eighteen holes around a golf course. I had slept ten hours. Mary was long gone by the time I got downstairs for coffee. Her note read, *See you tonight at the condo*. So, I had loaded Jake and Junior and, much to their delight, taken them with me to the office.

Gretchen came in, patted Jake and Junior, sat down, and reviewed the events of the past week, which proved typically boring. I sat and thought about the blackmailer/kidnapper known as Kenny Stone, formerly somebody else. But who? And then something from the past came flooding back, and I had an idea. I called David Steele.

When I got him on the phone, he said, "Make it quick. I have a meeting in five minutes."

"Kenny Stone appeared on the grid about ten years ago," I said. "Before that, he was somebody else. Is it possible he was in witness protection and got bored with it?"

"Why would you think that?" David Steele said.

"My first big case was about a guy who was going into witness protection and took off before it happened. He changed his name and started a new life. I just thought it might be worth a look to see if anyone ditched their witness protection identity about the time Kenny Stone came on the grid."

"I'd say that's a long shot," David Steele said. "And the witness protection boys are very possessive of their cases. Once they get someone relocated, I don't think there's a lot of follow-up, and they sure as hell don't share who is where. Anyway, I'll nose around a little and see what I can find. Might take a few days. I've got to run." He disconnected without another word.

69

Midmorning two days later, I got a call from John Banks.

"The associate director informs me that I'm supposed to assist the hotshot FBI consultant slash private investigator with the witness protection files," John said.

"How long did it take you to rehearse that little opening?" I said.

"No time. It was extemporaneous."

"Extemporaneous. Big word for an FBI guy."

"Just testing to see if you know what it means," he said.

"Extemporaneous means spoken or done without preparation."

"Tough *and* smart," John said. "How can I help you, Agent Youngblood?"

"How did you get access to the witness protection files?"

"I think access came from the director himself. There is now an official file on Kenny Stone."

"Do you still have all the info you dug up on him?"

"Sure," he said. "I put all that stuff in my Youngblood file, figuring you'll have an epiphany one day and I'll have to access it again. What do you need?"

"I need you to go into the files and see if you can match Kenny to anyone who went into witness protection somewhere between ten and thirteen years ago."

"I see where you're going with this," John said. "You think Kenny bolted from witness protection and reinvented himself. Not a bad thought."

"I'm guessing it didn't take him long to get bored," I said. "I'll bet he took off in a year, two at most, from the time he went in."

"I'll start when Kenny Stone came on the grid and work backwards. I should know by tomorrow, or the next day at the latest."

"Thanks, John," I said. "I'll wait to hear from you."

◆ ◆ ◆

John called me back late that afternoon.

"You found something already?"

"It didn't take long for the asshole to take off," he said. "One month. I'll send you the file. Kenny Stone is a very bad boy. A sociopath, probably. You might want to take a shower after reading the file."

"Thanks for the warning. Send it now. I'll read it before I go home."

"You already have it," John said. "Check your email."

I checked. The file was there: *Kenny Stone-Tony Ballantine-Antonio Bella.pdf.* I opened it. There was a lot to read. Antonio Bella, his birth name, was a career criminal who had worked his way up in the New Jersey mob. He was suspected of killing at least a dozen people, including three women. He was a feared enforcer who liked to torture people. When they finally pinned a murder rap on him, he had flipped on the mob and given up enough information to send ten mobsters to jail and wreck the North Jersey mafia for years. Still, I couldn't believe the feds would put this monster back on the street. It made me angry.

Antonio's witness protection identity was Tony Ballantine. He changed his look by dyeing his hair blond and cutting it shorter. The dark beard from his mafia days was also gone. On first glance, two different men. Under closer observation, the same guy, without a doubt. The hair was even shorter for the Kenny Stone persona. He had also lost some weight.

The man with three names was worse than I suspected. I felt even more compelled to find him. I stewed for a few minutes, then called David Steele and told him what John Banks had found.

"Checking witness protection was a good thought on your part," he said.

I ignored the compliment. I should have thought of it sooner. "How could they cut a deal with this monster?" I said.

"Oh, you know what they'd say," David Steele said. "Greater good and all that bullshit. Maybe it is, but I couldn't do it."

"I'm going to find this guy and take him off the board."

"No, Youngblood, you are not. As your boss and your friend, I'm telling you to calm down. Find another way. Do not bring yourself down to his level. You are not judge, jury, and executioner."

"Part-time boss," I said.

He ignored me and turned up the heat. "You getting this?" David Steele was sounding a little like my old drill instructor.

I took a deep breath. "I got it. You're right."

"You're a smart guy," he said. "I repeat: find another way."

That night, Mary and I were finishing our dinner drinks, dinner having long been consumed. I told her about the Kenny Stone-Tony Ballantine-Antonio Bella file.

"Evil," she said. "You're not going to be able to let go of this, are you?"

I looked at her and said nothing. She took a drink of wine, then poured the rest of the bottle into her glass. I took a swig of AmberBock. I was drinking from the bottle, a longneck. We were quiet for a while, staring at each other.

"I have an idea," Mary said.

"Let's hear it."

"I'll bet Carlo Vincente would be interested to know what Antonio Bella has been up to the last ten years. Doesn't Carlo have some connection to the North Jersey mob?"

"You're a genius," I said. "Yes and yes. Carlo does have a connection, and I bet he'd be very interested. I'll call him tomorrow."

"I think I deserve a reward," Mary said, finishing her wine.

"Don't you think we're having too much sex?"

Mary looked at me like I was speaking in tongues.

I smiled. "Gotcha," I said.

70

The next morning, I was in the office early, waiting for an appropriate time to call Carlo Vincente. I had met Carlo, now a semi-retired New York mafia boss, on my first big case. I had done him a favor and then another, and he considered himself in my debt. He had done me a few minor favors but never considered the slate clean. Despite our being on opposite sides of the fence, I liked Carlo and trusted his word. At eight o'clock, I dialed his private cell phone, a number, I was told, known to only a few.

"Mr. Youngblood," Carlo answered. "What a surprise!"

"I hope I didn't call too early."

"Not at all," he said. "I'm an early riser. I don't sleep much these days. A product of getting older, I think. I hope this is not bad news."

"I think you might find it good news. At the very least, interesting news."

"Well, I like interesting, and I like good even better. Let's hear it."

"Does the name Antonio Bella ring a bell?"

There was a moment of silence. "Loud and clear," Carlo said, his voice a menacing growl. "A rat of the lowest order. There is still a price on his head. What do you know about Antonio Bella?"

"A lot. I stumbled across him in a case I was working. He did some very bad things to the daughter of a client of mine. I was able to get to her in time. I nearly had him in Memphis. I have a pretty good idea where he might resurface."

"Tell me," Carlo said.

"No."

His laugh was a low rumble. "I see you haven't changed. Still not afraid to poke the bear."

"I know the bear is an old softie," I said.

He laughed again. "When it comes to you, maybe. I consider you family. So, you're not going to tell me. What's the plan?"

"When Antonio resurfaces, I'll know about it. I'm not of a mind to turn him over to the authorities for punishment. I thought you, or some of your friends, might be interested."

"Very interested," Carlo Vincente said. "If I turn Antonia Bella over to the North Jersey mob, I'll be a folk hero. What do you need from me?"

"When the time comes, I'll let you know. I'll need Gino and Frankie, if you think they would want to be part of this." Gino and Frankie were two of the top enforcers in Carlo's organization. I knew Frankie well. Gino, not so much. I had once broken his nose.

"They would love to capture the rat and be part of the extermination," Carlo said.

"I thought as much. I'll be in touch at some point. It may be weeks or months, but the rat will surface sooner or later."

"Something to look forward to. I appreciate your thinking of me, Don."

"Stay safe and well, Carlo," I said, then disconnected before he could say anything else.

71

More than a week passed. February was in the history books, and March roared in like a lion, bringing a foot of snow. The snow came one week after I talked with Carlo Vincente. The lake house was a winter wonderland, and Mary and I spent the weekend isolated from the rest of the world.

That Saturday, after a late breakfast, we snowshoed a hiking trail around the lake, a workout that was exhilarating and exhausting at the same time. Upon our return, I shoveled a path to the hot tub, and we took our drinks and hurried in with nothing on but baseball caps to keep our heads warm. The scene was idyllic, with light, windless snow, 20-degree temperatures, and steam rising from the 102-degree water.

We had dinner at the bistro table in front of the fireplace and afterward made love on the couch.

Much later, as we turned in for the night, Mary said, "You sure know how to show a girl a good time."

"I loved every minute of it, Doll," I said.
Mary laughed and turned out the light.

◆ ◆ ◆ ◆

The temperature remained cold in Mountain Center and the surrounding countryside, which allowed the snow to keep a fresh look. I drove to the office Monday morning and enjoyed the early-morning silence as I fitted a Dunkin' Donuts K-Cup into my Keurig. A minute later, I was at my desk taking that first glorious drink while booting up my computer. I went straight to email. I had one from Laramie Sims:

Subject: He's back!

I opened it. The text was a two-word message:

Call me.

I called.
"Your boy is in town," Laramie Sims said. "I heard from Jimmy the Ghost last night. Word is, Kenny Stone is back in town and dealing drugs, high-end stuff."
"Not really Kenny Stone," I said. "He's had at least two other names that I know of. His real name is Antonio Bella. He ratted out the North Jersey mob, went into witness protection with a new name, got bored, and came out as Kenny Stone. Antonio Bella is a really bad guy."
"So, what do you want to do now?" Laramie Sims said.
"I want you to stay out of it. I'll handle it from here."
"Works for me. You coming soon?"
"Probably tomorrow," I said. "I need to make some calls. When the problem is taken care of, I'll call you and we'll get together for a meal before I head back. I'm buying."
"That works for me, too," Laramie said. "I'll wait to hear from you."

◆ ◆ ◆

I finished my coffee and took a long look at tomorrow's weather. A winter storm warning was in effect: one to three inches of snow in the mountains. Although I was experienced navigating in snow, I wasn't about to tempt fate by driving through the mountains on I-40. I trusted myself, but there was always some crazy who didn't know what he was doing.

I called Jim Doak. "Is Big Bird available tomorrow?"

"You mean the Silver Streak?" he said.

"I thought that was a train."

"Not in my world. We are at your service. Where are we going?"

"Charleston, South Carolina."

"What time?"

"Sometime after lunch," I said. "Let's say one o'clock."

"See you at Tri," he said.

I had a second cup of coffee, nuked a blueberry muffin that Mary had made, and called Carlo Vincente.

"You have news?" he said.

"To be confirmed," I said. "But it looks promising. Can Gino and Frankie be in Charleston, South Carolina, tomorrow for dinner?"

"They can and they will," Carlo said. "Where?"

"The Renaissance Hotel. Tell Frankie to call me when they land."

"Will do," Carlo said. "Good hunting."

72

At five o'clock the next afternoon, I was in a corner suite on the top floor of the Charleston Renaissance Hotel reading the latest news on my laptop when my cell phone rang. I didn't recognize the number, but I was guessing it was Frankie.

"Mr. Youngblood?"

"That you, Frankie?"

"We're here," Frankie said. "Just landed. What's the plan?"

"I'll meet you and Gino in the lobby of the Renaissance. You won't need to rent a car. I have one. Call me when you get here."

"See you when we see you," Frankie said, and disconnected.

◆ ◆ ◆

They called from the lobby an hour later, and I went down to meet them. We shook hands. I had seen Frankie a lot over the years, but I had not seen Gino since I broke his nose on my first big case.

"How've you been, Gino?" I said. "Long time, no see."

"I've been good," he said. "You're really hot stuff now, I hear."

"Gino," Frankie growled.

"No offense," Gino said.

"Sorry about the nose," I said. "Heat of the moment."

He shrugged. "Goes with the territory. Win some, lose some."

"We good?" I said.

"We're good," Gino said.

"You guys hungry?" I said.

"Yes," they said in unison.

"I know a place."

"Thought you would," Frankie said.

◆ ◆ ◆ ◆

We were in the back of Jimmy the Ghost's hangout, sitting with Jimmy at a table for four. Introductions had been made. Jimmy seemed impressed that my companions worked for Carlo Vincente. I was continually surprised at how many people knew or had heard of Carlo.

"Whatever you guys need," Jimmy said. "No charge."

"Right now, we need food," Frankie said. "Are the steaks any good here?"

"They are exceptional," Jimmy said, motioning for a waiter.

Orders were placed and instructions given. We engaged in casual conversation as we waited. I mostly listened. Jimmy, Frankie, and Gino talked about Charleston, New York, women, sports, and the business. At some point, Frankie said to Jimmy, "Mr. Youngblood is a close personal friend of Mr. Vincente. I've been driving Mr. Youngblood around for years."

I started to protest, but I didn't want to embarrass Frankie. I let it go, distracted by the arrival of our steaks. They looked and were superb.

When all of us were finished eating, I looked at Jimmy and said, "Where can I find Kenny Stone?"

"Probably at his girlfriend's apartment in North Charleston, or so I hear."

"Good information?"

"I think so," Jimmy said.

"I need to get him on the street. How can I do that?"

"You-all guarantee he's gone after tonight?" Jimmy said.

I looked at Frankie.

"Totally off the grid, never to surface again," Frankie said. "Guaranteed by Carlo Vincente himself, who would owe whoever helped to make it happen a big favor."

A smile, or maybe it was a smirk, passed over Jimmy's face and then was gone. "I never liked Kenny Stone," he said. "Why don't I call and tell Kenny I have a big-time buyer who wants all his product? I tell him the buyer will pull into the alley behind his girlfriend's apartment building at eleven o'clock. The buyer will be paying top dollar."

"That will give us time to get there and set up," I said. "You know his cell number?"

"No, but I know the girlfriend's number."

"Make the call," I said.

He took a little black book from the inside pocket of his jacket, found the number, and dialed it. He waited.

"Jasmine, it's Jimmy. I need to speak to Kenny." Pause. "He's not? Too bad. He going to miss out on a huge sale. I'll call another guy." He disconnected and smiled at me. "He's there. I'll bet he calls in the next minute."

As soon as the words escaped his mouth, his cell phone rang. He answered on the fourth ring.

"This is Jimmy." Pause. "You're too late. I got another guy on hold." Pause. "Okay, you owe me. Here's the deal. Whatever you charge this guy, I get ten percent." Pause. "Hey, take it or leave it. I thought of you first because the word is you got top-quality stuff." Pause. "Okay, deal. Where are you?" Pause. "Thought so. Okay, the buyer will pull up in the alley behind Jasmine's apartment building at precisely eleven o'clock. You come out, he'll hand you the money, you hand him the stuff, and he's gone. I gave him my word it's good stuff. Any funny business and you're in the kind of trouble you don't want to be in." Pause. "Very wise. How long will it take you to get it together?" Pause. "What's the price?" Pause. "As long as it's top quality, I can sell that. They'll be out in the alley at eleven. Black Escalade. Which street should the buyer enter the alley from?" Pause. "Okay. Third doorway. Got it. Pleasure doing business with you, Kenny. I'll expect you to come around tomorrow."

He disconnected the call.

"Well played," I said.

"If you think you're about to lose something, then you want it more," Jimmy the Ghost said. "Human nature."

"Ain't that the truth," Frankie said.

"You'll need ten grand," Jimmy said.

"Where can I get ten grand this time of night?" I said.

"From me," Jimmy said. "Return it when you're finished."

♦ ♦ ♦ ♦

We got the ten thousand from Jimmy the Ghost in a plain white envelope, along with an address for our GPS and directions for entering the alley. At ten forty-five, we pulled the Escalade over to the curb at the alley entrance. I was in the backseat on the passenger side. Gino was driving. Frankie was in front next to Gino. As Jimmy had promised, there was no traffic. It was not a neighborhood frequented at night.

The alley ahead was dimly lit. I could just make out three doorways, dark from the shadows cast by the streetlights on either end of the alley. Perfect hiding places. Frankie got out and silently moved down the alley, staying in the shadows, keeping as close to the buildings as possible. He took up residence in the second doorway, near the door where we expected Kenny Stone to emerge. He was invisible in the shadows.

We waited. At exactly eleven o'clock, Gino slowly rolled the Escalade down the alley with only his parking lights on. Frankie remained invisible. We were rolling toward the third doorway when I saw a sliver of light. Kenny Stone took one cautious step out as we pulled alongside. My window was down, my arm hanging out, envelope in hand. Kenny Stone looked around and took a few quick steps toward me with a package. He grabbed the envelope from my hand and said, "I'll need a quick look at this."

"Take your time," I said. "It's all there."

He began thumbing through the bills. While he was distracted, counting his bonanza, Frankie came out of the shadows, slipped up behind him, and zapped him with a Taser. Kenny went down. I opened the back door, and Frankie picked up Kenny and pushed him inside.

"Please get in the front, Mr. Youngblood," Frankie said. "I'll ride back here and keep our package secure."

I did as I was told, and fifteen seconds later we were rolling.

We set the GPS for another trip to Jimmy the Ghost's hangout to return his money. I heard grunts and moans from the backseat. Kenny's hands and mouth were duct-taped.

"Shut up or I'll zap you again," Frankie said.

Kenny went quiet. Gino drove on in silence.

We pulled up in front of the bar.

"I won't be long," I said. "Scoot over. I'll drive to the airport."

I went in. No one paid any attention to me. I found Jimmy at his usual table in the back and handed him the envelope.

"How'd it go?"

"Like clockwork," I said. "Would you like to say goodbye?"

Jimmy smiled. "I'll pass."

"Nice doing business with you," I said. I slid a hundred-dollar bill across the table. "For ole times' sake."

He nodded. "Come back for a steak next time you're in town," he said. "Bring your lady. On the house."

I nodded, turned around, and walked out.

◆ ◆ ◆ ◆

At the airport, I followed Frankie's directions to the private hangar. Frankie pulled Kenny from the back of the Escalade and turned him over to Gino. He handed Gino the Taser. "He gives you any trouble, zap him."

Gino looked at me. "Good work," he said. "I'll be seeing you."

I nodded, and Gino moved away, escorting Kenny Stone to Carlo Vincente's private jet.

Frankie watched them go, then turned to me. "Well done. Mr. Vincente will be pleased."

We shook hands.

"See you when I see you," Frankie said.

He turned and walked toward the jet. I watched as they pushed and pulled the man formerly known as Antonio Bella up the stairs and inside. The stairs rose from the tarmac and disappeared into the side of the jet. A minute later, they were moving out.

I called Carlo Vincente. "The package is leaving the airport as we speak."

"You never cease to amaze me, Mr. Youngblood. I am again in your debt."

"You're doing the world a favor," I said. "That's enough for me."

"Don't be a stranger," Carlo said.

He didn't wait for a reply.

73

I slept late. I shaved, showered, dressed, and called Mary.

"I'll be home this afternoon."

"That's good news. How'd it go?"

"As good as it could. The man formerly known as Antonio Bella is back where he belongs, with the North Jersey mob."

"I wouldn't want to be him," Mary said.

"Nor would I."

◆ ◆ ◆ ◆

I packed what little I had and called Laramie Sims. "Breakfast," I said. "I'm buying."

"There's a place called Millers All Day. It's six or seven blocks down toward the water on King Street. Can't miss it."

"I'm leaving now," I said.

Downstairs, I left my luggage at the concierge desk and headed right on Wentworth to King Street. I took a left on King and briskly began the half-mile walk. Laramie was in a corner booth with his back to me. He had left the seat against the wall for me. I sat.

"Thanks for saving me the primo spot."

"I eat here all the time," Laramie said. "I figured you should have the view of the street. Besides, you're paying."

The waitress arrived and poured coffee. "Hello, Laramie," she said, obviously flirting.

"Hey, Crystal."

"What can I get you-all?"

"I'll have the biscuits and gravy platter with eggs, scrambled," Laramie said.

She looked at me.

"Make it two," I said.

She smiled at Laramie and went away.

"Friendly," I said.

"Uh-huh."

"And good looking."

"That, too," Laramie said.

"Interested?"

"Maybe. How'd that thing work out?"

"Well enough," I said. "Kenny Stone will not be bothering Charleston anymore."

"Good riddance," Laramie said.

Our food arrived, and what talking we did was about life on the Charleston police force, my work with the FBI, and private investigating.

An hour later, I was heading to the airport to meet Jim Doak.

74

The following day, I was at my desk making a list of things to do. The trip home had been uneventful. The welcome I received from Mary was very eventful. I smiled thinking about it as I made my list. At the top was, **Call Jason Gildersleeve**. I dialed his private number. With a campaign looming, I knew he would be up early.

"Mr. Youngblood," he answered. "It's been awhile. To what do I owe the honor? Good news, I hope."

"The best," I said. "Your problem has been completely taken care of."

"You're one hundred percent sure?" the congressman said.

"Yes."

"Nice to hear. Send me the bill for your services."

"I will," I said. "I hope you win. You have my vote."

"That's much appreciated. I still wish you would join my campaign. I need someone to give me honest opinions."

"If I get really bored, I might just do that," I said. "Keep in touch, Congressman."

"I certainly will," he said. "Goodbye, Mr. Youngblood."

◆ ◆ ◆ ◆

Next on my list was the associate deputy director of the FBI. I called his private cell, and he answered on the second ring.

"It's been awhile, Youngblood," David Steele said.

"Two weeks. I did what you told me and found another way. You can close the book on alias Kenny Stone."

"How?"

"Don't ask questions you shouldn't know the answers to," I said. "Best if you don't know too much."

"Is he dead?"

"Probably, although the last time I saw him, he was alive and kicking."

There was a long silence while David Steele processed the news. I knew he would eventually figure it out, just not the details.

"Okay," he said. "Works for me. I'll close the file."

"Got anything good for me right now?"

"Nothing you would be interested in. Routine stuff. Take a couple of weeks off, and stay out of trouble. I'll be in touch."

◆ ◆ ◆ ◆

Next, I called Jessica Johnson's private cell. I let it ring five or six times and was about to hang up when she answered.

"Jessica, it's Donald Youngblood. How are you?"

"I'm much better, Mr. Youngblood. I want to thank you again for all you did. Silverthorn has been a lifesaver for me."

"You're not the first to say that," I said. "I'm glad it worked out."

"Did you call to check on me, or do you have news?"

"Both. I thought you'd like to know that Kenny Stone is dead. You don't have to worry about him anymore." I didn't know that as a certainty, but it was a real good bet.

"Good," she said. "I hope he burns in hell." She paused. "Sorry, that just kind of slipped out."

"Understandable," I said. "If you ever need anything, you have my number. Stay safe and well, Jessica."

75

About a week before the PGA Championship, I was in the office early when I got a call from an area code I didn't recognize. Things were quiet and I was bored, so I answered. "Cherokee Investigations, Donald Youngblood speaking," I said in a voice about half an octave lower than normal.

"Mr. Youngblood, my name is Brock Browning. I'm in charge of security for the PGA Championship. Claude Akers said you would be interested in joining us."

"Yes," I said. "Thanks for calling. Did Claude explain the circumstances?"

"Yes, he did. He said your daughter is caddying for a club pro who made the cut. That would be Tony Price, correct?"

"That's correct."

"We'd be glad to have you on the course," Brock said. "You would have to look like part of our staff. We're wearing all black—pants, short-sleeve T-shirts, windbreakers if the weather is too cool for short sleeves. I'll supply the windbreaker and a bulletproof vest. Both will have *PGA Security* imprinted on them. You'll also get a walkie-talkie tuned to a special frequency. You bring everything else, including your weapon. We carry Glock Nines. Do you have one?"

"Yes," I said.

"Is Mr. Price going to arrive early for a practice round?"

"That's the plan," I said. "We'll be there Tuesday."

"Okay," Brock said. "Check in with me at the security tent, and I'll get you squared away."

"See you then," I said.

• ♦ ♦ •

Later that day, I called Bradley Culpepper. I owed the general a call, and I wanted to stay in his good graces.

"Youngblood," the general said. "Are you staying upright?"

"Trying to," I said. "I wanted to tell you the rest of the sniper story and thank you again for your help."

"Hang on a minute," he said. I heard the general's muted voice, probably giving orders not to be disturbed. "Go ahead, Youngblood."

I told him step by step how I had gone about identifying Eli Wirkus. He listened silently. A couple of times, he interrupted to say, "Smart" or "Good thinking." I strung it out as long as I could, letting the general feel he was getting the full treatment. I finished with Eli's phone call.

"The assassin calling the target," the general said. "That's about as weird as it gets. So, are you going to close the book on Eli Wirkus or go after him?"

"The consensus of people I trust is that Eli Wirkus is sincere and will not try again. It fits with his background and beliefs. I don't think I have anything to worry about, and I'm told he would be nearly impossible to find."

"Sounds right," General Culpepper said. "But watch your six anyway. Never hurts to be cautious."

"I will," I said. "Thanks again for everything."

76

North Carolina weather in May is, for the most part, ideal—warm days and cool nights, not much rain, perfect for golf and golf courses. Pinehurst No. 2, the site of many major tournaments, was in pristine condition, ready to host the PGA Championship. Designed by the renowned Donald Ross in 1907, it was a legend among American courses.

I stood on the practice tee with my security badge and Glock Nine on full display, wearing my vest with the walkie-talkie attached. The weather was warm enough for short sleeves, so my windbreaker was in Tony Price's golf bag. I watched Tony rocket golf balls far down the range. In less than an hour, he and Lacy would make their way to the practice green and then the first tee. Brock Browning had made good on his promise, and I was now a member of PGA Security. I stood stoically, trying to act like I knew what I was doing. From time to time, I looked around, as if trying to spot potential threats. I didn't see any. Security was much more serious for the PGA Championship than it had been for the club pro event. I had my game face on.

Tony seemed relaxed and confident as he and Lacy went through their routine. I hoped it would carry over to the tournament.

◆ ◆ ◆ ◆

On the first tee, I stood in the background as the starter read, "Ladies and gentlemen, please welcome the head pro from Mountain Center Country Club in Mountain Center, Tennessee, Tony Price." Tony tipped his hat, stepped between the tee markers, and teed up his ball. He stepped back and waggled his driver a few times, then addressed the ball and drilled a perfect drive dead center in the fairway of the 402-yard par-four hole. The game was afoot. Tony was solid, Lacy supportive. They made their way around the front nine, securing seven pars, one birdie, and one bogey for an even-par thirty-five. Tony was a little less consistent on the back nine, with five pars, two birdies, and two bogeys. The last birdie, at eighteen, gave Tony an even-par seventy for the day and a tie for twentieth. Outstanding for a club pro.

◆ ◆ ◆ ◆

The mood at dinner that Thursday night was upbeat. I sensed relief from Tony and Lacy at having finished a fine round and being in position to make the cut.

"Great round today," I said.

"I felt good," Tony said. "Lacy kept me focused and really helped on the greens. She reads greens as good as any veteran."

Lacy smiled.

"I'm going to feel some pressure tomorrow," Tony said. "It's been ten years since a club pro has made the cut. If I make it, I'm going to get some attention."

"Relax and enjoy it," Lacy said. "We're going to make the cut. I'm not ready to go home."

"There you go," I said, looking at Tony.

"I guess that's settled," Tony said.

77

On Friday, day two, the scores were higher. The wind was up, the greens were faster, and the pin placements were trickier. I accompanied Lacy as she walked the course at first light, studied the greens, and took notes. Tony had an afternoon tee time and would meet Lacy on the practice tee an hour before. I was getting nervous. I could only imagine how they felt.

On the first tee, Tony drove into the rough. The PGA had let the rough grow higher than normal, and getting out required a Houdini-like effort. Tony's second shot was short of the green, but his chip was good enough to give him a decent chance at par. After much discussion with Lacy, Tony lined up the putt and stroked it in from twenty feet. I could feel us all relax a little. Seven more pars and a lip-out bogey later, Tony teed off on the tenth hole, one over par for the day. The tenth was a monster par-five, the longest hole on the course. A driver, a three wood, and a nine iron later, Tony and Lacy were surveying a fifteen-foot birdie putt. Lacy said something, pointed at a spot on the green, and Tony nodded. Lacy pulled the pin and walked away. Tony lined up the putt, stroked it, and watched as it disappeared into the cup. Birdie. All even for the day and for the tournament. It stayed that way until Tony made bogey on the par-four fourteenth. One over par. Three pars later, Tony was still one over as he and Lacy studied a twenty-foot putt for birdie at eighteen. Tony's putt looked good for almost the entire twenty feet, then slid right just at the last second, leaving him a tap-in par. Nevertheless, he carded a solid round of seventy-one and was well inside the cut line.

After Tony finished in the scorer's tent, an NBC Sports commentator asked for an interview. Lacy and I stood fifteen feet away and listened.

"I'm here with Mountain Center, Tennessee, club pro Tony Price. Tony, how does it feel to be the first club pro in ten years to make the cut in this tournament?" she asked.

"Well, I'm really happy," Tony said. "It's a great accomplishment on this golf course, and I had a lot of help from my caddie."

"At this point, it looks like you're going to be in the top twenty at the end of today. Any thoughts on the next two days?"

"Just enjoy myself and try to hang around par," Tony said.

"Thank you," she said to Tony, then turned to the camera. "That's Tony Price, the only club pro in ten years to make the cut at the PGA Championship."

◆ ◆ ◆ ◆

That night at dinner, Tony's cell phone was going crazy with text messages. He said his wife's phone was doing the same. Finally, he turned his phone off.

"TV time," Lacy said. "You're on the map."

"I was more nervous about that than the golf," Tony said.

"You did fine," I said.

Later that night, I called Mary.

"Having fun?" she said.

"You bet."

"How about Lacy?"

"Lacy is all business."

"Oh, I could see that," Mary said. "I watched the tournament as long as Tony and Lacy were on the course. They got a lot of airtime. Even got a glimpse of you in the background a couple of times. I recorded it for posterity."

"You can have my autograph when I get home," I said.

"I'll expect a lot more than your autograph, if you get my meaning."

We teased each other for a while, and then I said good night and went to bed. I was exhausted. Security is a tough gig, especially if you have to walk eighteen holes.

78

On day three, I could feel the energy level around the golf course rise, an excitement that hadn't been there the first two days. It was moving day; players were trying to make a move to improve their position for the stretch run on Sunday.

Lacy gave Tony some good advice. "Get there early," she said. "A lot of people are going to be congratulating you on making the cut. You'll be the celebrity of the day. It's going to take more time on the practice tee and putting green."

How she knew this, I hadn't a clue, but she was right. I think every pro who made the cut, and a few club pros who didn't, came by to congratulate Tony. I stood with Lacy as he talked to a couple of well-known pros.

"Is that going to hurt his game?" I asked. "All this attention?"

"Hard to tell," she said. "Might keep him loose."

"How did you think to tell Tony to get here early? That was a really good idea."

Lacy smiled. "I talked to Flip. He told me."

"You've been talking to Flip?"

"Every night for a week."

"Smart girl," I said.

◆ ◆ ◆ ◆

If Tony was distracted by all the attention, he didn't show it on the first tee. He drilled his drive dead center 280 yards down the fairway. An iron to the green, an easy two-putt, and he was off and running with his first par of the day. The sun was out for the most part. Small, puffy, fast-moving clouds dotted the sky. The steady breeze made golfing more difficult than usual, but Tony seemed to play well in the wind and turned the front nine in a one-under thirty-four. He got in trouble on the back with two bogeys but settled down after dropping a thirty-foot birdie putt on the par-three fifteenth. Pars on sixteen, seventeen, and eighteen left him even on the day.

I waited with Lacy as Tony completed his work in the scorer's tent. The same female commentator from the day before was conducting interviews with the leaders not far from where we stood. They were household names, past major winners in fierce competition with one another. Somewhere among the top five leaders, I expected, was the eventual winner.

Tony exited the tent and headed in our direction. The NBC interviewer glanced his way but quickly focused her attention on something else. Tony Price was old news, not close enough to the lead to warrant airtime.

"Where do we stand?" Tony asked Lacy.

"Tenth," Lacy said. "Four shots back."

"Damn," Tony said. "That's hard to believe."

"Believe it," Lacy said. "You're playing great. You're in the hunt."

We started to walk away when I heard a familiar voice: "Tony, hold up." We turned and saw Peggy Ann Romeo, local Mountain Center TV anchor, heading our way with a cameraman in tow. "Can I have a few minutes? You're big news back home."

"Sure," Tony said.

"I want all three of you on camera," Peggy Ann said. "This is a very big deal for the folks in Mountain Center."

"I don't—" That was all I got out.

"Quiet," Lacy said. "You stay right there and behave." She sounded exactly like Mary. My protest died in my throat.

"Okay," Peggy Ann said. "Ready. Roll camera." Seconds later, Peggy Ann said, "I'm here with Mountain Center Country Club head pro Tony Price, his caddie, Lacy Youngblood, and well-known Mountain Center private investigator Donald Youngblood, part of the PGA Security team. Tony Price became the first club pro to make a cut at a PGA Championship in ten years and currently is in tenth place after finishing his third round. He stands at plus one for the tournament. Tony, congratulations."

"Thank you," Tony said.

"How does it feel?"

"Like a dream."

"Did you think you'd get this far?"

"Not when I began the journey," Tony said.

"Any goals for tomorrow?" Peggy Ann said.

"Even par would be nice," Tony said. "We'll play one shot at a time and see what happens."

"Good luck tomorrow." Peggy Ann turned to Lacy. "What's it like out there?"

"Exciting," Lacy said. "The course is spectacular, and Tony is playing great. I'm really proud of him."

"Don," Peggy Ann said, "what's it like watching these two?"

"I'm in awe of what they're doing, and I have the best seat in the house to watch it," I said. "I've developed a whole new appreciation for the game of golf in these last three days."

"Tony and Lacy," Peggy Ann said, "continued success tomorrow."

"Thank you," they said in unison.

"From Pinehurst No. 2, this is Peggy Ann Romeo reporting."

◆ ◆ ◆ ◆ ◆

Late that night, Mary called. "Did I see you on the local news?"

"Wasn't me," I said. "A guy who looked like me."

"And sounded like you. Standing beside someone who looked like Lacy."

"Okay, I confess. I was railroaded."

"Tony is playing really well," Mary said. "It must be exciting."

"It's exciting watching them work together," I said.

"I think all of Mountain Center has shut down for three days, watching the golf tournament. Even the crooks must be fans. Calls have been way down."

"Speaking of shutting down, how about you taking Monday off and we spend it at the lake house?"

"Are you thinking what I'm thinking?" Mary said.

"Without a doubt," I said. "I've been gone too long."

"You certainly have."

79

On Sunday, the energy level was off the charts. There was a hum around the golf course like an overhead power line. A major champion would be crowned in the afternoon, and a half-dozen or so contenders were in the hunt. Tony seemed unfazed. He was a club pro in tenth position in the PGA Championship. He received a hearty round of applause when announced on the first tee. Tony rewarded his admirers with a perfectly struck drive down the center of the fairway. His fourth round had begun. Tony was on fire as he birdied the first two holes and pulled within two strokes of the lead. He came back to earth with a bogey on three and then started to grind out pars. On nine, he dropped a twenty-foot birdie putt and pulled back to within two strokes of the lead. His drive on the par-five tenth was perfect.

Then things unraveled.

The shooter came out of the woods. I saw him maybe thirty seconds before he opened fire. He was dressed in black, a dark silhouette in the shadows of the pine trees as he moved toward the fairway. He appeared to be carrying an assault rifle, maybe an AK-47.

"Get these people out of here!" I shouted at a nearby tournament marshal. "We have an imminent threat. Go, go, go! Lacy, you and Tony go now."

I headed toward the shooter as he opened fire. He was still a hundred yards away, spraying bullets randomly. Behind me, the gallery was beginning to realize what was happening, which started a stampede in the opposite direction.

"This is Youngblood. Shooter on ten," I said into my walkie-talkie. "I repeat, shooter on ten. Assault weapon. Approach with extreme caution."

I ran toward a sand trap that had a lip high enough for me to conceal myself. I didn't think the shooter had seen me yet. I peeked over the top. The shooter was in full body armor that included a helmet with a face shield. I assumed they were bulletproof. He emptied a magazine, ejected it, and loaded another. If memory served correctly, the magazine of an AK-47 held thirty rounds, but he could have had a modified clip. He continued toward the fairway, spraying rounds as he came. He was about thirty yards away when I rose up and fired three rounds. He staggered backward like he had been shoved. He looked around to see where the shots came from, saw me, and opened fire. I ducked back in the trap as rounds tore up the turf and sand around me. I heard other shots. A handful of security guards were crouched behind trees and bushes returning fire, but they weren't close enough to do any damage. I peeked out again. The shooter returned fire in their general direction, and then his magazine was again empty. I made my move, running at him, Glock drawn. He saw me coming. He ejected the magazine, started to load another, fumbled it, then dropped it. He bent to pick it up. I was within twenty yards when I stopped and took aim at the face shield. Whether it was bulletproof or not, I suspected nine-millimeter rounds bouncing off it would be quite distracting. I rattled off five shots. I don't know how many times I hit him. His head snapped back. He stumbled backward and fell down. He ripped off the helmet and mask like they were full of bees. He looked dazed and disoriented. He had the dark complexion, dark hair, and fine features associated with a Middle Eastern terrorist.

I was on the move as he pulled a pistol from his belt.

"Drop it!" I shouted.

Instead of pointing it at me, he tucked it underneath his chin and pulled the trigger. Just like that, it was over.

"Stand down," I said into my walkie-talkie. "The shooter is dead. Repeat, the shooter is dead."

A minute later, my cell phone rang.

"My God, I watched the whole thing on TV," Mary said. "Are you all right?"

"I'm fine," I said. "I can't talk now. Call Lacy. Make sure she's okay. We'll talk later."

I felt a presence at my side: Brock Browning. "Good work, Youngblood," he said. "What the hell just happened?"

Before I could answer, my cell phone rang again.

"I saw it all," David Steele said. "I want you to take charge. I'll have a team there within the hour."

"Yes, sir," I said.

I turned to Brock. "The associate deputy director of the FBI wants me to take charge of the scene."

"Fine with me," Brock said. "Tell me what to do."

"Tell your men to clear the area of any nonessential personnel. I don't want anyone in those woods. Get everybody off the golf course. There could be another shooter out there somewhere. I doubt it, but tell your men to stay alert. This may not be over."

"All PGA Security, this is Brock," he said into his walkie-talkie. "Clear the golf course. Send everyone home who doesn't need to be here. Stay alert."

"What's the damage?" I said.

"Don't know," he said. "Bunch of wounded. A few dead, I think. Ambulances are on the way. Jesus, I can't believe this."

"Get with your men," I said. "Make sure the course gets cleared."

"You got it," he said, and moved away, shouting instructions.

◆ ◆ ◆ ◆

Hours later, I stood with the FBI agent in charge of the crime-scene team. The area had been taped off, the body of the shooter removed, and lights set up. The agent's last name was Fordice. He was on his cell phone. The golf course was empty except for law enforcement and PGA Security personnel. Lacy and Tony were back at the hotel.

SAC Fordice disconnected and walked over. "Thirty-nine wounded and ten dead," he said. "Some of the wounded may not make it. It was a shooting gallery. Hard to miss with that many people to shoot at. That AK-47 can kill you from over three hundred yards."

"Damn him to hell," I said. "Ten people dead in a matter of seconds. They came out to witness a premier sporting event and went home in body bags. It's beyond my comprehension."

"It would have been a lot worse if not for you," he said. "Who knows how many people you saved? Go get some rest, Agent Youngblood. You deserve it. There's nothing more for you to do here."

I nodded and walked away.

◆ ◆ ◆ ◆

Lacy was waiting on me when I got back to the hotel. She was visibly shaken. I held her for a few minutes.

"I'm okay, you're okay, Tony's okay. Let's count our blessings," I said.

"We were lucky," Lacy said.

"Yes, we were."

"How many dead?"

"At least ten."

"My God," Lacy said.

I sat in a chair at the dining table across from her.

"Why has the world gone crazy, Don?" Lacy said. "I don't understand it."

"I wish I knew."

We sat there for a while, and then Lacy got up and went into her bedroom. A few seconds later, she came back out and handed me a little white pill and a bottle of water. "Mom said to make you take this. I'm taking one, too. We need to get a good night's sleep."

I didn't argue and did as I was told. Fifteen minutes later, I drifted off into a dreamless sleep and did not stir until midmorning.

80

I shaved, showered, dressed, and emerged from my bedroom a new man, wondering if the day before had really happened or was just a bad dream. I found a note on the table from Lacy:

Went for a run. Hot coffee in your Yeti. Breakfast sandwich in oven keeping warm. Call David Steele.

I sat at the kitchen table and drank the coffee and ate the sausage, egg, and cheese sandwich. I felt detached. In my head, Agent Fordice's voice kept saying, "Thirty-nine wounded and ten dead." I shook myself back to reality and called David Steele.

"How are you?" he said.

"I'm okay. I need to get farther away from this nightmare."

"I know what you mean," he said. "And I wasn't even there. Walk me through it."

So I did.

"I'm glad you were there, Youngblood. I don't know anyone who thinks faster on his feet than you do."

"I appreciate the compliment, but I just did what I had to do. What do we know about the shooter?"

"Nothing yet," David Steele said. "Middle Eastern, for sure. Fingerprints are not in any database that we have access to. We'll run his DNA."

"Anyone claiming responsibility?"

"No, and I don't think anyone will. There's a lot of outrage. There has been this unwritten rule that sporting events are off limits for this kind of thing. We're also getting chatter that even terrorist groups are outraged. I think this will turn out to be an individual acting alone."

"I'm not sure about that," I said. "He had on some really high-tech gear."

"That bothers me, too," David Steele said. "Hopefully, we can get to the bottom of it. For now, go home and get some rest. I'll let you know if anything develops."

◆ ◆ ◆

Lacy came back, said hello, and went straight to the shower. Five minutes later, Tony knocked on the door. I let him in.

"Want coffee?"

"No thanks," he said. "I've had my limit."

"Any news from the PGA?"

"Just got the word. There is no way we can finish the tournament. Too many commitments. A lot of players have already left town. The winner will be the third-day leader. The Saturday leader board will be the final leader board. They will award full prize money. That means I finish tenth and win two hundred ninety-seven thousand. Ten percent of that goes to Lacy."

"How do you feel about the decision?"

"I'm disappointed that we couldn't finish," Tony said. "But tenth place is great. It gives me an automatic invite to next year's tournament. The money is more than I could have hoped for. It's huge for me. But I feel so awful for those people who were killed and wounded. They were just there for a fun day, and look what happened. It's so senseless."

When Lacy came out a few minutes later, Tony told her what the PGA had decided.

"Too bad," Lacy said. "You might have won."

"Ever the optimist," Tony said.

"How much did we win?" Lacy said.

Tony told her. "Ten percent of that is yours."

"Too much," Lacy said. "I can't take that much."

"Yes, you will," Tony said. "No argument. You earned it."

Lacy looked at me and smiled. "Looks like you have another investment client," she said. "Me."

81

The first few days after the shooting were crazy. A number of national news networks wanted to interview me. Gretchen was adept at keeping them at bay when they called the office or showed up in person. When I did encounter them at my car or in front of our condo, all I had to say was the ever-reliable, "No comment. It's an ongoing investigation." Discouraged and bored after a few days, the press moved on.

I spent some time on the phone with Billy and Henry Cole, neither of whom pressed me for details. Mostly, they gave me pats on the back and told me to forget about it. I had a session with Roy and T. Elbert on Little Switz. T. Elbert probed for details but was cautious not to push too hard. Roy was more interested in the golf tournament.

I stayed away from the diner for a while, which annoyed Doris and some of her patrons, who were used to seeing me there three or four times a week. I knew I wouldn't get a moment's peace. The first time back, I had a seven o'clock breakfast with Big Bob. I waited until I knew he was there, then slipped in the back door to my table. Few were occupied at that early hour.

"I invited you here to keep the pests away," I said. "I'm buying."

"My pleasure," he said. "Anyone who bothers you, I'll arrest for stalking."

Doris arrived, beaming. "Haven't seen you since you got back. Where have you been keeping yourself? My, oh, my, that was something. All those people killed and wounded. And you right there to stop it."

"Doris," Big Bob said, "enough. We'd like to order."

"Oh, sure," she said. "Sorry. What can I get you?"

She took our order and scurried away.

"How are you coping?" Big Bob said.

"I'd be fine if everyone would just leave me alone."

"It's a small town, and you're a hero. It will pass. These people don't have a lot to be excited about. For a few weeks, it's going to be you. Deal with it."

Leave it to the big man to get straight to the heart of things. I abruptly changed the subject to sports, and a few minutes later our food arrived. Big Bob sitting at my table was like a mean dog in your front yard. Nobody wants to come to your front door. We ate in peace.

Epilogue

I was in the office early the day after having breakfast with Big Bob when David Steele called.

"How are you doing?" he said.

"I'm doing okay. I seem to have the ability not to think about things I don't want to think about."

"Well, I hate to bring it up again, but I have some news on the shooter. Do you want to hear it, or do you want to forget it?"

"Might as well know it all," I said.

"First of all, Homeland Security hijacked the case. No big surprise there. So, finding out information was difficult. I kept playing the Youngblood card."

"Youngblood card?"

"You know, that you, one of our agents, saved their ass. They were lucky you were there. They should have known this was coming. Like that. They got so tired of hearing it, they sent me a copy of the file. It might not be all there is, but there's a lot."

"I'm listening."

"The shooter," David Steele said, "was a twenty-six-year-old Iraqi. Homeland Security calls him Omar, but that's not his real name. He was the son of a high-ranking ISIS leader. His desertion from ISIS brought dishonor on the family. Omar was in the States illegally and without permission from his father. He came in through Canada. HS had tabs on him, and then they lost him. He was off the grid for six months before the shooting."

"Obviously, he didn't bring his gear with him. Where did he get it?"

"It's only a guess," David Steele said, "and we'll never know for sure, but Homeland Security thinks he got it from an ISIS cell here in the States, and that he staged his suicide mission as a way to restore his family's honor."

"By killing all those people?" I said. "Great way to restore family honor. Insanity, is what it is."

"Young men like Omar have been taught to hate the West since birth. They're brainwashed. We're the infidels, and we must be destroyed at all costs."

"We've brought this on ourselves, haven't we, Dave?" I said. "We're messing where we shouldn't be messing."

"I can't disagree, but that's beyond my pay grade, Don. I have to run. You take some time off. Hang out at the lake house, take the houseboat out, fish, swim, have some fun. Forget about all of this."

"Is that an order?"

"You bet," he said.

"Finally," I said, "an order I'm willing to follow."

◆ ◆ ◆ ◆

Days became weeks, and the shooting at the PGA Championship was old news. The final body count was twelve dead. Two died in the hospital. Nobody was safe anywhere. It seemed like every day I went online, there was another shooting.

Lacy returned to Arizona State, a celebrity in her own right. She was invited to be a guest speaker at a number of events. She was approached by agents to do modeling, TV commercials, and screen tests. She turned them all down. She was already set for life financially, and she had no desire to be famous. Slowly, her life returned to normal, whatever that was.

Business at Cherokee Investigations was booming. Nothing like the boss getting on national television to bring out the masses who needed a private investigator. They left disappointed when they found out the head man handled only a few unusual cases a year. But some had legitimate needs and were happy to let Gretchen or Rhonda solve their problems.

◆ ◆ ◆ ◆

Summer was approaching as I sat on the lower deck early one morning drinking coffee. The warm sun and the hot coffee were perfect therapy for lifting my spirits. I scanned the lake with my binoculars to see if any nearby craft contained a sniper with a rifle. There were no nearby craft. For now, I was safe. As if on cue, my cell phone rang. Henry Cole.

"Henry, how's the Pacific look today?" I answered.

"Beautiful as always," he said. "I'll bet you're on your lower deck having coffee and Mary is still asleep."

"Right on both counts. Are you spying on me?"

"No, you're just a creature of habit."

"Guilty as charged," I said. "What's going on?"

"A piece of news that will close the file on Eli Wirkus."

"What is it?"

"Eli Wirkus is dead," Henry said. "You don't have to look over your shoulder anymore."

"How?"

"Shot."

"Who?"

"His girlfriend."

"Why?"

"Someone put a sizable bounty on his head, and the girlfriend must have decided their relationship was not long term."

"Ouch," I said.

"Indeed," Henry said. "Anyway, I thought you'd like to know. Give my best to Mary, and come see us soon."

"It may be sooner than you think," I said.

"Tomorrow, next day, next week," Henry said. "We'll be here. Let me know."

"Will do," I said. "Tell Rosa hello."

◆ ◆ ◆ ◆

Mary joined me an hour later, looking her sexy best. She kissed me lightly on the mouth and sat down with a cup of coffee.

"Henry called," I said. "I'm to give you his best."

"How nice of Henry, but your best is good enough for me, Cowboy. What else?"

"Eli Wirkus is dead."

"Really?" Mary said. "Well, that's a relief. What happened?"

I told her.

"That's cold," Mary said.

"It is."

We drank coffee and stared at the lake.

"Henry wants us to come down," I said. "I think I could use a little beach vacation."

"Great," Mary said. "When?"

"As soon as possible. I was thinking Tuesday."

"You'll have to talk to Big Bob," Mary said.

"Chicken," I said.

◆ ◆ ◆ ◆

Big Bob whined like a dog with a thorn in his paw, but in the end, I negotiated two weeks off for Mary. I started with a month, hoping for a week, and ended up with two. Mary was amazed.

The Pacific Ocean was dark except for the light from the full moon and a few twinkling lights from faraway boats. Mary and I sat close on the Coles' front porch swing. We had arrived midday. The weather was absolutely perfect, accented by a soft breeze coming off the gulf.

"Two weeks," Mary said, snuggling closer. "You should have been a lawyer, Cowboy."

"No thanks," I said.

We rocked for a while in silence; one of those moments that I would like to freeze in time and pull out every once in a while, to enjoy again when I needed settling.

"Are you okay, Don?"

"I don't know," I said. "I wish I could understand why I keep getting put in these dangerous situations. I think I'm more foolhardy that brave."

"You're wrong," Mary said. "You are one of the bravest people I know. And you're on the right side. You need to come to terms with that. You've saved many lives. I'm so proud of you. Don't doubt yourself. I will not allow it."

I don't think I had ever heard Mary speak with more conviction. I felt settled by her words of support. "Thank you," I said. "I need to hear that every now and then. Thank God you're around to tell me."

Henry and Rosa had turned in for the night but were obviously still awake. Muted laughter and other sounds came from their bedroom.

"Sounds like those two are having some fun," Mary said.

"It does," I said.

"What do you say we go have some fun of our own?"

The End

Author's Note

I was about halfway finished with writing this book when the pandemic hit. I chose to keep the pandemic out of Donald Youngblood's world. We have had enough reminders.

My wife, Tessa, and I were in Utah for our annual ski trip when the country started shutting down. One by one the Utah ski resorts closed and our reason for being there vanished. We packed up and started driving home. We spent the first night in Farmington, New Mexico. Things seemed fairly normal. Our next stop was in Amarillo, Texas. Our hotel was noticeably unbusy. The third night was spent in Fort Smith, Arkansas at the downtown Courtyard Convention Center. They had closed the top two floors. Only seven rooms were occupied on the two remaining floors. We were lucky to find a restaurant that was open. Fort Smith was a ghost town.

Normally, Nashville, Tennessee would have been our last stop before heading home to Kingsport, but we chose to drive the final eight hundred miles in one day since Nashville was a Covid hotspot. Traffic thru Nashville was very light. Nashville, too, was a ghost town. A reminder of how fast things can change. Home never looked so good.

Over the next year we stayed home waiting for a vaccine. The burning questions each day were (1) "What day is it?" and (2) "What's for dinner?" We survived. We streamed, we facetimed, we read, we even joined a wine club. We were blessed and bored, but we survived. Many did not; hundreds of thousands.

In March, we were vaccinated. We drove to Santa Fe, New Mexico for a much-needed vacation. Santa Fe was nowhere near normal. We enjoyed it anyway. We meant to stay a week. We stayed three.

As I write this Author's Note, our personal world is still not normal but it is improving. I hope yours is too.

Acknowledgments

My thanks to:

My wife, Tessa who fussed over the proofing of this book like a knight on a quest for the holy grail. Readers might find a few errors but not nearly as many as there could have been.

Steve Kirk, editor supreme, who knows Youngblood and company as well as I do and cleans up the messes I make along the way to telling their story. Seven books and counting, Steve!

Todd Lape, Lape Designs in Madison, MS for making my books look like they belong on the best seller list. Nine books and counting, Todd. Great job as always.

Meri Saffelder, our original web master, welcome back. You continue to care for the Donald Youngblood Mysteries website with skill and professionalism.

Mary Sanchez, lady of mystery, who moves silently in the shadows working hard to bring Donald Youngblood into the spotlight. Well done.

Buie Hancock at *Buie Pottery* who has supported Youngblood Nation from the beginning and given Donald Youngblood a presence in Gatlinburg, TN. Drop in or visit www.buiepottery.com.

Dr. Glen Moody at *I Love Books* Bookstore, Kingsport, TN who has given Donald Youngblood a home in the Fort Henry Mall. Stop by and say Youngblood sent you.

Book lovers everywhere, especially Youngblood fans; buy books!